R.D. BRADY

TACKLE THE FEAR

BOOKS

Vinci Books

vinci-books.com

Published by Vinci Books Ltd in 2026

1

Copyright © R.D. Brady 2021

A CIP catalogue record for this book is available from the British Library.
Paperback ISBN: 9781036700898
The EU GPSR authorised representative is Logos Europe, 9 rue Nicolas
Poussion, 17000 La Rochelle, France contact@logoseurope.eu

By R.D. Brady

The Nola James Series

Surrender the Fear

Escape the Fear

Tackle the Fear

Return the Fear

The Belial Series

The Belial Stone

The Belial Library

The Belial Ring

The Belial Recruit

The Belial Children

The Belial Origins

The Belial Search

The Belial Guard

The Belial Warrior

The Belial Plan

The Belial Witches

The Belial War

The Belial Fall

The Belial Sacrifice

Prologue

The gray minivan pulled to a stop next to Nola James's blue-and-white 1988 Honda Civic8i at the rest stop just north of Route 6. The door creaked as Nola pushed it open, and she had to give it a little extra shove. It had been sitting on a used car lot for a year before she acquired it. No one had driven it in all that time. The dust inside it was proof of that. It would never be her choice of car, but she just needed it for a short time, and then she'd ditch it.

Closing the stubborn door shut, she pulled on her sunglasses against the bright light.

Cars rolled by along the highway, and there were only two other vehicles in the rest stop lot. One belonged to family of five. The parents had rushed the kids to the restroom when they pulled in five minutes ago. The other car belonged to a young guy in his twenties. He was walking a black lab along the edge of the rest stop, begging the dog to do his business so they could get back on the road. The human was in a rush. The dog, not so much.

The middle-aged couple in the gray minivan that had

just pulled in sat for a moment talking. Nola leaned back against her car, giving them time to pull themselves together, aware of the clock ticking away. She needed to get moving. But she also needed them to be ready.

Finally, the doors of the van opened. Paulette Kelly stepped out of the passenger side. Her short dark curly hair was sprinkled with gray, and she nervously pushed her glasses up from the edge of her nose.

Her husband, Paul, stepped out of the driver's side and cast a glance around. He pushed up his glasses as well. Nola noted he'd dressed almost identically to his wife. She wore a navy-blue sweater with khaki pants and sneakers. He wore a navy-blue fleece with khakis and sneakers. She wondered if they had planned it that way or if after thirty years together, they just naturally migrated toward the same look. Of course, being they were named Paul and Paulette, she supposed she shouldn't be surprised.

Paulette hurried over, wringing her hands. "Is everything all right? Are you still going?"

Nerves radiated off the woman. She reminded Nola of a hummingbird, zipping about, never staying still. Nola hoped for her sake it was just a temporary affliction. It must be an exhausting way to live.

"I'm still going," Nola assured her. "I just needed to make sure you two were here before I go get them."

Paul joined them on the sidewalk, an obvious tremor in his hands. "I feel like I should go with you. You shouldn't do this by yourself."

Paulette was an accountant and Paul was the manager of a small restaurant outside of Chicago. Together, the two of them had raised one daughter, Marcy, now twenty-eight years old. They'd scrimped and saved their whole life to send Marcy to college and had been thrilled when she'd gotten into the University of Chicago. She had been a top student the entire time she'd been there and had been easily accepted into the University of Chicago law school. Her future looked incredibly bright.

Then she got pregnant her first year in law school.

Chad Whitman, Marcy's boyfriend since senior year, who was two years ahead of her in the law school, insisted that she drop out and they get married. The plan had been for Marcy to only step back from law school for a little while. Then after the baby was born, she would finish up school and go on to her career in law.

But that never happened.

Over the course of their relationship, Chad had been slowly pulling Marcy away from her friends and activities. The girl who'd once had dozens of friends to call had no one to turn to when she became pregnant. At her wedding, there was no one to stand up for her. Not even Marcy's parents were there, as Chad had insisted on a justice of the peace. They received a call later that day to tell them that their only daughter was married.

Paul and Paulette had tried to be supportive, even though it broke both of their hearts not being there. Unfortunately, that was only the beginning of the heartache.

Over time, their beautiful, vibrant girl became nervous, anxious, and unsure of herself. Slowly, Chad pulled everyone away from Marcy, even her parents, moving her to Indianapolis, nearly three hundred miles away.

Nola understood the signs. Chad was controlling Marcy's every move. She had no doubt that he'd made sure that she'd gotten pregnant. At the time, Marcy's grades were outpacing his. He couldn't allow that to happen. And now, with two children, she was hidden away in a lovely home in Sandusky, Ohio. She had no bank account, no social media presence, and her driver's license had lapsed. She didn't even have an email account or a cell phone. He controlled all of the money. He controlled Marcy.

Paul and Paulette hadn't spoken to her in over a year. At that point, they'd driven out to Indianapolis. For weeks beforehand, they called and called, but no one picked up. Finally, they got a recording saying the number had been disconnected. So they hopped in the car, only to find a new family at their daughter's former address and no forwarding address. They'd tried to track them down but had been unable to.

And that was because they were no longer in Indianapolis.

Unbeknownst to Marcy's parents, Chad had taken a job in Sandusky and moved the family. The two of them had been searching for her for a year but had been unable to find any sign of her. They had turned to the police, but they said that Marcy was a grown woman, and if she wanted to cut off contact with her parents, she was allowed to do so.

Desperate, they wasted their money on private investigators who did little more than a few internet searches and then stopped. But finally, two months ago, they found their daughter, and they drove out to see her.

Chad was the one who answered the door, and he immediately ordered them to leave. And then he'd filed a restraining order against them to keep them away from his wife.

Paul nervously pushed back his glasses again. "It's just . . . you don't understand what he's like. It's not safe. I should go with you to help."

Nola knew he meant well, but if Paul had ever been in a fight a day in his life, she'd be shocked. Paul would be a hindrance and not a help if push came to shove at their daughter's home. And she was pretty sure shoving would be the least of Chad's responses.

Besides, Nola knew exactly the type of guy Chad Whitman was, so she shook her head. "No. I've got this. It'll be better if you stay at the rendezvous point."

Nola planned to leave Paul and Paulette around the corner from the house just down the street, in case there were any problems. "I'll bring Marcy and the girls to you. Just be ready to leave as soon as we get them in the van. I know you're going to want to hug and talk and do all of those things, but you can't. You need to get them into the van and get out of here. Do not go home. You have that address I gave you?"

Paulette nodded, her gaze shifting around the parking lot. "Yes. I have it. And I went shopping last night. The back of the car is full of groceries. Enough for at least a week."

Nola nodded. "That should be more than enough. By then Chad will be locked away."

Tears swam in Paulette's eyes, and she hastily wiped them away. "Okay. We trust you."

Nola wanted to warn them against that. They had trusted too many people and had lost so much money in the search for their daughter. But in this case, their trust was well placed.

"I'll get your daughter back to you. Just be ready."

Paul wrapped his arm around Paulette as a tear rolled down her cheek. Nola ignored it and headed back to her car. They were good people. They didn't deserve this. But as she well knew, the good people in the world rarely got what they deserved. Neither did the bad.

Unless, of course, Nola got involved.

The house was dark as Chad Whitman unlocked the front door. He pushed it open with a frown, reaching for the light switch. He flicked it, but nothing happened.

"Marcy? Marcy, god damn it, what's going on with the lights?"

The thud of his briefcase hit the floor next to the door, and Nola could imagine a shiver of fear running through Marcy at the sound.

When she'd arrived four hours ago to get Marcy and the girls, it had taken some talking to get her out of the house. The woman had been absolutely terrified. She'd lost weight, and her hair seemed to be falling out.

It wasn't until Nola told her that leaving was the only way to protect the girls that she finally moved. Marcy and the girls were already gone, heading for the safe house with her parents. There was only one last thing for Nola to do.

Chad walked down the hall, his footsteps loud and angry. "Marcy! Where are you?"

Nola flipped on the light in the kitchen.

A jolt ran through Chad as he stuttered to a stop. The fear that had slashed across his face at a stranger being in his house abated as his eyes raked over Nola. His shoulders relaxed. Nola knew exactly what he was thinking: no threat here. Just a woman.

He stepped forward, anger lacing his words. "Who are you? What the hell are you doing in my house?"

Chad Whitman was, by anyone's standards, a handsome man. He had thick dark-blond hair highlighted by the sun during his daily three-mile runs. His bright-blue eyes narrowed in displeasure at Nola.

In college and high school, he'd been the big man on

campus: popular, attractive. The guy all the girls wanted to be with, and the one all the guys wanted to be friends with.

But lurking underneath that attractive façade was the heart of a monster. A few ex-girlfriends had still been scared years later when talking about him. It had taken a lot of coaxing to get them to swear out depositions detailing his patterns of abusive behavior.

When Nola arrived earlier, bruises dotted Marcy's body, despite the long sleeves and pants she wore to hide them. She'd gotten so thin, the clothes were practically swimming on her. Through Bishop, Nola knew that Chad had given Marcy worse than the bruises. There'd been a few trips to the hospital. All out of town, of course. All different hospitals.

And from the crooked bend to a few of Marcy's fingers, it was clear that sometimes she hadn't even made it to the hospital.

Nola stood up from the kitchen table, rage roaring through her as she imagined this monster stealing the joy from Marcy's life until she became an absolutely terrified shell of the woman she used to be. It would take years to get Marcy back to some semblance of that woman, if she ever managed to at all.

And the only chance she had of that was if this monster was put away.

"I'm a friend of Marcy's," Nola said calmly.

"You need to get out of my house. Marcy!" Chad's nostrils flared as he yelled, puffing out his chest and reminding Nola of an ape asserting dominance.

"She's not here. Neither are the girls." Nola kept her tone even, although the mention of the girls sent a new shot of anger through her. The oldest was six, the youngest only four. Both of them already showed signs of abuse. They were terrified of new people.

And why wouldn't they be? They'd never met anyone. They spent all of their time in this house with their mother. Instead of allowing Marcy to go to the store to pick up groceries, Chad had them delivered. The oldest was home-schooled. Doctor visits were done by Chad. In fact, anything involving the outside world was handle by Chad.

From what Nola could tell, Marcy had quite literally not stepped outside of this house in a year. The home record-ings supported that. Because Chad had installed cameras so he could keep an eye on his wife and girls while he was at work. Bishop had looped some of the old recordings to keep Chad from seeing Nola arrive and his family leave.

"What do you mean they're not here? Get out of my house."

Nola smiled, stepping around the kitchen table, rolling her neck until it cracked. "I don't take orders from you. And neither does Marcy. Not anymore."

Chad narrowed his eyes, and Nola could see the anger beginning to burn inside of him. Guys like this didn't like when women told them what to do. They believed women had their place, and they certainly didn't tolerate women ordering them around.

"You have trespassed in my home. In the dark. I didn't know who you were." He smiled. "But accidents happen."

He darted forward to grab Nola by the shirt. But he was used to people who didn't fight back.

Nola always fought back.

Side-stepping his sloppy reach, Nola grabbed his wrist, turned it ninety degrees, and then slammed it without mercy toward the floor. She heard a crack but knew it wasn't broken, merely sprained.

Chad let out a screech. "My wrist. You broke my wrist!"

Nola rolled her eyes in disgust. "And how much worse have you done to your wife? And all the other women in your past."

"I don't know what you're talking about." Chad's voice trembled.

She scoffed. The big man was practically crying the first time someone actually fought back. "Well, I'm sure the district attorney will explain it to you."

Chad froze. "What are you talking about?"

Anger poured through Nola, needing a release. She slammed her fist into his face. He cried out. "My nose, you broke my nose."

Nola conceded that might be possible, given the blood now rolling down the man's face. But it didn't calm the anger boiling inside of her. If anything, it made it boil higher. How many times had he made Marcy bleed in their years together? How many times did his girls have to watch their mother hobble around, barely able to stand?

She twisted his arm more. "All those security cameras you have around the house? I had a friend tap into them. They've documented abuse going back years. We found all of the hospital records too. You're going to be going away for a very long time."

Chad stared up at her, his anger dissolving into fear. "You can't. That was all Marcy's fault. She just wouldn't listen. I had to. It was for her own good."

Dragging him along the floor, she hauled him up and then slammed his face into the wall. She growled, speaking through gritted teeth. "It wasn't for her own good. It was for you. You did all of that to control her, to make yourself feel like a big man." She pressed his face harder against the wall. "Well, how does it feel, Chad? Do you feel like a big man now? Or am I the bigger man now?"

His shoulders shook, and tears leaked from his eyes. "Stop. Please stop."

Nola imagined just how many times Marcy probably said the exact same thing to him until, after years of futility, she stopped begging, knowing it was of no use. In all likelihood he would soon turn that anger toward the girls once they started to talk back.

Or just breathe wrong.

With a growl, Nola whipped him away from the wall and away from her. He tripped over a kitchen chair and crashed to the floor. He got slowly to his feet, holding out his hands. "Look, what do you want? Do you want money? I can give you money."

She stalked toward him. "I don't want money. I want you in jail. I want you to be locked up. I want you to have a cellmate that knows what you did and does to you every day what you've done to Marcy for the last six years."

Chad shook his head, backing away. "No, no. I didn't do anything wrong. She just wouldn't behave. It was for her own good."

Nola slammed a foot right into his groin. His knees buckled and his eyes went wide as he cupped his privates before sinking to his knees.

Leaning forward, she glared down at him. "And that was for your own good."

She grabbed him and crushed him face down onto the ground. Pinning him in place with her knee, she pulled out the zip ties from her back pocket and secured them around his wrists and ankles.

Trembling with anger, she stepped back to take some deep breaths. Guys like him always got under her skin. He was an entitled jackass who'd had everything handed to him: the best schools, the best advantages. He took and he took and he took. And whenever something went wrong, it was somebody else's fault.

But when push came to shove, like most abusers, he fell apart when someone fought back. And right now things had most definitely fallen apart for him.

Nola took another step back, her anger not diminishing at the sight of him immobilized. She wanted to step forward and slam her fists into him over and over again for all the damage he'd done to Marcy and the other women from his past.

But if she started wailing on him, she wouldn't stop. And she wasn't an executioner, at least not for this guy. Marcy was safe, the girls were safe, and the district attorney now had all of the information they needed to put this piece of dirt away for a very long time.

"The cops will be by in a few hours. Why don't you stay there and think about what you've done?"

Chad squirmed on the floor, trying to look up at her. "You can't leave me here. You can't—"

Ripping off the piece of duct tape that she'd placed on her sleeve earlier, she slammed it over Chad's mouth, careful to keep his nose free so that he didn't suffocate. Although she was tempted to save the system the bother.

"You will go away," she said as murderous images danced through her mind. "And you will never go near Marcy or the girls again. If you do, I will come back. And if I come back, you'll end up six feet under. Is that clear?"

Tears rolling down the side of his face, Chad looked up at her with big eyes. He blinked.

She leaned down closer. "Is. That. Clear?"

Chad nodded quickly. Nola gripped him by the hair and

yanked his head back before dropping it forward. Shaking, she stood and headed for the door, knowing if she stayed a moment longer, she would not be able to restrain herself.

And she wasn't sure she would regret it either.

Stepping out into the cool night air, she walked toward the car. Leaning back against it, she pulled out her cell and quickly typed a note to Bishop.

He's trussed up. Everything good with the DA?

Nola stared up at the night sky as she waited for a response. The cool air rolled over her, calming some of her anger.

We're good. I reached out to one who's got a track record of taking down these guys and not folding. She's swearing out a warrant for him tonight.

A little faster than Nola would like, but she supposed it was for the best. *Okay. What's next?*

You got a call from an old friend. He wants to meet up.

Nola raised her eyebrows at that. She didn't have a lot of friends. And she certainly wasn't going to waste her time with someone claiming a connection to her that did not exist. Back in her CIA days, she was constantly getting asked to work with different agents. They all tried to play the "friend" angle. It never worked. *Who?*

Jack.

Her heart hitched. She typed back immediately. *Send me the details.*

Chapter One

NOLA

Located just northwest of Scranton, Pennsylvania, Clarks Summit was a small mountain town set just off Interstate 81. The history of Clarks Summit dated back to the Revolutionary War when the founder, William Clark, fought in the Battle of Bunker Hill. As a reward for his service, he was given 800 acres in Pennsylvania. Later, the gift was ruled illegal, and Clark ended up buying the land himself. He and his sons erected a log cabin in the woods, and that was the beginning of Clarks Summit. Its more recent claim to fame was as a location in the "Threat Level Midnight" episode of *The Office*.

For most people, though—besides the five thousand plus who called the town home—Clarks Summit was a convenient stop off the highway in between Scranton and New Jersey.

Which was exactly its purpose for Nola today. She pulled off I-81 onto the main road, her gaze flicking to the spot where Friendly's had once stood. She, David, and Molly had once gone there on their way up to Santa's workshop in northern New York. Friendly's had been Molly's favorite restaurant. She loved their desserts. Her eyes would grow bright, and her smile would be wide as she looked at the laminated menu, trying to decide which sundae she was going to get. Yet each time it was always the same one: Monster Mash.

The Clarks Summit Friendly's had closed down years ago. The building that had housed it was now just an empty husk, all its memories locked inside.

Averting her gaze, Nola continued down the road to the large McDonald's. The McDonald's was a newer addition to the Clarks Summit area. Its golden arches stood as a beacon for weary travelers, much like a lighthouse would have been for weary sailors in days long past..

Pulling into the parking lot, she reversed into a spot at the back of the lot so that her hood was facing out. Then she settled back to wait.

Jack DiMeola. She hadn't spoken with him in years, but what he'd said to Bishop was correct: He was one of the few people she considered a friend. They'd met at work. He'd been on his way out of the CIA while she'd been on her way in. Jack had been around for decades, and for the first two years had shown Nola some tricks of the trade. He'd been a rare find in the CIA: a good man. He was loyal to his country and to his fellow agents.

A few years before he planned on retiring, he hurt his knee and ended up on desk duty. That had been the end of it for Jack. He was not a desk jockey. He took early retirement.

But Nola had kept in touch with him during her years with the agency. He'd been a great sounding board. The last time she'd seen him had been at Molly and David's funeral. He'd told her he was there if she needed him. A lot of people said that at the time, but she knew Jack meant it. She'd never called him, though.

She'd never called anyone.

A paint truck with *Two Jacks Painting* on the side rolled into the lot and then reversed into a spot a few down from Nola.

Nola stepped out of the car as Jack stepped out of his. He'd put on a little weight in the last few years, but he still looked pretty good, considering he was pushing sixty. His brown hair had yet to show any evidence of gray, and his build still looked solid. There were a few more lines around his eyes. Nola hoped they were from laughing and not worrying. Jack was one of those people who deserved a good life.

He walked around the car toward Nola, a smile on his face. "Aren't you a sight for these old eyes."

"Old? You're never going to be old, Jack."

Jack smiled as he gripped Nola's hand with his lightly paint-splattered one. His white painting pants and top were similarly dotted with paint, although there were only a few specks here and there. Apparently Jack was a relatively neat painter.

During his downtime, Jack used to paint landscapes. But Nola supposed landscapes didn't exactly pay the bills. "So, house painter, huh?"

Lifting his large shoulders, Jack shrugged. "It's a living. Got bored pretty quick after leaving the agency and trying to find some hobbies. Needed something to fill the time, so my brother-in-law and I started a painting business. It actually pays pretty well. And you know I don't like a desk job."

"That I do."

He nudged his chin toward the restaurant. "I'll go grab us a few things. Be back in five."

Nola just nodded as he headed away. Jack didn't want two agents to be indoors at the same time. He always wanted one outside. Apparently that still counted even when you were no longer in the business.

Nola made her way over to one of the picnic tables set up at the back of the lot. Ten minutes later, Jack joined her, placing a bag and a disposable cup in front of her.

He looked down at her, his eyebrows raised. Nola pulled open the bag and looked at the double cheeseburger and fries inside. Then she took a sip of the drink. Chocolate shake. "I should have known you'd remember."

Jack chuckled as he took a seat across from her. "Hard to forget. Most people change up their order every once in a while. You were a slave to the double cheeseburger."

Like mother, like daughter, Nola thought. "I don't have them as much anymore. The weight doesn't stay off quite as easily as it did when I was younger."

Patting his slightly rounded belly, Jack smiled. "Don't I know it."

The two of them ate in silence for a few minutes, and Nola enjoyed just sitting there with someone that she hadn't seen in a while but who she knew incredibly well.

She hadn't lied earlier: Jack still looked good. He could easily pass for late thirties. He'd been an avid triathlete before the knee injury. But it looked like he'd found some other way to keep himself in shape.

Taking a bite of her cheeseburger and relishing the taste, she studied the man who sat across from her. Jack looked the same, and he acted almost the same. But she could feel the sadness around the edges, even though he tried to hide it. "So what's going on?"

Rolling up his finished wrapper, he pushed it back into the bag. "We had a bit of a rough patch. Still in a bit of a rough patch, my family and I."

"Terry?"

Jack shook his head. "No, for some reason that woman is still standing by me. Kids are good too. No, it's, uh, it's my sister. Well, my niece, really. Cindy."

Nola knew Cindy. Jack had been so excited whenever he talked about her. The apple of his eye. He had all boys, so Cindy was his unofficial daughter. Even though he had his own kids, he still bragged about Cindy like she was one of his. "How's she doing?"

His lips tightened as he shook his head. "She's gone, Nola."

Nola sucked in a breath, even though she should have expected the response. "What happened?"

With troubled eyes, Jack stared out over the parking lot. "She took a handful of pills about two months ago. She was in a coma for a few days, but then the doctor said there was no hope."

Frowning, Nola tried to do the math. "How old was she?"

"Twenty."

Nola closed her eyes, feeling the weight of such a loss. When she opened them, she was unsurprised to see Molly had slipped onto the bench next to her. Eight years old, her dark hair was in two long braids with red ribbons at the ends. She wore her navy-blue sweatshirt with HAPPY stenciled across the front, each letter in a different color. Red leggings and chunky Ugg boots completed the look. Nola had always loved her in that outfit.

"She's okay, Mommy," Molly said, her dark eyes peering into Nola's.

Nola looked down at her daughter for a moment and then back at Jack. "Is that why you called me?"

He leaned forward. "I've heard some things in the last couple of years. Since you left the agency. I have an idea of what you do with your time these days."

"Oh, do you?"

"I don't take exception to it. Molly, she was—" Jack cut off. "Whatever you need to do to get through that, I get it. That pain, it's a place that I didn't even like to visit for long when I thought about what happened to your family. But now, I feel like I live there too. "

A lump formed in Nola's throat, and this time she was the one who looked away. She glanced back down at the bench next to her, but Molly was gone.

Jack took off his cap and ran a hand through his hair. "God, I'm making a mess of this. I swear I'm making a mess of everything these days." His voice and his hands shook.

"Why don't you start at the beginning?"

"Yeah, yeah," he said. But he didn't start talking right away. Nola finished up her sandwich and was halfway through her fries before he started to speak.

He cleared his throat. "Cindy was a sophomore at Indiana University at Richmond. She had a full soccer scholarship. She was good, really, really good. The whole family would trek up to see her games. Even the US team had come asking about her plans for the future. She looked really, really happy."

Placing his hands on the tabletop as if to brace himself for the words yet to be said, he took a breath.

"And then everything changed. She started doing badly in classes. She was barely training. Something had happened, but she wouldn't tell any of us what. Her mom and I went up to go see her one weekend, and it was like she was a different person. We brought her home at the end of the semester. And that's when she finally told her mom."

Nola knew what he was going to say before she said it. "She was raped," she said softly.

Jack rolled one of the napkins from the table into a tight ball in his fist. He gave a short nod. "Yes. She'd actually tried to get him charged. But the university forces those kinds of complaints through a mediation process."

The mediation process: an absolute end run around the criminal justice system. Companies and corporations often forced employees to go through the less-formal process, which benefited the corporation rather than the complainant. For college and universities, it was no different. Rather than go through a formal police department, cases of sexual assault were brought to a committee on campus.

The committee was staffed by administrators, faculty members, and maybe one student. The student then had to explain to these college representatives what had happened. And more times than not, the college would argue that there wasn't enough evidence and therefore there was nothing they could do.

Which meant that the perpetrator got away with it while the victim was left devastated.

"When Louise brought her home," Jack said, "she thought maybe things would get better. And they seemed to. In fact, right before, she seemed really happy." He broke off, his chin trembling.

Nola closed her eyes. It wasn't unusual for suicide victims to be happy just before they took their life. The pressure was gone because they'd already made the decision.

Jack continued. "Louise found her. She started screaming, and I swear she didn't stop for hours. I was there picking up my brother-in-law. There was nothing we could do. We called the ambulance, but her heart had stopped. My brother-in-law and I managed to get it started again, but her brain, it had been deprived of oxygen for too long."

Nola's heart went out to him. Jack had always been a huge family man. When he'd worked for the agency, he hated being away for the holidays. He tried to get home as much as he could.

During Nola's first year as an agent, he'd actually brought her home with him for the holidays. It had been a Christmas like she'd never seen. There'd been kids running around, presents everywhere, and garlands wrapped around the long banister in the hall and draped from all the doorways. It had been her first Hallmark Christmas. She honestly thought those type of holidays only happened in the movies. And Jack's family had treated her like she was one of them.

And she remembered Cindy. Back then, she had curly pale-brown hair in two pigtails. She'd had these dark-brown eyes that were huge and that seemed to light up every time she smiled. Wearing a bright-red velvet dress, white tights, and black patent leather shoes, she looked like she'd stepped out of a Christmas movie too.

In Nola's mind, that was always the picture of Cindy that came to mind whenever Jack mentioned her, even years later. And a feeling of warmth would flow through her at the thought of that bright smile. The image of Cindy had stayed so strong in her mind, the wholesomeness of that little Christmas girl, that Nola had bought Molly a similar dress, complete with white stockings and black patent leather shoes.

And now both Christmas girls were gone.

Rage had started to curl around the edges of her mind as she thought of how alone Cindy must have felt to take that final step. "What do you want me to do?"

Jack took a deep breath. His gaze met hers straight on. "I want you to make them pay, Nola."

"Them?"

"Anyone who pushed her to the point where she couldn't face another day. As far as I'm concerned, they're all responsible for what happened to Cindy: the monster who did this and everyone that helped keep him hidden." Jack's gaze speared into her.

Nola didn't look away as she nodded, "I'll take care of it."

Chapter Two

Nola and Jack didn't speak for much longer after she agreed to track down those responsible for Cindy's rape and suicide. As Nola pulled out of the parking lot, she took some deep breaths, trying to stem the rage she'd kept locked down while talking to Jack. Rape on a college campus was practically endemic. More than a quarter of all college women experienced sexual assault. Yet instead of that being a call to action, a call to change the mindset of men, the onus was put solely upon women to protect themselves. It infuriated Nola how the responsibility for preventing rape was placed upon the victims.

It wasn't just college campuses where they urged women to be vigilant. During the pandemic over in Great Britain, a rape case resulted in the police department strongly suggesting all women stay inside for their safety. The women staged a rally instead, questioning out loud why women should be told to stay in and not men. After all, the one thing the police agreed on was that the perpetrator was male.

But that was how it went. Women were told not to walk alone, not to drink too much, not to be too rude when turning down a guy, not to dress too provocatively, and not to flirt too much, lest a guy get the wrong idea. As if a single glance wouldn't be enough in certain cases for a guy to get the wrong idea.

And then even with all those warnings, when a woman spoke up and told what had happened to her, one of the first responses she had to deal with was doubt. Somehow in a society that constantly told women they needed to protect themselves from becoming a victim, claiming to be a victim was not believable.

The idea that Cindy was victimized and then re-victimized when the school essentially told her that her word was not enough made Nola see red. Society was failing women on so many levels.

It took a good hour for Nola to calm down enough to shove the anger to the back of her mind, where it lay simmering. And she knew it wasn't just this case. There were pockets of her life that she had walled off, trying not to think about them. But this case would start battering at some of those walls.

For that alone, she wondered for just a brief moment if she should consider turning this down. But almost as soon as she had the thought, she discarded it. Jack asked her for help. And she was damn well going to give it to him. She'd just have to shore up those walls of hers.

Her thoughts turned to Indiana University at Richmond. It was a big football school if Nola was recalling correctly. If Nola was going to head out to IUR, she was going to need some resources and to do some research first. Normally, Bishop found her most cases and sent her a case file of what she'd compiled. But since Nola found this case, things were going to work a little differently this time.

She wasn't, however, starting off completely blind. Jack had two sources for Nola to tap: Cindy's former roommate and a physical trainer who Cindy had liked a great deal. The former roommate, a girl named Jen Winfrey, had been at the funeral but had been avoiding Jack's calls for the last few weeks. But she was still on campus. She picked up her phone and dialed Bishop.

"You're going to the university in Richmond?" Bishop asked when Nola explained what her plan was.

Nola popped the phone into the cup holder after placing it on speaker. "Yeah. I need some background on the school, its structure, who's in charge of sexual assaults on campus."

"There's probably a sexual assault office of some type. Normally, it falls under affirmative action or student development," Bishop mumbled. Nola could picture her at her laptop, her mass of blonde-brown curls tied haphazardly above her head. Her face highlighted by the glow of the screen. "Looks like, yeah, they have a student issues coordinator. They cover a lot of ground: sexual harassment, sexual misconduct, student grievances. Huh."

"What's huh?"

"Looks like they used to have a position focused on sexual misconduct exclusively. But that got weeded out in a reshuffling of the administration. The former person in charge left the college during the restructuring. She would have been the one that Cindy reported the incident to."

"I'm going to need her name and contact info."

"No problem. I've started a file for you."

"Good. I'll need a cover too." She knew if she was just

24

wandering around campus asking questions, it could cause problems.

"Well, you won't be able to pass for an undergrad. You might work as a graduate student," Bishop mumbled.

Nola rolled her eyes. "I wasn't suggesting I go undercover as a freshman. And are you saying I'm old?"

"What? No, of course not. You look really good for your age."

"Maybe you should stop talking now," Nola said dryly.

"I think I should have stopped a while ago," Bishop muttered, and Nola could picture her wince. "But seriously, I think a grad student would be the best cover. A professor would require a lot of interaction with other professors. I can create a fellowship, or maybe there's one I could utilize that no one's using. Anything else?"

Nola mulled the question over for a minute. "Yeah, actually. For the cover, make sure my research targets sexual assault. It'll help when I start asking questions."

"Okay, good. That's a good idea. No problem. You, uh, heading right there?"

"No, I'm stopping by the estate. I need to grab a few things."

"Oh, good. I'll be around for dinner. When will you be here?"

"Should be around that time."

"Awesome. See you then." Bishop hung up.

The estate was the home of Nola's mother-in-law, Ileana Hamilton. It was also the closest thing to a home that Nola had these last few years. But on the occasions she was there, she only stayed a few days at a time.

From her current area of Pennsylvania, it was only a few hours away. She supposed she could head right to Richmond. It was going to be a long drive. But she found she didn't relish the solitude of the drive. The idea of stopping by the estate held more than a little appeal.

She didn't look too closely at those feelings. She just accepted that they were there, even though they were a radical break from her way of working ever since a terrorist had taken her husband and daughter in a bombing that had been targeting her.

For years, she'd been tracking down the people the criminal justice system couldn't touch. She'd been the one that finally got justice for the victims. And she still had a passion for that. That hadn't changed at all.

But the need to close herself off from everyone *had* started to change. She still preferred her own company, but now there were a select few she wanted in her orbit more often. Most people looking at her situation would probably think it was Rafe and his family that had stirred the change. And perhaps they had sped it up.

But the truth was it had been that case down in Georgia. Meeting Rascal and Anna Mae's brother, something about that case had started the shift. And then Rafe, Sofia, and Enzo had accelerated that change.

"They're your home base now."

A quick glance at the rearview mirror revealed her daughter, forever age eight, now sitting in the backseat.

"Hi, sweetheart. What did you say?"

"Rafe, Sofia, Enzo, Grandma, Bishop, Avad—they're your home base now. You didn't have one for a long time. But together, they all made you want one. It's good. It means you're healing."

"That's some pretty in-depth analysis for a little girl."

Molly met her gaze in the mirror. "I'm not a little girl anymore. That's just how you see me."

A lump formed in Nola's throat. Molly was her world.

She had been since the moment she'd been born. Even before their deaths, Nola had kept her circle small. She'd learned earlier in life how letting someone in opened the door to pain. But with Molly, there'd been no walls with her. Walls had been an impossibility. Molly had become her heart, one that walked around outside Nola's chest.

Then someone destroyed her heart.

But maybe she was wrong and Molly was right. Maybe her heart hadn't been completely destroyed. Maybe it was actually starting to heal.

And part of Nola, a part that she rarely acknowledged, could admit that she liked the idea of that.

Chapter Three

The drive to Maryland was shorter than a lot of Nola's drives over the last few years. When a case was too far away, she would fly. But if possible, she preferred to drive. She'd gotten used to the long stretches of road, even looked forward to them. Locked in the car, away from people, it was perfect solitude. Drives took on an almost meditative quality for her.

Today, though, the long drive only served to fan the anger she'd been keeping a lid on. She couldn't help but think about what Jack and his family had been through. Rarely did Nola wander into the world of what-ifs, but her mind couldn't help but question how she would have handled the same situation with Molly.

And the answer? Badly. In fact, homicidal would probably be a better word. Jack never had that same killer edge that Nola had. And time and grief had dulled that kind of fire in him.

The death of Molly and David had only fine-tuned those impulses within Nola. And picturing Molly as Cindy wasn't helping calm her anger. Even without that link, she couldn't get the picture of Cindy as a little girl out of her mind. What right did anyone have to attack, to destroy the innocence, the trust of such a beautiful soul?

No one had that right. Which meant Nola was going to make someone pay.

By the time Nola reached the edge of Ileana's driveway, she'd pulled that anger back again, another good reason for the long drive. As her wheels touched the asphalt surface, Bishop sent her a text to let her know she was at the house.

Nola didn't bother responding, knowing Avad would let Bishop know she'd arrived. Instead, Nola focused on the estate grounds. It was stunning. Summer was nearly over, but the estate was still in full bloom. Ileana had hired an exceptional landscape architect who made sure there was always something blooming with color during the warm seasons. Right now, everywhere she looked, she spied irises, snapdragons, black-eyed Susans, and a new addition: sunflowers.

She smiled at the tall flowers that soared upwards of ten feet. In the early spring, she'd brought the seeds home and started them with Enzo and Sofia in the greenhouse. Each time she'd been back, the kids had shown her the seeds' progress. The kids had been in charge of watering them. Back in late May, they had finally put them in the ground, dotting a few here and there across the estate. Not all had survived, but enough had that they brought smiles to the kids' faces.

And now, seeing a group of six full grown, they brought a smile to Nola's as well.

As Nola made her way along the long drive, Ileana's home came into view. The homes Nola had grown up in were dilapidated, just a step shy of condemned buildings.

The two-story home in front of her now was something from a story book. Brown and white stone covered the exterior with white shutters. The house extended out on each side, and a side porch on the left acted as a three-season room. In front was a circular driveway where a well-manicured hedge encircled a fountain. It looked like a perfect English estate.

Pulling to a stop near the front door, Nola stepped outside as a squeal of laughter erupted from the back of the house. With a glance at the front door and a thought to Bishop waiting inside with the details she'd managed to find on Cindy, Nola still found herself heading around the side of the house.

Following the limestone pavers, she stepped into the backyard a moment later. A patio was to her right, a blue-and-white-striped awning extended over it. A new outdoor kitchen, which had been created earlier in the summer, stood along the back end.

Avad, standing at six and a half feet, his blond hair just beginning to gray at the age of fifty-six, had his back to Nola as he oiled the grill in preparation for the night's meal. Avad was Ileana's head of security, but he was more than that. He was family, and he also was someone Nola could call on to help with when she needed it. And like family, he sometimes showed up to help even when he wasn't called.

A tire swing had been added to the weeping willow not far from the patio. Sofia, her long dark hair flying behind her, sat on the swing and was being pushed by her younger brother, Enzo. And helping her was Rafe Ortiz. Tall, with broad shoulders and an even more tanned complexion than usual, he laughed as he watched his children's antics.

And Nola realized she'd been mistaken. Enzo wasn't helping push his sister. He was trying to catch her. Each time Rafe pushed the swing, Enzo sprinted to the other side to catch her before sprinting back again.

An adult would pay good money for a personal trainer to make them do such an exercise. But like most kids, Enzo looked completely unbothered by the physical activity.

With another push of the swing, Rafe looked up, his dark eyes smiling as he caught sight of her. "Nola."

Pushing through the dropping branches of the willow, she smiled. "Hey. I'm just stopping in to pick up a few things."

Enzo immediately stopped playing with his sister and sprinted over to Nola, wrapping his arms around her, burying his head into her side.

A feeling of warmth rolled through her, along with the feeling of rightness. She didn't know exactly what her role was in Rafe's family, but she knew she enjoyed having one. She leaned down and rubbed Enzo's back. "Hey there."

This had been Enzo's standard greeting every time Nola came home. And Nola found that she looked forward to it. Still clinging to Nola, Enzo leaned his head against her thigh and looked up at her. "Are you staying for dinner?"

Originally, Nola had planned on just zipping in, grabbing what she needed, and heading out. It was going to be a long drive out to Indiana.

But there was such hope on Enzo's face. She couldn't destroy it. "Yes, I'll stay for dinner, and I won't leave until tomorrow morning."

He grinned. "Good."

Nola looked up and caught Rafe's eyes. He smiled back at her, echoing his son. "Good."

Chapter Four

Bishop wanted a little more time to finish up her file before she discussed it with Nola. So Nola did some laundry, had dinner with everyone, and just basically enjoyed her time at home. She was just zipping up her bag when there was a knock at the door.

Nola turned around to find Bishop standing there. Biracial, with a Nigerian mother and Iranian father, Bishop had pale-brown skin and a riot of freckles across her nose and cheeks. Her eyes were a pale green and her hair a mass of curls she rarely, if ever, tamed. She was also brilliant and worked as an analyst for the CIA.

Her smile disappeared as she caught sight of the bag. "You're not leaving tonight, are you?"

Nola dropped the bag on the bench at the end of the bed. "No. I promised the kids we'd watch a movie. I'll head out first thing in the morning."

Bishop's relief was quick. "Good. They'd be really disappointed if you left before then."

That was true, but Nola knew the kids weren't the only

ones who'd be disappointed. Bishop had lived with her before she'd met David and had been there for Molly growing up. She'd only moved into her own place shortly before the two of them passed away. Molly, David, and Nola had been Bishop's first real family. Losing David and Molly had been so tough for her. And Nola hadn't been there for her. She hadn't been capable of being there for her. Luckily, Ileana and Avad had stepped in.

She still felt guilty about that, but at the time, there was nothing she could do. It took everything in her just to keep breathing.

Bishop held up her tablet. "I finished compiling your file."

Taking a seat on the bed, she patted the spot next to her. "What have we got?"

Making her way around the bed, Bishop kicked off her slippers and hopped up on the bed next to Nola. Then she handed her a small envelope. "I got you a cover. You are Nola James, sociologist grad student doing research on sexual assaults on campuses. You're working on your PhD and are visiting from Canada."

"I'm Canadian?" Nola asked, pulling out the documentation.

"It's an international fellowship. The applicant dropped out at the last minute, and it was a good fit."

Nola smiled. "I'm not complaining. I'm impressed you were able to do all of this so quickly. Do I have to report to anyone or anything?"

"Nope, that's the great thing about fellowships. It's basically money for doing research. No taking classes. No teaching them."

"There must be some oversight."

"Yeah, you're supposed to report to a professor about

your progress. I chose Dr. Avian Landing. He is on a research trip to England. He won't be back for two months."

"By which time I will be long gone." Nola paused.

Bishop was staring at her tablet with a frown.

"What is it?" Nola asked.

"Just thinking about college. It's a strange beast. Ostensibly, the goal is to educate the student body, but with a school like IUR, their priority is often less focused on educating than money making, through sports in particular. And IUR is rolling in dough." Bishop's frown deepened as she flipped to another screen. "They have one of the most lucrative football programs out there."

College football was never something that interested Nola. "So it's a good team?"

"Actually, it's only okay. But they have some huge contracts with merchandising and TV. The football team brings in fifty-two million annually."

Nola nearly choked on her water. "Fifty-two million? That's insane."

"And that's only what the college makes. The boosters, advertisers, they make bank too. Football programs like IUR are a cash cow."

Nola knew football programs made bank, but that was a whole other level. "Does the college make that much from tuition?"

"Not even close," Bishop said.

"So the sports program is more important."

Bishop nodded. "Sports programs at schools like that are on a different level to the point that they are a different world. Education is not a consideration. In fact, many have gotten in trouble for helping their star athletes to the point of grade manipulation and even substitution. Sports are *the* priority."

Nola frowned. "But most of these kids don't go on to play professional sports."

"Correct. Of college players, less than 2% will go on to play professional. For the kids that don't make it, college is the high point. And for many, it's a very quick downward slide after that. They may have the degree, but not the knowledge that goes with it. It's a complete disservice to the students. America is the only country that puts such an emphasis on sports. To the rest of the world, that emphasis is confounding: education is so much more important."

Nola knew that was true. And she herself never understood it. Even in high school, football players were often at the top of the social hierarchy, regardless of their grades. Smart kids were never lauded for their achievements on the same level. There were no pep rallies or cheerleaders for the debate team or the mathletes.

Sitting next to her, Bishop flipped through different web pages, her eyes shifting across the images quickly as she took in the info. "How do you know all of this? I didn't think college sports would be of interest to you."

"Oh, it's not. But foreign adversaries who despise the US still want to send their children here for college. So there have been a few cases that have extended to US universities. We've kept our eye on some of the comings and goings. As a result, I had to see what makes colleges work."

"And what does make colleges work?"

"Money," Bishop replied without hesitation. "So if you're looking for what's behind Cindy's death, don't forget to follow the money. And right now, that might be your best bet because I can't find any indication of Cindy even filing a complaint."

Nola frowned. "Really?"

"I'm not sure that means that she didn't. Apparently they bury the reports that go nowhere, and although I've only done a quick search, it seems like *all* the reports go nowhere. I get the feeling the university wants to make sure they don't get any bad press."

"How much would bad press cost them?" Nola asked.

"It could be millions. They have a standing TV contract that allows their football games to be broadcast every weekend, same with basketball."

"And claims of rape, even if not from a member of the team, would make advertisers nervous," Nola replied.

"Yup." Bishop nodded. "And they've got a lot of boosters who are pretty powerful. I ran a few names, and they're all well-connected, wealthy and influential."

"The type who could make cases disappear?" Nola asked.

Bishop shrugged. "Can't say for sure. But doesn't seem impossible."

"What about the college itself?"

Her eyes flicking to the screen, Bishop said, "Well, the president's only been in place for three years and spends a lot of time talking about the their impressive sports teams. Legendary is a term he uses a lot. And he's brought a lot of money into the university, so it's safe to say they like him."

"What about the two names Jack gave me?"

"The roommate is on the tennis team. Was a good student, her grades took a little dive at the beginning of the semester right after Cindy's ," Bishop paused, searching for a word, ". . . incident. But they seemed to have stabilized. She called Cindy a lot this summer and texted too. The texts were just the checking-in type. Cindy stopped responding two weeks before . . . well, before."

"She's still at the school?"

"Yeah," Bishop said.

"Okay, what about the trainer?"

Flipping through a few files, Bishop nodded. "Leslie Barrack has been with the university for ten years. She's a physical therapist and works with all the athletes. She worked with Cindy after she pulled her hamstring two years ago. They seemed to get along real well. From what I could tell, I got a bit of a big-sister vibe from her."

"Jack says he thinks she'd be of some help."

Bishop shrugged. "Could be. She texted Cindy a few times over the summer as well, same kind of checking-in type of texts. It seemed Cindy was pulling away from her people."

Sighing, Nola imagined Cindy closing herself off. Bishop was quiet next to her. A glance showed she was staring at the tablet, but her mind seemed a million miles away. And Nola wanted to kick herself. This case was probably bringing up some bad memories for her. Before Nola had found her, she had not had an easy time of it.

"Hey, thanks for all this. But why don't I use Avad or Rafe for this case? You don't need to be—"

"No," Bishop said quickly and firmly. "I'm good. And Cindy, from what I could tell, she was a good person. Whoever did this needs to pay. And I want to help make that happen."

The commitment was in Bishop's gaze but also the pain she was trying so hard to mask. But wasn't that how it was? They all walked around trying to keep others from seeing the darkness that was trying to worm its way through them.

Nola wrapped an arm around Bishop and pulled her head onto her shoulder. "And I'm glad to have you."

And then the two just sat in the quiet, both trying to tamp down the darkness they rarely let anyone else see.

Chapter Five

True to her word, Nola stayed and watched a Disney movie with the kids. It was about second-born royals with supernatural powers. The kids had enjoyed it, as had Bishop. It wasn't exactly Nola's cup of tea, but watching the rest look happy, that had been good.

The drive to Richmond the next morning was uneventful. Nola listened to a murder mystery for the car ride. She guessed the killer three chapters in, but it had been a good way to pass the time.

As she drew closer to the city of Richmond, she saw more and more signs of the university: bumper stickers, billboards, T-shirts, and souvenir stores. Almost every car seemed to have something associated with the university attached to it.

Never mind the sports teams, the university must be raking it in hand over fist from all the merchandising. The university was so large it actually spanned three exits. The third was closest to the house Bishop had arranged for her, but Nola pulled off at the first exit. She wanted to get a feel for the area before setting up shop.

A massive wrought-iron sign greeted her only a half mile from the exit, heralding the entrance to the university. Pristine sidewalks outlined the tree-lined drive. Different buildings, most in red brick, were scattered on either side. Students and a few parents wandered along the campus, making Nola realize that Bishop had been correct: She would never pass as a college kid. These kids looked way too young.

And way too excited. Each kid seemed to be beaming, looking forward to the year ahead. The semester had started yesterday. No one looked worried or scared. And the campus helped with that, being so big and bright.

In a strange sort of way, the clean lines of the place almost made it feel more trustworthy. What could possibly go wrong in such a place?

Driving through the campus took a good thirty minutes. The place was expansive. And the longer Nola drove, the less appealing the space seemed. Besides the expected dormitories and classrooms, there were restaurants, bars, apartments, massive gyms, and athletic fields. Lots of activities for people who might legally be adults but emotionally weren't. That seemed like a recipe for disaster, especially with the amount of money the college was making. Add in that it was a city populated by kids aged between eighteen and twenty-two, not exactly the most level-headed of ages, and you had all the ingredients for some really poor decision-making.

By the time she left the campus, Nola was feeling slightly nauseated. She left by the west entrance over by the absolutely massive football stadium. It was true she knew little about sports, even less about college sports, but she had to think that that stadium was supersized.

Like many colleges and universities, the neighborhoods surrounding the university weren't quite as well-kept. Nola drove through street after street of rental properties. College kids were everywhere here as well, taking advantage of the leases that allowed them to be around campus long before the dorms were open.

Three blocks from the campus, music blared from a two-story home with wooden porches both on the first and second floor. Mattresses had been stacked on the front lawn, and kids—because she simply couldn't classify them as young adults—took turns diving off the second-floor porch onto the mattresses below.

It was only men who were taking the leap. Yet again, Nola wondered how on earth anyone ever thought they were the smarter of the genders. With a shudder at their antics, she drove by quickly before one of them broke their necks and she was a witness to a crime of stupidity.

Two more turns, and Nola pulled onto Meadow Lane, wondering about the name. Perhaps the row of rundown houses had replaced a once gorgeous meadow. If so, the current state of the place was an insult to that meadow.

Nola pulled into the driveway of number 37. Turning off the car, she stopped and peered over the steering wheel at the single ranch in front of her. It had a peaked roof and two small windows on either side of a small in-need-of-some-paint wooden door. A porch had been constructed what looked like decades ago and was bowing under the pressure of time.

For the first time in a long time, instead of quickly stepping out and getting herself set up, Nola sighed and leaned back against the driver's seat. She couldn't help but think of waking up in Ileana's home this morning. She'd thought she'd sneak out before everyone woke up. But everyone seemed to know her plan. They'd all been up, and a huge breakfast had been waiting for her along with everyone still in their pajamas to see her off. For the first time in a long time, it had been hard to leave.

And now it was hard to get out of her truck. Giving herself a mental shake, she gripped the door handle and shoved the door open. *Get it together, James. Jack is counting on you.*

Remembering why she was here did the trick. She quickly headed to the front door and unlocked it. Running a sweep of the house, she found it was pretty clean. There was a living room, kitchen, one bath, and a bedroom. That was it. But that was all she needed. Grabbing her cleaning stuff from the truck, she spent an hour cleaning the place and then headed back outside for the rest of her gear.

And she learned she wasn't alone.

A gray-and-white pit bull stood quietly at the front of the drive near the house. Nola spied her after she closed the back of her truck, her arms filled with her weapons crate, computer bag, and her small duffel.

Stopping short, Nola studied the dog looking for any signs of aggression as the dog studied her back, just as intently. The dog's ribs were clear under her dirty coat. The white scars all over her body indicated that she'd been in a lot of fights. And the prominent teats indicated she'd had at least one litter of pups. Her ears had been cut short, and not cleanly. Nola wasn't sure if another dog or a human was responsible for that cruelty.

"I don't mean you any harm. I'm only going to be staying for a little bit," she said as she approached the dog.

The dog tilted its head as if listening and then turned

and walked slowly to the backyard before slipping through the fence. Nola watched the dog go and then turned for the house. Probably just a stray. There hadn't been a collar.

She secured her stuff in the house and headed back to the car. She had an appointment on campus. She'd just stepped outside when she pictured the dog again.

After a moment's hesitation, she headed back inside and into the kitchen. Pulling out an old stainless steel camping bowl, she filled it with water. Unlocking the back door, she set the bowl on the first step of the deck. Then she headed back inside, locking up again before climbing into the car and promising herself she'd see if the dog stopped by while she was out. Maybe she'd leave it some food.

But then she pushed thoughts of the dog from her mind and focused on the reason she was here: Cindy. It was time to find the monster that pushed her to the edge and then over it.

Chapter Six

The campus was busy. Some upperclassmen had been allowed to move in today, although most athletes had been on campus for a few weeks. Students were taking advantage of the unusually warm afternoon sun. A few sat or walked alone with their eyes on a screen and earbuds in. But most were in groups standing, laughing, or chatting with one another. One group of four girls sat in a circle on the ground and ignored each other as they all stared at the screens of their phones.

Nola felt like she'd stepped onto another planet. She'd never gone to college. She'd never really wanted to. This kind of world was completely foreign to her. She didn't understand the easygoing nature of the young people she saw walking around her. Even when she'd been the same age, her soul had been years older. These kids look completely immune to the dangers and realities of the world. She wondered what that would be like, to just walk through the world not knowing about the darkness at its edges, not knowing, or perhaps not focusing, on the fact that

that darkness could reach out and snatch your happiness away at any moment.

The students weren't that much younger than Bishop. She supposed Bishop could slip into this world and be part of it. She'd actually gone to college. She'd done the normal classes in an abbreviated time. But she hadn't lived on campus. At that point, she didn't feel comfortable doing so. But now Nola supposed she might be okay with it. Bishop had been through a lot in her young life, but she hadn't come out quite as scarred as Nola had, and for that Nola was grateful.

Originally, Nola had intended to speak with Cindy's roommate first. But the trainer Leslie Barrack could only meet this afternoon. With school starting, she was booked solid. If Nola didn't meet with her today, it would be a few days. So after going to the main office and getting her student ID, Nola walked into the large campus center eating area. It was nothing like the one she'd had in her high school. This one looked like a high-end food court. There had to be more than two dozen restaurants represented. Scanning them, she made a beeline for Jamba Juice.

Tables lined the walls and center of the room, but there were only a few people at them. Discounting the ones who looked barely old enough to drive and the few kids with their parents, Nola had no trouble picking out Leslie Barrack. According to the file, she was thirty-two and had been with the university for five years. She had a strong muscular build and her long light-brown hair was pulled back into a tight ponytail.

Wearing an IUR T-shirt and shorts, it was clear the woman was a believer in exercise. She looked up as Nola approached. "Nola?" she asked.

Nola nodded as she slid into the seat across from her. "Yes. Thanks for meeting with me."

Flicking a glance around, Leslie leaned forward. "I wouldn't have, except Jack called me. He asked me to talk to you. But I don't know how I can help. I feel horrible about what happened to Cindy. She didn't deserve any of that."

Nola studied the woman across from her. She could feel the grief around her, and so Nola discounted her original plan of playing up the research angle. She decided to get closer to the truth. "No, she didn't. I told Jack I'd ask around and see if I could find out who hurt her."

Leslie met her gaze and then looked away, shaking her head. "I don't know who raped her."

"But you knew about the rape." It wasn't a question.

Leslie sat back with a sigh, running a hand over her mouth. "Yeah. Cindy told me maybe a month after it happened. She had changed. She wasn't coming to her sessions, and her grades were dipping. I showed up at her dorm, pushing for answers. She burst into tears and told me what happened. She was . . . destroyed. But she wouldn't give me a name."

"Someone threatened her," Nola said.

Leslie's eyebrows rose. "You figured that out pretty quick. Took me longer. At first I thought she was in denial, but then one day she told me she wasn't allowed to tell. That someone associated with this asshole had threatened to sue her and her family for libel if his name ever came out." Leslie made a sound of disgust.

"What about her roommate?"

"Jen? She probably knows. Those two were really tight. But I don't know if she'll talk to you."

"Why not?" Nola asked.

"Jen . . . she took Cindy's death really hard. She's kind of shut a lot of people out."

"I need to speak with her."

"I'll give her a call. Tell her you'll be coming by. It might help."

"Thanks," Nola said, studying the woman across from her. "Now what aren't you telling me?"

Surprise flashed across Leslie's face, along with guilt. "What? Nothing. I told you, I don't know who hurt Cindy."

"But you know something," Nola said not letting the woman look away.

Leslie sighed. "No, not exactly. I mean, Cindy's not the first case on campus, obviously, but all the cases seem to disappear. Nothing ever happens, and it never makes it to the media. Someone's got to be covering them up."

"Any idea who that might be?"

Leslie threw up her hands. "Honestly, it could dozens of people. A lot of people with a lot of money count on IUR's squeaky-clean image. But for the cases to disappear, it has to be more than one person." She paused. "I know this is your research area. But you need to be careful. You start kicking around this hornet's nest, it's going to come back to you."

"That's okay. I've grown immune to their stings."

"I hope so." Leslie stood up. "I'm sorry, I've got to run. I'm meeting one of the students."

"No problem. But if you could call Jen?"

"I will. I'll do it right now." Leslie pulled out her phone, then stopped. "What are you going to do when you find the person who did this?"

"Make them pay."

Pausing, Leslie met her gaze, her jaw tightening. "Good."

Nola watched her walk off dialing the phone as she went. Once she disappeared through the doors, Nola turned and studied the other people in the cafeteria. She couldn't help but contrast it with her own experience in a school cafeteria.

Night and day, she thought as she stood.

Chapter Seven

NOLA
TWENTY-ONE YEARS AGO

The aroma of hamburgers and fries wafted out from the cafeteria as fifteen-year-old Nola James pulled the door open. She wrinkled her nose at the smell. A rumor had gone around last year that the hamburgers were delivered in boxes labeled "Grade D but edible." She could never bring herself to eat another one. It wasn't a huge loss. They tasted like ketchup-drenched hockey pucks.

As Nola stepped inside, the cafeteria was a buzz of voices. A quick glance around showed the usual high school suspects. The jocks had taken up their position along the windows to the right. Half a dozen football players in their jerseys sat on tabletops while their admiring fans sat nearby.

Nola rolled her eyes at the display. The football team had lost about 75 percent of their games so far this season and yet somehow they still walked around with their chests puffed up, acting as if they were kings of the school.

She supposed she couldn't really blame them. After all, everyone treated them like they were.

On the left-hand side of the cafeteria were the more studious, quiet kids who broke off into groups of three or four. In the middle were the kids who straddled those two lines, sometimes hanging out with the cool kids when there was a big enough party and sometimes hanging with the quieter kids at the same events.

Nola belonged in none of those groups. She certainly wasn't a jock. And while she was quiet, it wasn't due to shyness. Plus, she had zero interest in any of the parties that were being held by her intellectually starved peers.

Wistfully, she stared at the rain pouring down outside the windows. Normally she would eat outside, but today's weather had made that all but impossible.

As she wove her way through bodies and tables, barely anyone even glanced at her. She was fine with that. She knew all their names. But she had a feeling only about a half a dozen or so really knew her full name, even though she had been in this school district almost since kinder-garten. Her father might not have been the best, but he'd at least managed to keep her in the same district for most of her life, if not the same house.

For two years, she'd gone to school in a district neigh-boring this one. Her father had been locked up, and the foster system hadn't asked which school district she preferred. She was pretty sure that almost all of the kids she was looking at never even realized she'd been gone and then magically reappeared. Or at least, no one had said anything.

A hand waved at her from the edge of a table on the left-hand side of the room. The hand belonged to the person who made all the difference as to what school district she attended. Nola gave Beth Landry a nod and headed toward her.

Beth, at least, had noticed. She and Beth had been friends for as long as Nola could remember. In her early life, Beth lived five houses down on the opposite side of the street from her. After her father had gotten locked up, they'd had to move a few blocks away to a different house. But Beth had been thrilled to see Nola back.

Nola slumped into the seat across from her, placing her brown paper lunch bag on the table. "I hate when it rains," she grumbled.

Beth smiled. "You hate everything that has to do with school."

Nola shrugged. "You're not wrong."

Beth gave one of her trilling laughs, and Nola was once again amazed that the two of them were friends. They were as different as two people could be both in looks and appearance. Nola's hair was a pale, nearly white blonde, while Beth's was a dark drown. Beth's skin was also darker, thanks to her father's Kenyan roots.

But their physical appearances were really the least of their differences. Beth had a Pollyanna view to life. She never seemed to see the dark side of things, only the light. Nola was the complete opposite. If there was even a hint of a shadow in a situation, Nola teased it out until it covered her entire view.

And yet somehow the two of them had met when they were young, and they clicked. Nola supposed it was a perfect example of opposites attracting.

Digging the peanut butter and jelly sandwich out of her bag, she grabbed a milk off of Beth's tray. "Thanks."

Beth nodded at her, not replying. Every day, Beth bought her milk. Nola's father more often than not forgot to give

Nola money for lunch. Her peanut butter and jelly sandwich was made with the ends of a loaf that she had managed to secret away in her room before her father came home in one of his drunken stupors and finished the damn thing.

But luckily, last night she'd managed to find twenty bucks in his pocket when he passed out on the couch. She'd pick up a few supplies at the supermarket on the way home and stashed them away. She planned to ask him later if he had any money for groceries and get some for the house.

It was not an easy way to live, but Nola had grown accustomed to it. After his stint inside, her father hadn't exactly turned over a new leaf. Although now that she thought about it, she supposed he had in his own sort of way. He was no longer into anything illegal because he definitely didn't want to go back to prison, but he hadn't come out a better man. If anything, he'd come out a worse one.

Nola just had to make it to the end of high school, and then she was out of there. She'd already decided that she was going to sign up for the Marines the day she turned eighteen. It was the only guarantee she had of getting out of her house.

Sitting across from her, Beth had a very different existence. She had two parents who loved her and a grandma who doted on her. Her grades had never dipped below a B plus, and that was only in music. She was tone deaf. Colleges would one day be fighting over her. She had a bright future ahead of her.

Nola was determined to make sure that she had just as bright a future, although she had a feeling that her idea of what would make a good future would once again be radically different from Beth's. Nola had no illusions that she was a normal girl. She was attracted to the darker side of life, to the more violent. Beth wouldn't even step on a spider.

Chewing on her sandwich, she looked around the cafeteria, knowing she would not miss a moment of being in the school except for the lunches with Beth.

Barely touching her own lunch, her friend sat across from her, practically rocking in her seat. Nola frowned. "What's up with you?"

Normally Beth was a happy person, but right now she looked like she was about to burst. She let out a squeal as she leaned forward. "I have a date tonight."

Nola couldn't help the surprised look that flashed across her face. "You do?"

"Gee, thanks." Beth rolled her eyes.

"I don't mean it like that. I mean, I just didn't know you were interested in anybody. Who is it?"

Leaning forward, Beth nudged her chin toward the other side of the cafeteria. "Jerry Whitmore."

Nola managed to school her impression so her shock didn't show through, but she felt it to her bones. Jerry Whitmore was hands down the most popular senior in Gradia High School and one of the football players. He wasn't the best football player by any measure, but that did absolutely nothing to temper his popularity. His family's money and the confidence that came with it assured him a prime spot in the Gradia social scene. He was also, as far as Nola was concerned, a complete arrogant ass. But she knew that Beth had had a crush on him for years.

Which meant this was an area she was going to have to tread very carefully. "How did that happen?"

Shooting a glance across the cafeteria, Beth leaned forward, her eyes bright and her smile wide. "He asked me after English class. It was so cool. He's going to pick me up and everything."

Nola nodded slowly, not sure what to say. She did not like Jerry at all. There was something in his eyes, something shifty. Of course, she felt that way about most of the boys in her grade, but with Jerry and his friends, there was something a little extra there.

And apparently Nola hadn't been doing a good job of keeping her feelings hidden because Beth's face fell. "What? What's wrong?"

"Nothing, nothing. That's great."

Beth crossed her arms over her chest. "You say 'that's great,' but your face says 'that's horrible.'"

Nola winced. She really was blowing this. "It's not horrible. It's just . . . you know I've never really liked Jerry. I don't think you can trust him."

If Beth had laser eyes, Nola would be dead. "You don't think that anyone can be trusted."

"No, that's not true."

Her mouth in a thin line, Beth stared at her. "Tell me one kid you trust in this school besides me."

Nola's mouth opened and then shut. Beth was right. She couldn't think of a single one.

Hurt flashed across Beth's face before her chin started to tremble. "I don't know why I thought you'd be happy for me. You know I've liked him forever. Couldn't you at least pretend to be happy?"

Guilt rolled over Nola. Beth was right. She had no reason to dislike Jerry, not really. It was just a gut instinct, like when she knew one of her dad's friends was bad news. But Beth was also right that she didn't trust anyone but her. Yet her gut still gnawed at her at the idea of Beth placing her trust, even a small amount, in Jerry.

But one look at Beth's face made it clear how important this was to her. Her chin had stopped trembling, and she had that hard look to it that Nola had only seen a few times.

Stubbornness was something in their personalities that they both shared, although Beth's stubbornness rarely emerged. Taking a deep breath, Nola exhaled her mistrust and forced a smile to her face. "I'm sorry, really. That's great."

Apparently neither her words nor her smile were convincing. Beth shook her head and grabbed her tray. "Whatever. I'm going to go meet Mrs. Harper. She wanted to talk to me about some band thing."

"I'll go with you." Nola grabbed her lunch bag and started to crumple it up.

"No. I'm good. I'll see you later." Without waiting for a reply, Beth headed toward the exit, emptying her tray at the garbage can as she passed it.

A heavy feeling settled in Nola's chest as she watched her go.

Raucous laughter broke out from across the room. Nola turned and watched as a group of football players guffawed, a few slapping Jerry on the back. Jerry flashed a smile at them, pushing his dark-brown hair from his face. His green eyes caught Nola's gaze, and he gave her a smirk.

The hackles along Nola's back rose. She really did not like that guy. Jerry turned his attention back to his friends. Nola knew he'd dismissed her from his thoughts already.

Beth had received no more thought than Nola did. He'd never shown her even the slightest amount of interest. So what had changed? He and Beth had no classes together, not with the two years in between them.

Nola couldn't shake the feeling that despite Beth's

hopes, this date with Jerry wasn't going to be everything she dreamed. And for once, Nola really hoped she was wrong.

Chapter Eight

NOLA
PRESENT DAY

Cindy's former roommate still lived in the dorms on campus. Floors and sometimes entire wings of dorms had been set aside just for the college athletes. Nola made her way across the campus toward them. This side of campus was different, but the kids were still the same: carefree. Nola was pretty sure she had never been that carefree in her life.

Harriman Hall was just up ahead. It was a long two-story brown brick building. A set of wide white cement steps led to its four doors. There was a group of both male and female students sitting along the steps to the right. They barely glanced at Nola as she passed. She stepped into the main lobby, which had a large sitting area on the left side. On the right was a long conference table, although the chairs had been pushed back against the wall.

Nola stepped inside, seeing a young guy sitting behind the main desk. He didn't even glance up as she entered.

Earbuds in his ears, he bobbed along as he listened to music, staring at a notebook and doodling.

Turning to the left, Nola took the stairwell up to the second floor. Stepping out onto the floor, two girls walked around her, not even sparing her a glance.

"I checked out the syllabus for my psych class, and we have a paper due in three weeks. It was going to be so easy. It's so unfair."

"It really is," the other girl said.

Not rolling her eyes at the conversation was difficult. Such problems these youths faced. Instead, Nola focused on her surroundings. The hall was wide and each of the doors was wooden with no window on them. Most doors held a whiteboard that people could leave messages on. A few residents had decorated their doors. But when Nola stopped at room 212, there were no extra decorations, and the whiteboard sat empty.

Nola knocked quickly. Movement from inside indicated that someone was home. A few long moments later, a quiet voice called out, "Who is it?"

The question alone was unusual. College kids tended not to be overly security conscious, especially when they were in their dorm. Usually they would just fling open the door to see who was there. But apparently Jen Winfrey wasn't a typical college kid.

Jen and Cindy had been assigned as roommates freshman year. But they had clicked almost instantly and asked to be reassigned as roommates sophomore year. Jen was on the tennis team and they were both regular attendees at each other's events when their schedules allowed. Cindy's social media accounts were littered with pictures of the two of them smiling up at the camera.

But those smiles had stopped last March.

A check of Jen's social media had shown that she'd stopped her social media posts at about the same time Cindy did. The two of them went through this together.

"It's Nola James. Leslie told you I'd be coming?"

A moment later, the door opened. A tall, slender extremely pale redhead stood holding onto the handle. Her pale-brown eyes looked out from underneath red bangs that she'd obviously straightened, because the rest of her hair was a mass of long red curls. She wore no makeup, and her freckles stood out against her pale skin.

Shifting from foot to foot, she flicked a glance toward Nola's eyes before her gaze quickly darted away. "Oh, yeah, she mentioned that you'd be coming by. I just I didn't realize it would be today."

Nola moved so that her foot was in the doorway. "Mind if I come in?"

Flicking a glance behind her, Jen nodded reluctantly as she stepped back and pulled the door open wider. "Yeah, sure, sorry about the mess."

The room had two beds, one on each side of the room, with dressers tucked along the walls opposite the base of the bed. There was one large closet and a door that led to what looked like a small bathroom.

Half the room was indeed a mess. It was littered with clothes, books, and papers. But that was undeniably Jen's roommate's side. Jen's side was extremely neat. Her bed was unmade, but that was the only thing that wasn't immaculate. Jen sat on her bed and gestured toward a chair next to it.

Nola pulled it over from the desk and took a seat. "Where's your roommate?"

"She's not really here much. She just kind of comes, dumps her stuff, and takes off again." Jen's gaze darted toward a picture on the board next to her bed. Cindy and Jen stood with their arms wrapped around one another, grinning up at the camera, a bright sun and blue water behind them. Whoever this new roommate was, she definitely had not entered the friend category.

Dark circles were under Jen's eyes, indicating that she was not sleeping well. But her tennis game had improved. According to the file from Bishop, Jen had redoubled her efforts at the sport. Now that Nola had a look at her, she had no doubt that that was in part because she was exorcising her demons through her athleticism.

Grabbing a pillow, Jen crushed it to her chest. "Leslie said you wanted to talk about Cindy. She said it has something to do with your research." She swallowed nervously after she said her deceased friend's name.

Nola knew that the stereotypical approach would be for her to offer her condolences, but Nola had a feeling if she went that route, she would lose Jen. So, she decided to try a different tack. "So, you two were roommates freshman year, is that right?"

Jen nodded. "Yeah. We were assigned. Sometimes that's a complete and total disaster. But for us, it was awesome. We just kind of clicked, you know?"

From personal experience, Nola did not actually know what that felt like. But she got the gist of it. "And you were roommates last year?"

Her shoulders stiff, Jen just gave an abrupt nod.

Nola leaned forward. "I know this is difficult. But I am trying to find out what happened to Cindy. She didn't deserve what she went through."

"No, she didn't," Jen said softly.

Deciding straightforward was the best approach, Nola said, "She told you about the rape?"

With a flinch, Jen squirmed, but she nodded.

"And do you know who the assailant was?"

Jen nodded again, this time more slowly.

"Can you tell me?"

Tears forming in her eyes, Jen looked up at her. "Why? Cindy's gone. What does it have to do with your research?"

"Because I'm not just doing research. I'm also looking to get justice for victims. And yes, Cindy's gone. But that doesn't mean that he gets to get away with the harm he did to her."

A bitter laugh erupted from Jen. "He's not going to get punished. His type never gets punished."

After taking a deep breath, the words poured from her as if they had been bottled up, just waiting for a release. "She tried that, you know. And now Cindy's dead, and he's just walking around, king of the campus."

Jen's anger was palpable, and Nola couldn't blame her. "Why don't you tell me his name, and then I'll see what I can do."

"There's not anything you can do. And the college already knows his name. They've known it from the start. And I was told if I said anything about it that I would get kicked out. Not him, *me*. They'd pull my scholarship and I'd get booted." A tear leaked from the corner of her eye, and she wiped it away furiously.

Nola would like to say she was surprised by the threat, but she knew how much these big universities protected their money-making sports franchises. "How did they threaten you? Did they send you something?"

Jen shook her head. "No. I testified against the jerk in that stupid thing they called a trial. But it's not a trial. I wasn't even done speaking, and the head of security warned me that I could be sued if I said anything about him. I mean, they were saying all these horrible things about Cindy, and I'm the one who got threatened, not any of them. They lined up player after player who lied about her, and they all just got away with it. But as soon as I spoke up and told what actually happened, I was told I would lose my scholarship."

Nola didn't have to ask why she didn't just switch colleges. It was one of the things she and Cindy had in common. So it wouldn't be easy for her to switch schools. And if she did, she definitely wouldn't be able to play tennis. And it was entirely possible with the way the school was handling this situation that they might destroy her academic record, or at least make her flunk out of classes. Nola had read about it in some of the cases she had researched last night.

"Jen, I need you to listen to me."

Looking completely and totally defeated, Jen's gaze met Nola's. And Nola's anger spiked. God, she hated people who used their power this way.

"I'm not the cops. I'm not someone who's going to put your name in an official report of any kind. In fact, I'm not going to put your name anywhere. My job, my one and only job, is to bring the person that did this to Cindy to justice by whatever means are necessary. I won't get you involved, but I am going to find him. And I am going to make him pay."

Hope appeared behind Jen's eyes.

"You don't know me," Nola continued. "And you have no reason to trust me. But I promise you, I will make sure that your name isn't mentioned. I just need a name. I just need a place to start."

Flicking a gaze at the door, Jen bit her bottom lip.

Nola let the silence drag out, knowing that Jen had to

come to this decision on her own. Then there was a knock at the door.

Jen stiffened.

"Who is it?" Nola asked.

"Security. We just need to make sure that everything's all right. Can you open the door, Ms. Winfrey?"

Jen's face paled three shades as she stood up. She walked to the door like she was heading to a firing squad. She pulled the door open. Two officers stood there. The younger one flicked a glance at Jen before zeroing in on Nola. "All guests need to register with security before coming on campus."

Nola stood. "I'm not a guest. I'm a grad student."

"ID," the officer demanded.

Slowly, Nola slid the ID from her back pocket and handed it over. The officer, whose name tag said Dobson, scrutinized it like he didn't believe it was real. Finally, he handed it back. He turned to Jen. "There any problem here, Ms. Winfrey?"

Jen shook her head. "No, no problem."

"Good. If there ever is, you just give us a call," he said.

"What actually brought you guys to this door?" Nola asked. "Did someone call in a complaint?"

Dobson smirked. "Something like that." He returned his attention to Jen. "You ever have any problems, you call us. We're always around. We're always watching."

Jen paled even more at his words. She nodded slowly, and the officers headed back down the hall. Jen kept the door open and turned to Nola. "I think you should go."

"Who hurt Cindy?" Nola asked.

A tear trailed down Jen's cheek. "It doesn't matter now. You can't fight them, and neither can I. Can you please go?"

Nola wanted to press her more, but the poor girl looked like she was on the edge. And questioning her further would only push her over it.

"Okay, but I'm going to be around, and if you want to talk, you just need to call." She placed her business card on Jen's desk and then walked out. The door closed softly behind her.

And Nola knew that campus security's message to Jen had been received: keep your mouth shut.

Now Nola just needed to figure out who they were sending the message for.

Chapter Nine

Nola spent the rest of the day trying to get information from the college about sexual assaults. Each year, they were supposed to put out a report detailing the assaults on campus. For the last five years, there had been a grand total of zero cases reported on the official form.

A conversation with the new director in charge of student issues offered no further clarity. Plus, the woman kept getting interrupted as issues popped up across campus. Finally, Nola was set up in a small office with an undergrad who showed her the system and how to look for info herself. After four hours, all Nola had was a raging headache. She managed to reach Melanie Price, the previous women's advocate, but Price wouldn't be able to see her until later tomorrow.

Returning home, Nola checked the water bowl on the back deck and found it empty. Taking it back inside, she refilled it with water and grabbed the extra takeout she'd picked up. She placed the bowl back in the same spot and unwrapped the burger and fries. Not the healthiest of meals, but the dog could definitely use the fat.

After unwrapping the food, she looked around the backyard. The gray-and-white head peeked back through the hole in the fence. Nola nodded. "It's for you, girl. Enjoy."

Then she turned and headed back inside. After finishing her own dinner, Nola curled up with the info on the Sexual Misconduct Task Force, as they were now known. There was one student representative. The last one had graduated the year before, so chasing them down wouldn't be easy. But the other members were still on campus. She could speak with them tomorrow and see what they had to say for themselves.

By eight, she found herself yawning. Walking into the kitchen, she got herself a glass of water and then downed it, thinking over the events of the day. Jen had been scared, and those security officers showing up had only reinforced it. The timing was beyond suspicious. Someone was keeping an eye on Jen.

Movement in the backyard caught Nola's attention. Nola peered through the window and saw the dog stretched out on the grass. Filling up a glass, she headed outside. Keeping her movements slow, she poured the water into the dog's bowl. The dog looked over but made no move to leave. Nola nodded as she straightened. "Well, looks like you enjoyed dinner. I'll fix you something tomorrow morning. Have a good night."

It had not been an auspicious beginning to her case. In fact, it had been dreadful. She'd run background checks on the security office and the members of the committee that Cindy had spoken to. Nothing really stood out, so she'd sent the names to Bishop, hoping she'd have better luck.

Then she pushed back from the kitchen table with a

frustrated sigh. She was no closer to finding Cindy's attacker, although she was convinced that Jen at least knew his identity. She decided to call it an early night. Crawling into bed a short while later, visions of Jen and Cindy wandered through her mind. But that wasn't the last face she saw as she drifted off to sleep.

No, the last face was her first friend, Beth.

Chapter Ten

NOLA
TWENTY-ONE YEARS AGO

Nola didn't see Beth for the rest of the day. She stopped by Beth's locker as soon as the last bell sounded. Leaning against the locker for a while, she waited as the hall started to clear. Finally, she slid down to the ground, her head turning this way and that, hoping to catch a glimpse of Beth's familiar face. Fifteen minutes after the final dismissal bell had rung, it was clear Beth wasn't coming.

The hurt was quick and fast. Beth hadn't waited for her to walk home. They always walked home together. Rolling her hands into fists, Nola took a deep breath. Damn that Jerry. He was already causing problems. Pushing up off the ground, she headed for the exit.

Outside, the rain had shifted from a downpour to a medium drizzle. It wasn't too bad if you weren't going far. Unfortunately, that wasn't Nola's situation. The buses were long gone, meaning she had a two-mile walk ahead of her.

She flipped up the hood of her sweatshirt, but the rain and wind kept blowing it back down. After only a few minutes of fighting with Mother Nature, she conceded defeat. She was going to get soaked.

A trip to the supermarket had been her after-school destination when the day started. The argument with Beth though changed all that. She really needed to see her.

Skipping the grocery store wasn't such a big deal. The way her stomach was tied up in knots, she wouldn't be able to eat anyway. She and Beth had gotten into fights before, but this one felt different. They'd never fought about a person. It felt like Jerry was standing in between their friendship.

Nola didn't know what to do. She didn't trust Jerry, that was for sure. But was making sure Beth knew that worth their friendship? No.

Thirty minutes after she left the school, Mrs. Landry opened the door at Nola's knock. There was a softness to Mrs. Landry. Maybe it was her shorter stature or the few extra pounds she always seemed to be trying to lose, but to Nola, she looked like the perfect mom. Her dark-brown hair was pulled back into a bun, and she was wearing her usual dress pants and sweater combo. This time, the pants were dark blue, the sweater a deep maroon. She gave Nola a tight smile. "Hi, Nola."

Trying to ignore the squishy feeling in her drenched Converses, Nola shifted from foot to foot. "Hi, Mrs. Landry. Is Beth around?"

Mrs. Landry shot a look over her shoulder. "She's actually busy right now. She needs to finish up some homework before she's allowed to go out tonight."

Nola's heart plummeted. Mrs. Landry was an old softie. She would never make her daughter finish up her homework on a Friday night, which meant that Beth didn't want to see her. "Okay. Just tell her to give me a call when she gets home tonight, okay?"

"I will, dear. Do you want an umbrella?" she asked, reaching toward where the umbrellas were stored in the front hall.

Nola shook her head. "I'm already soaked. A little more rain won't hurt. Just tell Beth to call me tonight. It doesn't matter how late it is."

Mrs. Landry gave Nola a look of pity that made her squirm, even though with Mrs. Landry she knew the feeling was one of genuine compassion. "She might be late. But I'll tell her. Take care." She closed the door.

Hurrying down the stairs, Nola started to jog as soon as her feet hit the path. She hated that Beth was mad at her. She was the only one, well, almost the only one, in the whole world who wasn't a complete jerk to her.

Minutes later, she stopped on the sidewalk in front of a formerly white Cape Cod. The gutters hung off the roofline, and the screen door sat at an unnatural angle. The yard was overgrown, and the landlord had been calling, telling her father he needed to cut it. She knew that would never happen, which meant she'd have to so they didn't get booted.

A whistle sounded from the house next door. Standing under the small overhang above his front door, wearing track pants and a dark-blue T-shirt, fifty-six-year-old Nico Ramirez waved her over.

With only a quick glance at her cold, dark house, Nola headed next door.

Nico had been Nola's neighbor for the last four years. He was probably the only other person besides Beth who she truly trusted. She could have smacked herself. Nico. She could have told Beth she trusted Nico. Granted, he wasn't a student at the school, but he had to count, right?

He opened the door wide, and Nola stepped inside, closing the door behind her.

Nico shook his head. "You look like a drowned rat."

"Well, that's perfect, because that's exactly how I feel."

"Get those shoes and socks off. I'll throw them in the dryer. Then go throw on some spare clothes and we'll throw the rest in the dryer too."

Nola did as he asked and then made her way to the second bedroom, closing the door behind her. About three years ago, Nico had started keeping some extra stashes of clothes for her in his home. Sometimes when her father got drunk, he got a little violent. So on the nights when Nola knew he was going to be out drinking, she stayed over at Nico's house.

She stayed with him a lot.

Stepping out of the room, Nola padded her way down to the laundry room and dumped her clothes in the dryer along with the sneakers and socks that Nico had already tossed in. After turning it on, she closed the door to the laundry room and then made her way to the kitchen.

The kitchen was small but immaculately clean. In fact, the whole house was spotless. Nico hated mess. The yellow cabinets stood against the left-hand wall, and in front of her were a few more along with the sink, and the fridge right next to it. A small white table with three chairs was pushed up against the wall to Nola's right. Nico stood at the stove pouring boiling water into a teapot.

He never did a teabag in a cup. Even if it was just him, he made a "proper cup of tea," as he said his grandmother had always called it.

Nola took a seat at the table and stared at the rain

through the kitchen window, trying to figure out what she could have done differently with Beth. She wanted a do-over. She wanted to go back in time and just slam a hand over her big fat mouth.

Bringing the tea over when it was ready, Nico set a cup in front of her and then sat across from her with his own mug. "What's wrong?" he asked.

Fidgeting with the mug handle, she felt the emotions clawing up her throat. She really needed to get Nico to tell her how he did that. He could always tell exactly the kind of mood she was in without her saying a word. She shrugged. "Beth's mad at me."

"Why?"

Taking a sip of the tea, which burned the top of her mouth, she pushed it away. "She's got a date tonight, and I just I don't like the guy."

"Why?" He asked again.

Nola shrugged. "I don't know."

Nico leaned forward and stared into her eyes. "That's not true. You know why you don't like him. So, why?"

He was in Mr. Miyagi mode. Years ago, Nola had watched the movie *Karate Kid* late one night in her foster home. Mr. Miyagi had seemed like such a cool character. She'd wanted her own Miyagi, and then like a miracle, she'd ended up living next to Nico. He was a former Special Forces soldier, and then he'd been a cop after that. He'd long since retired. But ever since he saw the black eye her father had given her one night, he'd taken it upon himself to show her how to fight.

But his lessons hadn't been all about fighting. They'd also been about trusting your gut. Nico was a firm believer that your senses told you a lot more than you realized and that she really needed to listen to those nagging voices that more often than not picked up on what was actually happening.

Nola didn't answer his question right away. Nico would have been disappointed if she did. So she sat back and thought about Jerry. She'd known him since elementary school. Back then, he'd been the kid who'd pull a girl's hair when the teacher wasn't looking. Then as soon as the girl cried out and the teacher looked around, he would be sitting somewhere else far from the girl he'd just picked on. He also wasn't bothered with picking on kids younger and smaller than him. In fact, that seemed to be his preference.

She supposed that had been his behavior pattern for as long as she could remember: Find someone small and vulnerable, cause them pain, and then avoid being held accountable. One time he'd even started beating on a kid who'd just moved into the district. That time, Nola had hit him with a garbage can lid to get him to stop. Then she'd gotten detention for hurting him. The kid he'd hurt never came back to school. Nola never even learned his name. Jerry always seemed to be doing something sly on the side, and there was never anyone that held him accountable.

"He's arrogant, and he's a bully. But he's never been called on the carpet for any of it. He gets away with it all the time."

Nola pictured Sylvia Bradford from a year ago during an assembly. Nola's class had been seated behind Jerry's, and Jerry had been sitting right behind Sylvia. Sylvia was painfully shy. She didn't like anyone talking to her. She just couldn't seem to see why anyone would focus on her.

That day, they'd had a substitute, and Jerry kept snapping Sylvia's bra strap. She was in tears when she went up to the teacher to ask for help. But the teacher simply told her to ignore him.

How exactly was a fourteen-year-old girl supposed to ignore a guy that was literally abusing her in plain sight? Even now Nola, got angry thinking about it. It seemed that boys were allowed to do whatever they wanted, and girls just had to put up with it.

"What's his family like?" Nico asked.

That was an easy answer. Jerry's dad was all over the TV with his commercials for his lighting store. He had three lighting stores as far as Nola could remember, and he was definitely one of the richest kids in school, if not the richest. "His family's rich. He's got a gorgeous sports car that he was given as soon as he got his license. The parents made a big deal about it and had it brought to the school so everyone could see him get it."

"So Mommy and Daddy are arrogant showboats who give him whatever he wants. He's a bully who doesn't get called out for it, and you really don't think there's any reason that you don't like this guy?"

Nola gave him a small smile. She knew he'd understand. "Okay, he's a complete tool. But Beth, she's liked him for as long as I can remember, and now he's asked her out." Nola fell silent.

"And why does that bother you?"

"I don't trust him. I don't think he's going to be good to Beth. I don't know. I can't see why he would ask her. I mean, Beth is quiet and sweet, which is the exact opposite of Jerry. And I mean, they don't even have any classes together. I don't think I've even seen them speak before."

Nico was quiet for a moment. "You might not have seen them speak, but Jerry sounds like the type who would notice when someone was interested in him."

Nola grunted. That was undeniably true. And Beth hadn't exactly been subtle about her crush. Nola remembered one school assembly when Beth brought one of those disposable cameras. She must have taken twelve pictures of Jerry alone. "Yeah, I think it's safe to say he knew or knows that she had a crush on him."

"So what are you going to do?"

"What am I going to do? Nothing. I mean, what can I do? She likes him. He asked her out. She's going, and she's already mad at me because I didn't jump up and down with excitement when she told me."

Taking a long sip of his tea, he then placed it carefully on the table, arranging it so it aligned perfectly with the condensation ring. "Sometimes when we see a problem, we can't always stop it. You'll just have to be there for her when this goes badly."

"Maybe it won't go badly," she said in an unusual burst of optimism.

Her friend's gaze didn't let her look away. "You don't really believe that, do you?"

Nola sighed, slinking further into her chair. "No. This is definitely going to go badly."

Chapter Eleven

NOLA
PRESENT DAY

The campus was much busier when Nola arrived the next day. In fact, it was a mob scene. There seemed to be a sea of students milling around the front of every building and more stepping out of cars at the curb.

Surprised to see so many, she then realized that the rest of the students were allowed to start moving in today. SUVs lined up along the sidewalk. Parents helped kids pull bag after bag and suitcase after suitcase out of the back of them. A few older students headed inside, with friends helping rather than parents.

Nola held the door open as an older man carrying two large plastic crates filled with god knew what headed toward her.

"Thanks," the guy mumbled from behind his tower of plastic.

She let the door close behind him and then looked up,

feeling eyes on her. Behind a group of about six squealing underclassmen, who apparently had just seen each other again after a long break, a tall girl with long waist-length wavy brown hair stared at her. Her light-brown eyes caught Nola's and didn't look away. It was weird, even though she was staring right at Nola, she couldn't quite make out her face with all the shifting of people in front of her.

A chill rolled over Nola's skin. Even as everyone hustled and bustled around her, the girl kept her gaze locked on Nola. It was clear the girl wanted to tell her something. Hustling down the stairs, Nola had to jump back as a kid on a skateboard zipped toward her. "Heads up."

Nola jumped back just in time.

She looked toward the group of girls, but the girl with the long brown hair was nowhere to be seen. Nola looked around the area, trying to see if she could spy her but there was no sign of her.

Casting another glance around, Nola knew she was gone. If she really had something to tell Nola, she'd find her again.

A heaviness settled in Nola's chest, and she rubbed at it. Ghosts weren't usually something she saw in such a crowded setting. As she walked, she looked at all of the coeds milling about some hurrying but most looking like they were in a rush to go nowhere.

Such a strange existence, she thought again. Would this have been Molly one day? Walking around carefree? Would she have been carefree or would Nola's demons have infected her daughter as well?

An undercurrent of upset reached her ears. Nola slowed looking toward one of the dormitories ahead of her and to the left. A couple obviously much older than the students— probably someone's parents—stepped out of the dormitory escorted by the same two security officers who'd come to Jen's door. Nola stopped where she was and watched as the man and woman argued with the officers. One of the men reached out and grabbed the woman's arm. The male who was with her pushed the officer away.

A shout went up from farther down the path. Leslie sprinted toward the group, her hands up. She joined them, talking to the two officers, her arms waving in the air, but she was too far away for Nola to make out what she was saying. Then Leslie wrapped her arms around the man and the woman and led them toward the parking lot. Arms crossed over their chests, the security officers stayed behind and watched them go. Nola followed the couple and Leslie.

Leslie led the couple to the edge of the parking lot. The woman burst into tears, and Leslie pulled her in tight for a hug. Then she stepped back as the man took the woman from her arms, saying something softly before the two of them headed through the cars.

Her eyes worried, Leslie stood in the same spot, watching as the couple made their way to the car. The man helped the woman into the passenger seat before moving around to the driver's side. The trainer stayed where she was until the car pulled out of the lot, and then she turned, her shoulders drooping.

"Leslie?" Nola called.

Leslie's head jolted up, her gaze zeroing in on Nola. She wiped self-consciously at her eyes and gave a small laugh. "Hey, didn't see you there."

Nola nudged her chin toward the couple. "What's going on?"

With a sigh, Leslie shook her head. "Honestly, I'm not really sure." She took a seat on a nearby bench and gestured for Nola to join her. Nola did and waited.

It didn't take long. Leslie pointed to the parking lot. "That's Amy and Mike Blevins. Their daughter Julie is a junior here, or at least was. I had an appointment with her this morning, but she never showed. She's a smart kid and an incredible runner. She hurt her knee last semester, and I've been doing a lot of physical therapy with her for the last few months. I like her."

"So what's the problem?"

"Like I said, she missed her appointment. It was supposed to be just a quick check to see how she's faring. I thought maybe she just got caught up with everybody returning to campus. So I came to check, to see if maybe she slept in or got her times wrong." Leslie sucked in her breath. "Her roommate told me."

Nola's stomach bottomed out. "Told you what?"

"She left. Sometime Saturday night, she packed up her whole room and left a note saying that she just needed some time to figure out what she wanted to do with her future, and she left. There's not a stitch of her clothing left in the room, not any of her bedsheets or anything else belonging to her. Everything's gone."

"Did she tell anyone? Did anyone see her go?"

Leslie shook her head. "No. Her roommate wasn't here yet. She's not an athlete. When she arrived, she saw that half the room was empty. She knew that wasn't right, that Julie should have been here. She went down to the main desk to see what was going on and even called Julie's cell phone but didn't get an answer. It went right to voicemail. When she went back to the room, she found the note."

Nola frowned. She did not like the sound of that. "There must have been something that the security cameras could reveal about her leaving."

Frustration laced Leslie's words. "Security claims that

there was something wrong with the cameras that night and that they have no footage from ten p.m. Friday night until noon on Saturday. Which just so happens to be the time when Julie left."

"Was there a problem in any of the other cameras on campus?"

"Just the cameras covering the dorms."

Nola eyed her, not sure how much she should say.

"I don't like this," Leslie said. "Julie wasn't the type to just turn tail and run. I think something happened to her. Her parents want to know what's going on, and I don't blame them."

"There are no problems at home or a boyfriend or anything like that?"

Leslie shook her head. "Boys weren't an issue. She was focused on her rehab, getting her physical shape back to where it was, and acing her classes. She had plans for law school and she wanted to get into an Ivy league. Yale's been her goal since she was a kid."

"She never contacted her parents?"

"No. The roommate called them, and that was the first they'd heard of it. They called the college to see what was going on. The college said there was nothing they could do. That Julie was an adult and therefore entitled to leave. They called me right as I heading for Julie's dorm. I spoke with them a few times over the course of Julie's rehab. I told them to wait for me, but they got here faster than I thought they would."

"What was with security?"

Leslie glared over her shoulder at where security had been, but the two men were gone. "They told the parents they were trespassing. That if they didn't remove themselves from campus immediately, they'd have them arrested."

"Well, that's one way to deal with scared parents," Nola said dryly.

"Yeah, a horrible way. They just want some answers. This isn't like Julie. She wouldn't just disappear like that without a word to anyone. Her parents know something's wrong, but the college is sticking by the idea that there's nothing they can do."

Nola looked back toward the dorm. There might not be anything the college could do, or rather, would do, but there was something Nola might be able to do. She could have Bishop see what she could find.

"Sorry to dump all this on you. I just . . . you caught me at a bad time. So, uh, how'd it go with Jen?" Leslie asked.

"It didn't. Security showed up just as I was leaving." Nola paused. "Any chance they're watching Jen?"

"What? No, I don't think so." Leslie sighed. "Actually, I don't know. I feel like I don't know anything anymore. A few days ago, I would have said Julie would never just disappear, so I don't know if my judgment counts for anything anymore. But I was thinking about Cindy, and if anyone besides Jen knew what happened to her, it would be Melanie Price."

Recognizing the name, Nola said, "The previous women's advocate."

Leslie nodded. "Yeah. She was a big get for the university. She has a huge name in the women's movement. But then she was slowly shoved more and more to the sidelines. The restructuring was the last straw."

"I already have an appointment to see her."

"That's good. Melanie's good people." Leslie stood. "I should get going. I have a meeting. But I hope you find what you're looking for, for Cindy's sake."

With a nod of agreement, Nola watched Leslie leave,

but her gaze shifted back to where she'd last seen Julie's parents. It was entirely possible Julie Blevins *had* just decided to step away from her life. But Nola thought she'd do a little digging just to confirm it.

So she headed to the library after seeing Leslie. She did a quick online search of Julie. The first thing that struck Nola when she looked into Julie Blevins was that she looked a lot like Cindy, but with longer hair. She was also a good student and a top athlete. There was nothing in her social media posts that indicated a problem, but that wasn't unusual. People put on their best face when on social media.

Her emails didn't indicate any issues, though, or at least not ones that would result in a radical life change. Her text messages were similarly unremarkable. If Julie had been planning this for a long time, she had kept it hidden from those around her. And if it was a spur-of-the-moment thing, it was decidedly out of character for her.

By the time Nola was ready to call it a night, she was feeling decidedly frustrated. Nothing was panning out the way she'd expected it to. She thought she'd at least have a name to target by now.

But she had nothing. Nothing for Cindy, and nothing for Julie.

Climbing into bed, their two images rolled around in her mind. But they kept getting supplanted by one other: Beth's. All of this was bringing up memories of Beth, and try as she might, Nola couldn't seem to keep them away.

Chapter Twelve

NOLA
TWENTY-ONE YEARS AGO

Nola stayed at Nico's for dinner at his insistence. They had a long, strenuous workout before that, which involved a long run, push-ups, squats, and core exercises. After that, they went over knife defenses which were definitely some of Nola's favorites.

Spending time with Nico was great because it helped pass the time much more quickly than if she'd been home on her own. But by 9:30, she knew she needed to get back to her own house. Nico offered for her to stay the night in the spare bedroom, but Nola wanted to be home in case Beth called.

Once home and after a shower, she grabbed the phone and dragged it down the hall, pulled it into her room, and closed the door. Her dad wasn't home yet. It was Friday night, so in all likelihood, he wouldn't be home until the early morning hours.

Grabbing her dog-eared copy of Sun Tzu's *The Art of War*, Nola curled up in her bed to read while she waited for Beth to call. For the first two hours, she glanced at the phone every few minutes and even checked it a few times to make sure it was still working. It wouldn't be unheard of for their phone to be turned off.

As the clock crept closer to Beth's curfew of eleven, Nola found herself unable to focus on the book. She started pacing her room, tossing laundry into the laundry basket and rearranging her small collection of books. Finally, the clock struck eleven. Beth would be on time. She never violated curfew.

Okay, she'll need time to get inside. Her mom will probably want a big rundown. Maybe even snacks at the kitchen table. Twenty minutes.

As the clock headed to 11:45, Nola curled up in bed to wait. *Maybe she's grabbing a shower or her mom is making her repeat every moment of the evening.*

Nola grabbed Sun Tzu's book again and forced herself to keep reading even as she yawned. She would call. She had to call.

Birds chirping woke Nola. Squinting at the blinds, bright light peered in from its edges. Wincing, she picked up *The Art of War*, which she had rolled over onto sometime during the night.

Rubbing her ribs, which would no doubt sport a bruise, she glanced at the phone that sat quietly next to the bed. Her heart dropped.

Beth hadn't called.

Nola knew Beth was mad, but deep down she really thought she'd call. But then maybe she thought Nola wouldn't be excited and that she would take some of the glow away from her date.

Her stomach tied up in knots picturing Beth with Jerry. She was probably right. Even if Beth had called, she didn't know how supportive she could pretend to be. At the same time, she didn't see how a date with him could possibly have gone well. She rolled out of bed and made her way quietly down the hall.

Maybe she was wrong. Maybe Jerry had seen what a good person Beth was and was good to her. Nola clung to that idea even as part of her brain mocked her fantastical thinking.

Snoring from the living room indicated that her father had made it home alive. She supposed that was good.

She walked into the kitchen and opened up the fridge, but there was nothing there. *Right, I didn't make it to the supermarket yesterday.* There was still the small stash of food in her closet, but closing the fridge, she realized she wasn't really hungry, at least not for anything here.

Heading back to her room, she quickly got changed into her running clothes and tied her shoes while sitting on the edge of her bed. Slipping the twenty she'd gotten from her father into the pocket of her shorts, she headed to the park.

As she started to run, doubts and worries about Beth filled her mind. But after about five minutes, she shoved them away, letting the rhythm of the run sync up with her heart rate and gave herself up to the emptiness of the feeling.

She always seemed to be able to clear her head of thoughts and just focus on her breath when she was on a run. Picking up the pace, she headed into the park and finished the loop around it before heading toward Main Street. Golden arches appeared in the distance, and she slowed her pace. The run had been a full five miles. A glance at her watch showed that she'd done it in just over thirty. Not bad, especially being she'd skipped breakfast.

Dropping to a walk, she pulled open the doors of McDonald's, knowing she couldn't really afford it, but needing a little comfort food. Five minutes later, she was heading back outside with a breakfast sandwich in a bag. Heading toward Beth's house, she ate it on the way.

God, it was good. She tried to make it last, but her appetite had reemerged on the run. Licking her fingers as she approached the Landrys' house, she rolled up the wrappers. Dumping the evidence of her breakfast in the Landrys' garbage can, she climbed the steps and rang the doorbell.

This time it was Mr. Landry who answered. Tall, with dark skin and hair that had brown just turning gray, Nola rarely saw or spoke with him. He was a lawyer, and usually when she was over, he was working in his office downtown or in the one down the hall. She didn't think he'd ever answered the door before.

His whole body was stiff as his haunted eyes caught sight of her. Mr. Landry wasn't as warm and bubbly as Mrs. Landry, but he was a very nice man. But right now, he looked stressed. Something was wrong. "Nola, good morning."

"Uh, hi. Is Beth up yet?"

His hands trembled as he shook his head. "No, not yet. But I'll have her call you when she gets up." He started to close the door.

Nola put out a hand to stop the door from fully closing. "Is everything okay, Mr. Landry?"

He swallowed, his gaze meeting hers for a moment before it darted away. But in that one moment, she saw the fear and anger in his eyes. "Yes, yes. Everything's fine. I'll have her call you later."

Nola removed her hand, letting the door close. She stepped back, her focus on the closed door. Something was definitely wrong. It was possible it had nothing to do with Beth's date last night, but the gnawing at her gut told her it had everything to do with it.

Slowly, Nola walked back down the steps, stopping at the base to look back up at the house. It was early. It was entirely possible that Beth was sleeping in, but she'd always been an early riser, even on weekends. It was one of the few commonalities they had between the two of them.

No one was really around this early, and Beth's neighbor on the left-hand side had gone to Florida for a few weeks. The Landrys were watering their plants and taking care of their cat.

Nola quickly walked over to the driveway, and then as quiet as she could, she rolled the garbage can over to the side of the porch. With one more quick glance around, she climbed onto the garbage can and balanced on the edge of the porch.

Taking a breath, Nola straightened and slowly reached up for the roof. Using the trellis on the left side of the porch, she climbed up until she was on the porch roof. Quickly, she made her way across to Beth's bedroom window. Carefully, she lifted the sash. Beth always left the window open for Nola in case she ever wanted or needed to get out of her house.

Pushing the drapes aside, she quietly climbed into the room and then stood, giving her eyes a moment to adjust to the dim light. The room was pretty big, at least three times the size of Nola's. The walls were a pale pink—Nola had helped Beth paint them last summer. Posters covered one entire wall. On the right side was a tall wardrobe with Beth's desk next to it. Above the desk was the friendship board she'd made: pictures of Nola and Beth across the years. Nola didn't have any pictures of the two of them. Beth was the keeper of their friendship.

Nola dragged her eyes from the smiling pictures to the big bed, covered in a thick white comforter. The large mound under the comforter meant Beth was still in bed. She was turned away from the window, only her dark hair above the covers.

Unsure, Nola stayed where she was, not making a sound. If Beth was sleeping, she certainly didn't want to wake her. After all, if she was still mad at her, that certainly wasn't going to help.

But something felt wrong. Something was going on with Mr. Landry, and in her gut she knew it had to do with Beth.

Quietly, she walked to the bed and sat at the edge. Beth didn't stir, but Nola knew she had to know she was here. Reaching out a hand, Nola lightly touched her shoulder. "Beth?"

"Go away, Nola," she said, her voice muffled by the blankets. She didn't look at Nola.

"Are you okay? Are you sick?"

"Just go away, Nola." Beth sounded like she was on the verge of tears.

Nola pulled her hand back, not sure what to do. She knew she should probably leave. Beth had told her to go.

But Nola needed to know what was wrong. Nola stood up and walked around the side of the bed. Beth's eyes were closed, or at least the right one was. The other one Nola couldn't see with the way the blankets were pulled up.

Nola knelt down next to the bed. "Beth, what's wrong? Are you okay?" Nola asked quietly.

Beth shook her head, her curls moving above the blankets, and then her shoulders started to shake. "Nola." The name came out as a wail.

The sound broke Nola's heart. Raw heartbreak and devastation was encapsulated in that one word. Gently, Nola reached out and pulled the blankets down.

A gasp escaped her lips before she could even think to hold it back. Beth's lip was cut, and her left eye was swollen shut.

Nola stared at her even as the truth of what had happened slammed into her. Compassion was quickly replaced with white-hot rage. Her words came out clipped and harsh. "Did Jerry do this to you?"

Beth yanked the blankets back up. "Just go away, Nola. Go away!"

Nola winced, knowing her tone had been all wrong. Reaching out a hand, she placed it on Beth's shoulder. "Beth, I'm—"

"Just go away, Nola! I don't want you here!"

Nola bolted to her feet, her heart breaking. Part of her knew Beth didn't mean it the way it sounded. She knew that Beth's side was one of the only places where she belonged. *She's hurt. She doesn't mean it,* Nola told herself even as she backed away from the bed, not sure what to do.

The door flew open. Mrs. Landry burst inside, her eyes wild. Her gaze flew to Beth, who'd pulled the blankets back over her head. Then Mrs. Landry's shoulders dropped as she caught sight of Nola.

"Oh, Nola." She reached out and wrapped an arm around Nola, pulling her from the room.

Chapter Thirteen

Instead of showing Nola to the door, Mrs. Landry led her to the kitchen table. She bustled about making eggs and popping two pieces of bread into the toaster. Nola sat at the table, feeling numb, picturing Beth's face.

Mrs. Landry placed the food in front of her along with cutlery and a drink. She ran a hand over Nola's hair and then kissed the top of her head. "Eat, Nola."

Picking up the fork, Nola ate without thinking and without even tasting. All she could do was picture Beth's face. Jerry had done that to her. Nola was sure of it.

By the time Nola was finished, Mrs. Landry was sitting down across from her, a mug of coffee clasped in her hand. Nola looked up, surprised. She didn't know when she'd sat down or how long she'd been there.

"What happened?" Nola asked, not even recognizing her voice. It sounded so small, so scared.

Mrs. Landry shook her head, placing the mug on the table. "She won't tell us. She called us last night from a pay phone outside the fire station. She was so distraught. We rushed over there, and she was—"

Tears sprang to Mrs. Landry's eyes, and she wiped them away. "Her clothes were all disheveled and she had red marks on her arms, legs, and her face . . . but she wouldn't say what happened."

Nola gripped the edge of her chair as anger rolled through her. He did this to her. He hurt her. "Do you know who she went out with?"

"The Whitmore boy. Her father went over to speak with his parents this morning. But he—Mr. Whitmore—said that Jerry said Beth had run off at some point during their date, and Jerry couldn't find her."

Nola scoffed. Right, like Beth would ever do that. She was too polite and too timid. "You don't believe that, do you?"

Mrs. Landry shook her head. "No, of course not."

"So what's going to happen now?"

Mrs. Landry sighed. "I don't know. Unless Beth tells us what happened, I don't know that there is anything we *can* do."

Nola knew she was right, but she hated it. Beth was such a soft, kind person. But it wasn't like her to stand up for herself. Nola didn't know if she'd ever be willing to testify about what had happened to her.

Nola stood up. "I should go."

Mrs. Landry nodded, her gaze far away. "Yes, of course, dear."

"If Beth gets out of bed later, or I don't know, if she wants to talk to me, can you tell her to give me a call? I can come back, or we can just talk on the phone. Whatever she needs."

"I'll tell her. Thank you, sweetheart," Mrs. Landry said.

The words were meant for Nola, but her gaze was far away. Her thoughts were obviously already gone from the room, no doubt focused on her daughter upstairs.

Hesitating as she stood there next to the table, Nola nodded. Mrs. Landry looked so lost. She'd never seen an adult look that lost before. Nola wanted to do something to help her, but she couldn't think of a single thing that would help. So she just turned and headed for the front door. And for the first time that she could ever remember, Nola was glad to be leaving the Landry house.

The phone was quiet all weekend. Beth never called. Nola stopped by again on Sunday, but Mr. Landry said that she didn't want to talk. Nola contemplated climbing up the trellis again but felt like it wasn't right to push Beth if she didn't want to talk, not yet at least.

At the same time, Nola really needed to know what happened to her. She needed to know what Jerry had done to her. She didn't need to know why. There was no why in this situation. Guys like Jerry did things because they could, and because something was twisted up and rotten inside of them.

The weekend dragged by incredibly slowly. By the time Sunday night rolled around, Nola was more than ready to head back to school on Monday morning. Even though Nola knew there was practically no chance Beth would go to school, a small part of her held out hope she would.

Unfortunately, Sunday night, she was awake more than asleep. As a result, when she walked into school on Monday morning, her brain was working a little slower than usual. On the way to school, she stopped by the Landrys, but Mrs. Landry told her that Beth wouldn't be in school that day and probably not for the rest of the week.

So it looked like Nola would be facing the hallowed halls solo. As she made her way down the hall, it took her a little longer than necessary, being her mind was elsewhere, to notice the whispers and giggles that were accompanying her. She stopped and noticed more than a few people talking behind hands, flicking gazes at her before looking away.

What was going on?

Brett and Colin, two other football team members, walked down the hall toward her. Brett looked Nola up and down with a smirk. "You as much fun as Beth?"

Nola's blood ran cold as she whirled around. The bell rang. Brett and Colin slipped into a classroom. Nola wanted to march in there and demand to know what they were talking about. But it was Mr. Hanover's class, and he would more likely than not have her in detention for the rest of the day if she interrupted his geometry lesson. So instead she rolled her hands into fists and headed to her English class.

Already late, she slipped in the back while Mrs. Shaffer was glancing down at the attendance sheet. As soon as she was done, Mrs. Shaffer started in right where she had left off: droning on about *To Kill a Mockingbird*. Nola's mind though was far away from the American classic.

Although she supposed it shouldn't be. In the Harper Lee tale, an African American man was falsely accused of rape, and Atticus Finch defended him, even facing down a mob.

When the bell rang, Nola jumped out of her seat and headed into the hall. People rushed by her as she glanced down the hall, but she didn't catch sight of Brett or Colin.

She turned and headed toward the gym, although she

was definitely going to beg out of class today. There was no chance she was suiting up and playing some state-required sport while her mind was like this. In all likelihood, she'd kill someone.

The gym was located on the first floor, but the locker rooms and the office of the gym teacher, Ms. Haliburton, were located on the basement level. Hoping she could catch her before class started, she headed quickly down the stairs. Her mind focused on Beth and the need to find out what had happened, she didn't even notice Harris Kingsley until she nearly bumped into him.

Nola stepped to the side, but he stepped with her, mirroring her movement. "Where are you going?"

Nola glared up at him. Harris wasn't a football player, but he was definitely the size of one. In fact, he was easily the largest guy in the senior class. He was also one of the dumbest. He'd tried out for the football team, but his primitive brain couldn't even figure out the basics of catch ball and run.

"Get out of my way, Harris."

He reached out one of his meaty paws and placed it on her shoulder. "No need to be like that. Now that I've seen what Beth's like, I'm guessing you're probably just the same."

The anger that clouded her brain at the mention of Beth's name was the only thing that made her hesitate. But Harris apparently took it as some sort of sign that she was okay with his hand being on her. He leaned forward. "Why don't you and I—"

Reaching up, Nola yanked his two middle fingers back practically to his wrist. "Why don't we what?" She spit out.

He let out a yell, but Nola didn't let go, continuing to pull the fingers back toward his wrist. Her teeth gritted as she glared down at him. "What do you know about Beth?" She demanded.

"No-nothing," he stammered as his knees bent until he was below her eye line, trying desperately to contort himself into a position that would relieve the pain she was causing to his fingers.

Nola didn't care. She yanked down harder. "Wrong answer."

He crashed to his knees, his eyes tearing up. "Let me go."

She leaned forward, glaring into his big, fat, stupid face. "Not until you tell me what's going on. Why did you say that about Beth?"

"It wasn't me. I wasn't part of it."

His cheeks red, a tear rolled down his cheek. If it was fake, it wouldn't work. And if it was real, it was a wasted effort. She wouldn't care if he started bawling and apologizing all over the place. His emotions meant nothing to her. Answers were all that counted.

"Part of what?" she demanded.

He flicked a glance at her and then shot his gaze back to the floor, his shoulders hunched. "The tape. I just saw it. Jerry and some of his friends, they were playing it this morning before school. Everybody's seen it by now."

"What tape? What are you talking about?"

"Jerry, he had a date with Beth, and he videotaped it."

Nola's stomach bottomed out. She knew he'd hit her. But she didn't think . . . He couldn't have. She applied more pressure to Harris's fingers. "What did he do to her?"

Harris blanched, his gaze once again darting to her and then away. "It just, I mean, at first, I thought she liked it, but then she started to cry. They hit her, and then, then they . . ."

"They? Then they what?" She said.

"They had sex."

Nola's mouth dropped open. She wrenched back on his fingers even more. "Beth had sex with Jerry?"

Harris winced, all but whimpering. "Yes. With Jerry and Brett and Colin."

Shock sent her stumbling back from Harris, and she released him. "Oh my God."

She could feel the blood drain from her face. She pictured Beth's face under the covers. All the conversations they'd had about love and Beth waiting until she'd found the right guy. And then Nola pictured Jerry's smug face.

Harris crawled away from her and got to his feet, cradling his hand. "You're psycho."

His words yanked Nola back to the present. Her gaze lasered into him. She stepped forward, her hands rolled into fists, anger rolled over her like a tidal wave. "Where. Is. Jerry?"

Chapter Fourteen

The hallway was quiet as Nola strode down it. Blood pounded in her ears. All she could picture was Beth's face and the horrible images that Harris's words had created.

Those bastards. I'm going to kill them. And I'm going to start with Jerry.

Collin and Brett deserved punishment as well, but they were lackeys. Without Jerry, it never would have happened.

She'd left Harris in the hall. He wasn't sure where Jerry was, but then she remembered that he was in history class during second period. Beth had always been excited because she had math in the room next door and always rushed to make sure she caught a glimpse of him before and after class.

Except Beth wasn't there today because he and his friends had raped her. She winced at the word but then made herself repeat it—rape. They were rapists.

She climbed to the second floor of the school building and made her way down to room 221.

The door to Mr. Gonzalez's room was open, and his

voice rang out into the hall. "Okay, now you have twenty minutes to finish the quiz. Use your time wisely."

Nola didn't pause as she strode through the open doorway.

Standing at the front of the room, Mr. Gonzalez frowned, pushing his glasses up his nose as he caught sight of Nola. "Nola? Do you need something?"

Nola ignored him. Standing by the first desk in the front row, she scanned the room. Then her gaze locked on Jerry, who sat toward the back in the middle row. He smirked at her. "Hey, Nola. How's Beth?"

With a growl, she launched herself down the aisle and slammed her fist into his cheek. The kids nearest Jerry's desk sprang to their feet and scrambled away. The classroom exploded into yells.

But Nola barely heard them. They were distant background noises as Nola slammed her fists into Jerry over and over again.

Arms wrapped around her as Mr. Gonzalez pulled her back. "Nola! Nola! What are you doing?"

Nola had enough presence of mind not to lash out at Mr. Gonzalez. He didn't deserve it. But Jerry deserved all she had done and so much more. Seething, she struggled against Mr. Gonzalez. Jerry struggled to his feet. Nola didn't even realize she'd knocked him out of his chair. She'd been so focused on connecting her fists with his face.

His lip was cut, and blood dripped from his nose into his mouth as he wiped at it. The skin around his eyes was red and already starting to swell. It wasn't enough. She hoped she at least fractured some of the bones in his face.

"What the hell?" Jerry demanded, wiping at his nose.

Struggling against Mr. Gonzalez, she growled. "You bastard! I want that tape."

Narrowing his eyes, Jerry snarled, "She got what she wanted."

Nola leaned her shoulders back toward Mr. Gonzalez and lashed out with a front kick that slammed between Jerry's legs. The class roared as he grabbed his groin and dropped to the ground.

Mr. Gonzalez yanked Nola down the aisle. "Nola! What on earth has gotten into you?"

He pulled her out into the hall and dragged her toward the stairwell. Nola barely felt him. She kept her focus on the classroom. That was just a little taste of what Jerry deserved, and she was going to make sure he got the whole damn meal.

Chapter Fifteen

NOLA
PRESENT DAY

The incident with Beth was at the forefront of Nola's mind for the rest of the day. She spoke with the faculty and administrative members of the committee. Since she didn't want to tip them off that she was looking at Cindy's case specifically, she had to ask them about their experiences on the committee. They all towed the line when speaking about their experiences. How it was an honor to be able to help students through this difficult time period and that they really felt they were helping the victims, certainly more than the legal system would. When Nola pressed them on how many cases they actually voted to go to a trial, they all of a sudden got hedgy or remembered a prior commitment. Those who didn't run out of the room cited confidentiality in their refusal to reveal information.

Attempts to speak with the security chief hadn't even gotten to that level. The security office said she needed to make an appointment and wouldn't be available until late next week. Melanie Price would be unavailable until tomorrow, although Nola didn't get the impression she was giving her the runaround like the chief was.

All in all, it turned out the be a wasted day. She was basically spinning her wheels. At home, she tried and failed to come up with an approach that might yield her results. She had to settle for combing through the data she already had.

The sports program generated over $50 million each year. That was a lot of money. What she didn't know was how that changed the college experience for the students who attended. Was it like high school, where the football team were the kings of the school? Who was the royalty, then, of the non-sports-orientated schools?

Nola truly didn't understand the appeal of college. She had left home when she was seventeen and gotten odd jobs in a little apartment to pay the rent in a horrible section of New York. It hadn't been much at all. And then she had been discovered and brought into the fold of the CIA. The lack of college had never been an issue. When it came to infiltrating terrorist groups overseas, no one really worried about whether or not you had a bachelor's degree in something.

For her line of work, college didn't add anything to her skill set. And from what she knew of college, it wouldn't be a place where she would exactly feel comfortable.

But part of the problem now was that her ideas about college came strictly from what she read and saw on TV shows. She had no firsthand knowledge of the college experience. And she needed to have a better understanding of that if she was going to figure out how to help Cindy's family.

Zipping up her jacket, she pulled a black cap over her hair, which she'd already pulled into a low ponytail. Grabbing her keys, she locked the front door and headed for her truck.

Movement from the driveway caused her to slow down, and she flicked her gaze in that direction.

She was there again, the little gray pittie. Slowly, Nola reached her hand into her pocket and pulled out the little baggie of chicken that she had put together after her dinner. She turned and slowly walked toward the dog.

The dog let out a soft growl.

Halting, Nola nodded her head. "I get not trusting people. But you still look hungry." She emptied the food onto the driveway and then nodded toward the backyard. "I left some fresh water up there and an old blanket too. It's not much, but it's yours if you want it."

Slipping the baggie back into her pocket, she then backed away from the dog before climbing into her truck. As the truck roared to life, the headlights caught the dog, who was moving cautiously toward the food. As Nola put the car into gear, the dog had started to eat.

The drive to campus was short, the roads relatively empty of traffic. It was eleven o'clock. One thing she did know about college kids was they tended not to go out early. This was, in fact, early for some of them. She had already passed at least a dozen people walking toward campus.

After a brief review of some social media accounts associated with the university, she knew that Fraternity Row was where most of the parties would be held tonight. Apparently on Friday nights, at least one of the fraternities threw a party. It seemed people tended to gravitate over there before heading to the bars downtown. And then they would often end up back at Fraternity Row for after parties.

Nola turned slowly into the campus and made her way toward the row of fraternity houses. She pulled over to the side of the row at the beginning of the block, knowing that she wouldn't be able to see as much from the car.

She sat behind the steering wheel for a little while, just taking in the scene. There had to be at least sixty people out on the street milling about with bright-red Solo cups. Most of them stood chatting in groups, although occasionally there'd be one or two walking down a sidewalk together. It looked like two of the fraternity houses were having parties tonight. The houses were old Victorians that had probably been gorgeous in their day. The original owners would probably turn over in the graves if they knew what the frats were up to in their beloved homes.

Light spilled out of large windows and open doors. Nola had no interest in going in. Her ability to blend in would be sorely tested with this younger crowd.

For a moment, she contemplated calling Bishop to see if she might be interested in joining her. But then she discarded the idea. At this point, the fraternities were just a curiosity and not directly related to her case.

But then her eyes narrowed as she recognized the shape of four guys making their way down the sidewalk. They were football players, although she couldn't remember their names.

Although there were two houses with their doors thrown open, most of the other houses had lights on. Apparently, all the frats were busy at home today.

A crowd of four girls hustled down the sidewalk toward the party, giggling and talking loudly. As they passed Nola, one of the girls with long brown hair stepped away from the group and stared at Nola. Goosebumps rose along Nola's arms as she met the girl's gaze. It was the ghost from earlier.

Without thinking about it, Nola stepped out of the car. The girl turned and hurried to catch up to the other girls, casting a glance back at Nola.

Nola frowned and started to follow.

The group of girls headed toward the fraternity house with the open door on the right-hand side. A few people called out to them as they made their way up the stairs. But the girl with the long brown hair continued on the sidewalk toward the darker part of Fraternity Row. None of the girls had even noticed her step away.

The girl scooted around a group of guys, laughing and shoving one another as they drank from their cups. Nola picked up her pace as the girl made her way toward a house two from the end. The lights were on in the second floor, but no lights were on at the front.

The girl slipped along the side of the house and made her way to a window low against the ground. The girl pointed at the window, and Nola nodded her understanding as the girl faded from view. Nola crouched down and peered inside.

The window was only about a foot tall and two feet wide. It looked into a concrete basement. The light was on inside, providing Nola enough to see two guys holding a girl up by her arms. The girl's head rolled from side to side.

Behind him, two more guys carried in another female. She was completely out, her head hanging back.

The four guys who carried the two girls in grinned at one another as they placed the girls on beds tucked into the corners of the finished basement. Then one of the guys nodded to a guy who took up position at the bottom of the stairs. A second guy joined him while the other one went to the other bed. The first guy looked back at the girl and smiled as he started to unbutton his pants.

Pulling her phone out of her pocket, Nola quickly set it to record and placed it against the glass. Then she sprinted around to the front of the house. She tried the front door, surprised to find it unlocked.

Opening it, she slipped inside and closed it quickly behind her. The first floor was bathed in shadow, although a dim light came from the hallway above. Nola headed straight down the hall, knowing that the basement stairs were most likely underneath the stairs leading to the second floor.

She stepped into the kitchen, her feet sticking to the floor. She didn't want to know what had been spilled there, although from the smell, it was obviously a mix of beer, alcohol, and vomit. Dishes and takeout containers lay piled along the counters.

A door to her left was closed. Nola opened it slightly to reveal a staircase leading down. For a moment, she thought of calling the police, but the anger that she'd been pushing away all day was still burning bright within her.

And it looked like she'd just found a good target for it.

Chapter Sixteen

Taking a breath, Nola rolled her neck and then flung the door open. Speed was going to be her best weapon at this point. She bolted down the stairs.

The heads of the two guys guarding the basement whipped around just as Nola reached them. She placed one hand on the banister and the other on the opposite wall and launched both her feet into one guy's chest. With a scream, he went flying back, his head slamming into the bookcase behind him.

His partner looked over, his mouth hanging open as he turned just in time for his face to meet Nola's right hook. She followed it up with an uppercut, and the kid sank to the ground.

Jumping over the kid, Nola pulled her baton from the back of her jacket and whipped it open. The two other guys in the basement already had their pants hanging at their ankles.

"Get away from them," Nola growled.

The two guys' heads jolted up. One of them took a step

forward, tripping as his pants got caught around his ankles. The other guy quickly pulled his pants up.

Nola strode toward him as the guy's face flared with anger. "What are you doing here? You're not allowed to be in here. Get out."

"Not without those girls."

The guy smirked. "And how are you going to take them? It's two against one."

Nola rolled her eyes. "Yes, I know it's not really great odds for you, but you can give it a shot if you'd like."

With the arrogance bred from youth, the guy took a swing at Nola's head. He telegraphed his move from a thousand miles away. Honestly, Nola could have sat down and had a bite to eat watching him take that swing, it was that slow.

She ducked the haymaker and slammed her fist into his stomach and then another one into his kidneys. The kid cried out. Nola brought her third punch, an uppercut, to his chin.

He dropped to the ground, holding his jaw, and Nola really hoped it was broken. His buddy from across the room finally managed to get his pants up and bolted toward her, ducking low as if he was going to try and tackle her.

Nola took one step back as he reached her, grabbed onto his shoulders, and then twirled in a 180. The guy let out a scream as his feet came up off the ground. He slammed onto his back. Nola followed him down, slamming her fist into his face. Twice. His eyes rolled up in his head, and he went quiet.

After she was sure the boys were incapacitated, Nola walked over to the two girls and quickly checked their pulse. They were breathing, but their pulses were awfully slow.

Damn it. Nola didn't want to call attention to herself. But these girls needed help. She glanced at the four guys on the ground. They needed to be in jail. She pulled out her backup phone and called 911.

Chapter Seventeen

Campus security arrived before the ambulance. Two officers stormed down the stairs. By the time they arrived, Nola had put ropes around all of the guys' wrists and retrieved her phone from the window upstairs. The girls were still unconscious.

The security guards, one a man with an Italian accent and the other a big beefy guy, stopped still when they reached the bottom of the stairs, looking between the four guys who were now trussed up, the two girls on the beds, and Nola.

Nola pushed off of the beam she'd been leaning against as they met her gaze. She nodded to the four men. "They were trying to rape these two. These two girls need to get to the hospital. I'm sure if you check their blood, they'll be some sort of roofie in it."

The officers looked again at the four young men and then back at her. The beefy guy placed his hand on the gun at his waist. "And who are you?"

"Nola James. I'm a graduate student. I was walking by

when I saw through that window what was happening. I came in to help."

The beefy guy looked like he wanted to say more, but the guy with the Italian accent cut him off. "Looks like it's a good thing you were walking by. Do you mind hanging around so we can get your information once we get these guys taken care of?"

Nola really didn't want to wait around. But in this situation, she didn't have much choice. "Sure."

The ambulance arrived five minutes later, and the EMTs hurried down the stairs with their bags. They quickly got the two girls onto stretchers and up the stairs into the waiting ambulances. They flicked a glance at the four guys. "Do you need us to check them out as well?"

Before either of the cops could speak, Nola shook her head. "Maybe send another ambulance for them. You need to get the girls to the hospital. You need to do a rape kit as well."

The beefy guy from campus security scowled at her. "I thought they didn't have time for that?"

Nola's eyes drilled into him. "I don't know how long they've been here. And I don't know what happened to them *before* they got down here. Their clothes look like they've been disturbed."

The beefy cop flicked a gaze toward one of the girls and finally noted that her shirt was buttoned incorrectly.

The EMTs headed up the stairs with the stretcher. Nola followed them, and the Italian cop walked with her. A crowd had gathered outside as the girls were placed on stretchers and then rolled toward the ambulances.

Nola and the cop stayed on the porch, and then he turned to her as the door closed. "My name's Rosario. I'm going to need your statement."

She quickly ran through what happened. Rosario took notes on his notepad, asking only a few questions before he nodded. "I'm going to need you to sign this."

"That's not a problem."

"You did a good thing here. I don't like to think about what could have happened to those girls if you hadn't intervened."

Nola eyed the cop and the intense look on his face as he watched the ambulance pull away. "This happens a lot, doesn't it?"

"Once is too much. But yeah, it definitely happens more than I like to see."

Another security car pulled up to the curb. A wince flashed across the officer's face before he covered it up.

"Problem?" Nola asked, eyeing the car.

"That's Dobson. He's going to want to speak with you. Can you stay here a minute?"

Nola nodded, leaning against the porch railing to watch as the cop hustled down the stairs toward the new car.

One of the officers who had tried to intimidate her at Jen's dorm stepped out of the driver's side door. She watched as Rosario gave him a rundown of what had happened.

Dobson flicked a gaze at Nola on the porch, his eyes narrowing. He gave Rosario an abrupt nod and then strode past him, heading straight for Nola.

Well, this should be interesting. Nola straightened up from her spot against the railing.

She stood with her arms crossed as Dobson strode toward her and then lumbered up the steps. "So, you're the one who found our alleged victims?"

"Alleged?" Nola asked.

Dobson ignored the question. He straightened his shoulders to try and make himself appear taller. At six foot three, he already towered over Nola, but apparently, he was going for a little extra intimidation. "You know, in situations like these, civilians shouldn't get involved. You should have called campus security."

It was an effort for Nola not to scoff. "It took you ten minutes to get here. If I'd waited, those girls would have been raped."

The officer didn't even flinch at the use of the word rape. Nola filed that away. He did, however, glare down at her. "You'll be lucky if you don't get charged with breaking and entering."

"Front door was unlocked. And due to the fact that there was a crime in progress, I don't think any judge would actually charge me."

Dobson leaned forward. "You don't know all the judges."

The threat was clear in his tone.

Nola wanted to say that she was surprised that Dobson seemed to be angry at her and not the frat dicks inside. But college campuses tended not to like when things like this were made public. And she had no doubt that that was exactly what Dobson's focus was right now. Still leaning forward, he continued. "I don't want to hear that you've gone to the newspapers with this. This is a police matter now. You need to keep your mouth shut."

Eyebrows raised, she looked him straight in the eye. "Oh, do I now?"

Surprise flashed across Dobson's face as he straightened. Apparently, the man wasn't used to people not being intimidated by him. "Yes, you do. Now why don't you get out of here?" He all but growled. "The police will handle this from here out. Like we should have from the beginning."

Nola didn't say anything else. There was nothing to say. She knew his type. She had to skirt around him, as he didn't even step out of the way to allow her to pass. *God, what a dick.* She made her way down the stairs.

Ahead, Rosario pushed off from Dobson's car to head back inside. He slowed as he approached Nola, and Nola slowed her pace as well.

"You did good tonight. Thanks," Rosario said quietly, keeping his eyes on the porch.

She gave him the slightest nod. But instead of heading to her car, she made her way over to the ambulance to make sure the girls were okay. A glance back showed Dobson laughing on the porch with one of the other officers. The sight made Nola's skin crawl.

Most of the crowd that had gathered when the ambulance had been here had dispersed. They seemed to have completely forgotten the two students who'd been pulled away on stretchers.

As Nola approached the ambulance, she had to step off the sidewalk to avoid a group of guys weaving down the path, their arms slung around each other.

She stopped just short of one of the ambulances to take in the street. One of the parties had spilled out onto the lawns of both houses. Bright lights flashed out into the night. Music blared across the street.

Kids stood standing in groups drinking beer from red Solo cups. She saw more than a couple throwing up in bushes. Nola shook her head. Nope, she hadn't missed anything by not going to college.

Chapter Eighteen

It had been a tough night. Nola waited with the girls until the ambulance headed to the hospital. She might not have liked the look of the security officers, but the EMTs seemed competent and concerned about the girls' welfare. She felt much better leaving the girls in their hands. Plus, a young woman had shown up, her face ashen as she took in the two girls on stretchers. She'd hopped in one of the ambulances with one of the girls.

Nola had left the scene feeling disturbed on multiple levels. She didn't like that she'd had another run-in with security so soon. She definitely had hoped to be a little bit more under the radar than that. Getting her name out there this quickly was not part of the plan, but she sadly knew what they said about the best-laid plans.

Driving away from Frat Row, she'd been too keyed up to go home right away. Instead, she'd found herself driving around campus and then around the downtown area. Everywhere she looked, she saw oblivious college kids out enjoying their night. A few stumbled out of bars with the help of friends. Most seemed to be voluntarily and happily drunk.

You idiots, she thought. Chances were most of them would be fine, but those girls on Fraternity Row should have been fine as well. They should have been able to go over to the guys' house, had fun, and then gone home. But those men had taken that choice from them.

After an hour of driving around the town getting the lay of the land, Nola turned in the direction of her rental, her hands clenching the steering wheel. Despite her attempts to clear her mind, the drive had only brought into greater clarity what the future held in store for those young women. They were in for a world of difficulty as they tried to move past what happened to them.

And the almost nonchalant attitude of the campus security wouldn't make that any easier. There'd been a definite "it's just Saturday night" kind of air about them rather than concern that the event would haunt those young women for years, if not the rest of their lives. Those young women's lives were forever changed.

The sad and beyond aggravating reality was those young men's lives probably wouldn't be. There might be a little blowback, but eventually it would die down, even though the women had been physically impaired. Less than three percent of all sexual assault cases resulted in some sort of punishment for the offender. And that was only of the third that were even brought to the attention of authorities.

God, it was infuriating. No one questioned if a person said they were mugged. But sexual assault? All of a sudden everyone was full of doubt.

With a sigh, Nola shoved the thoughts from her mind. The sexism rampant within society was nothing new, and it certainly wasn't something she was going to fix tonight.

Instead, she gripped the phone that she'd placed on the window and tapped it against the steering wheel that she turned onto her street. Pulling into the drive, she quickly put the car into park and hopped out. Climbing the steps of her porch, movement caught her eye. The dog lay curled up on the blanket, watching her carefully. She must have dragged the blanket around to the front of the house.

Nola eased her shoulders down. "Good girl."

Heading inside, she walked to the kitchen and poured herself a glass of water, part of her wishing she could be like those college kids and drink something that would make her forget for a while.

But that was not a part of her life.

Downing the drink, she booted up her laptop and refilled her glass. Taking a seat, she quickly attached the recorder and brought up the file.

In the time it had taken her to place the recorder on the window and then reach the basement, the two boys had each run their hands all over the young women's bodies. They then dropped their pants, and both had fondled themselves, big smiles on each of their faces.

Nola gripped the edge of the table, wishing she had done more damage to the boys.

She watched as she came down the stairs and took out the two at the base of the stairs first and then the other two.

The girls on the bed didn't even stir.

Nola took a breath and then stood up and walked across the back of the kitchen, trying to rein in her anger.

Boys like this thought they were entitled to do what they wanted. And society had told them that they were. She couldn't help but think of a feminist scholar she'd read once that said that rape wasn't illegal, it was regulated.

Nola knew that one out of four women experienced

sexual assault at some point in their lives. But younger women were at an increased risk for victimization. Research indicated that about a third of all college women were assaulted at some point during their college career.

Yet very few of those perpetrators were ever brought to justice. It always seemed to come back to he said, she said, as if women were just making up these accusations out of whole cloth.

She couldn't help but think of Judge Brett Kavanaugh's accuser Christine Blasey Ford. The woman was a respected professional in her field. She had a documented history that indicated abuse had happened at some point in her past. The woman even had an additional door placed on her house so she could escape, years later. And yet somehow at Kavanaugh's hearing, the committee found that his inability to remember anything trumped her ability to remember everything.

Retaking her seat, Nola made a copy of the file and then quickly edited it to end just as she opened the door to the basement. She didn't need *that* becoming a viral video. She took the file and sent it to Bishop with a note: *These two were taken in by campus police tonight. I need this video to find its way to someone trustworthy to make sure that they're brought to justice.*

She sent the email and then pushed back from the table.

Justice. She nearly scoffed. Justice in rape cases was not exactly a shining beacon of the criminal justice system. In most cases of sexual assault, when there was an actual conviction, the perpetrator was given a sentence of twenty-seven months.

Yet the victims were often sentenced to a lifetime of doubt, shame, and guilt. Almost all victims blamed themselves. And society had a nasty habit of blaming them as well. No one ever argued that someone's attractive house was the reason that they got robbed and blamed the home-owners. No one ever blamed the car owner of a flashy car for not getting a less-attractive option. But for victims of sexual assault, society often criticized their every move leading up to the assault, as if they had somehow welcomed it.

As if any woman would want that kind of attention. All women knew what happened after sexual assaults. It was the reason why so few women actually reported it to the author-ities. And some of the high-profile cases like Brock Turner and his pathetically meager sentence indicated exactly what judges were willing to do.

Rolling her shoulders, Nola's skin felt like it was too tight. Women always seemed to be the ones who paid the price for men's inabilities to control themselves. Whenever society talked about protecting women from sexual assault, the onus was always on the women to protect themselves. Yet there was one very simple instruction that should be emphasized: don't touch women without consent.

It was the equivalent of telling people that unless they boarded up their house with bars on the windows, got a high-tech alarm system, plus guard dogs, they were just asking for it and therefore they were responsible for the fact that their home got robbed.

Nola knew she was spinning. This kind of victimization and the entitlement of the perpetrators always got under her skin. Those guys in the basement hadn't looked remorseful or guilty—they looked annoyed that Nola had interrupted them.

They looked like Jerry.

She rolled her hands into fists, knowing she needed to calm down. Nothing good could come of her being in this kind of mood. She went into her bedroom and got changed, quickly lacing up her sneakers.

When she hit the road two minutes later, she took off at a fast pace. It was late, but she needed to run. She needed to let go of some of this anger or else someone was going to get hurt. She ran for sixty minutes. Then she walked for another mile, just to work off a little more steam.

By the time she made it back home, the streets had quieted. She walked into the house, grabbed a bottle of water, and then headed right out through the back door. She stopped at the bottom of the porch steps and stared up at the dark night sky. Wind pushed and pulled at her, and she welcomed it. She closed her eyes, breathing in deep.

Trying to get her heart rate to slow, she took ten deep breaths, . Small footfalls sounded from the driveway.

Nola didn't move, focusing on the sound and then calming her breath. By the time the dog appeared around the corner of the house, her breathing was back to normal. She walked to the edge of the porch and sat down on the top step, whispering, "Hey, girl."

The dog paused for a second as if not sure what to do. Nola held her breath, not wanting to make any movements or scare her away. The dog stepped forward and then climbed up the porch steps. She curled up only two feet away from Nola. She glanced over at her and then out into the backyard.

Nola took a deeper breath, this one more peaceful than any of the ones before it. And she sat there with the dog for the next hour as the wind whipped by. She said nothing, and the dog didn't move. The two of them just sat breathing together. Two lonely souls providing each other with the only thing that the other one was any good for at the moment: silent companionship.

Chapter Nineteen

Morning came too early. After finally going inside, and despite the run, Nola had struggled to fall asleep. Tossing and turning for hours, she dragged herself from bed feeling more tired than when she'd first laid down. First thing in the morning, she always liked to go for a run. But that wasn't happening today. She figured yesterday's counted as today's run. After all, it had been after midnight.

Besides, today the first thing she needed was caffeine.

She plugged in the coffee pot and set it to brew while she stared out the window overlooking the backyard. Letting her mind go blank, she just breathed. But as soon as the coffee machine beeped, her thoughts immediately shot back to the events of last night. The campus police hadn't looked as concerned as they should have when they arrived.

Maybe it was because it was campus police, but she didn't think so. A lot of larger universities these days had their own police force, with the powers of state and local police. Unfortunately, the priority of those forces sometimes became about what was best for the college and not the victims.

With the horrible stats on campus sexual assaults running through her mind, Nola knew she needed to make a little headway. So instead of pushing her already tired muscles, she sat down at the kitchen table and did some research on the Tau Alpha Sigma fraternity, or TAS as they were more commonly known on campus. It was not heartening stuff. Apparently there'd been rumors about sexual assaults for years, but the fraternity hadn't even been censured by the university. A look at the fraternity alumni page made it clear why that was. Their members included a bunch of movers and shakers within the business and state political communities.

Disgusted, Nola slammed the cover of her laptop shut and drained the rest of her coffee. Placing the mug in the sink, she flicked a glance out the back window. There was no sign of the dog, although the food that she'd left this morning had been eaten.

Grabbing her keys from the counter, she headed to the front door just as she heard steps walking up toward it.

Narrowing her eyes, she paused and moved into the living room, peeking out the curtain. A Jeep Cherokee, the type the university police used, was parked behind her truck, which meant until she got rid of whoever was at her front door, she wasn't going anywhere.

With a growl, she strode toward the front door and pulled it open.

It wasn't one of the officers that she'd met last night, but his face was familiar from the university's website. With a full head of thick white hair and a beefy face set on top of the bulky body of a former jock, the man stopped his hand, raised to knock.

"Chief O'Neil," she said without preamble.

The chief's graying eyebrows rose. "Have we met before?"

Nola crossed her arms over her chest. "No."

The chief tilted his head as if waiting for her to finish the statement, but she was done talking. He gave an awkward, huffed-out laugh. "Okay. Well, then, I'm Chief O'Neil, as I guess you know. And you are Miss James?"

Nola nodded without saying a word.

O'Neil started to step forward. "How about we have this conversation inside?"

Nola didn't move, and O'Neil had to backtrack quickly or risk bumping into her. "What conversation?"

Narrowing his eyes, O'Neil's mouth thinned as he displayed his unhappiness with her response. She had no doubt he was used to women getting out of his way and following his lead. Both as a result of the badge that he'd had strapped to his chest for twenty-five years before joining the university's security office and due to his status as a good old boy who'd been a football player at the University of Alabama before that.

"Well, now, I was just coming by to check and see how you were doing after last night's excitement."

Nola raised an eyebrow. "You call the attempted rape of two young women 'excitement'?"

The chief stared at her, raising an eyebrow. "Now don't go making it sound like that. We don't know exactly what happened yet. I'm just coming by to see how you're doing. You're new to the university community, and that's not exactly the best way to introduce ourselves."

"No, it's not. I was just heading out to see how the girls are doing."

"Well, they've been discharged now, and they're doing

fine. They probably won't appreciate having someone coming around and stir up all those unpleasant emotions."

"Is that so?" Nola asked, her gaze locked on O'Neil's face.

"Oh, yes, indeed. I'm sure those girls are embarrassed by their actions last night. I'm sure they just want to forget it the whole thing."

"*Their* actions? You think *they're* embarrassed?"

O'Neil settled back on his heels, a smug smile on his face even as he shook his head. "Of course, of course. They drank too much and got a little in over their heads. It happens a lot."

"For someone who said we didn't know exactly what happened, you sure seem to know a lot."

A glare emitted from his eyes, his tone getting a few degrees colder. "Those girls have been through an ordeal. Like I said, I'm sure they just want to forget everything."

"I believe them 'forgetting' is a big part of the problem," Nola drawled.

O'Neil shook his head, letting out yet another sigh. "I know. Young girls drinking to the point that they can't remember a thing. What is the world coming to?"

"So that's what you're saying happened? The girls drank too much? They didn't have a little help in that with, I don't know, maybe some GHB?"

The façade of friendliness dropped from O'Neil's face. "There's no proof of that. And you could get into a lot of trouble throwing those accusations around."

"Oh, I could get in trouble? What about the boys from last night? Any trouble heading their way, or is this just going to be swept under the rug like all the other allegations that have swarmed around the Tau Alpha Sigma house?"

The chief raised his hand. "Now, no allegations have

been swept under the rug. Everything has been fully investigated, and no wrongdoing has been found on the part of TAS. And in this case, a thorough investigation will be completed as well. But you have to remember, girls tend to get a bit emotional during these types of situations."

"Yes, well rape *will* do that," Nola said dryly.

The chief winced. "Now that is not a word we will be using. And I bet you this morning with the clear light of day, those girls are remembering things more accurately and are willing to accept ownership of their responsibility in last night's activities."

"Oh, will they?"

"Yes, indeed, he said, rocking back and forth on his heels, the good 'ol boy in his voice growing thicker. "And those boys, well, you know how it is. Boys being boys. But no harm was done, and I'm sure I can speak with them about your misreading of the situation."

This time Nola didn't have to fake her surprise. She leaned against the door frame, shoving her hands into her pockets so she didn't accidentally reach for the guy's throat. "My 'misreading' of the situation? How exactly did I misread the situation?"

"Well, breaking in like that. I mean, the fraternity is talking about pressing charges against you for breaking and entering, trespass, destruction of property, assault. The list goes on. I just don't think you understand exactly what all went on last night."

"Well, perhaps you could explain it to me," Nola said, struggling to keep her anger reined in.

"See, that's what I told the fraternity's president. That I'd come over and we'd just settle this." He nodded toward the door. "Might be best to have this conversation indoors, like I said earlier."

"We're going to have it right here," she said without moving an inch.

The chief grunted. "No need to be so unpleasant."

Nola didn't say a word, just stared at him.

Giving her a hard look, he shifted from foot to foot before he finally spoke. "Well, like I said, the fraternity's talking about pressing charges against you for breaking and entering and trespass and vandalism and all sorts of things. It's quite a bit of legal trouble you could have coming your way. And your fellowship could be at risk. Troublemakers tend not to be candidates that committees like to be associated with. I think it's in everybody's best interest if you just let things go."

"And by 'let things go' you mean not testify about the fact that I saw these poor girls strapped down to beds in the basement of the fraternity house?"

The chief shook his head as if disappointed in her. The patronizing sigh that accompanied the head gesture really got under Nola's skin. "See, there you go, misconstruing what happened. The girls, they reacted badly to all that they drank, and the boys just tied them down to make sure that they didn't get up and go hurt themselves."

Nola snorted. "Is that the best you could come up with? You want to go back and work that out a little bit better? Maybe workshop it with a couple other people?"

The chief glared at her. "You're being a might snippy for someone who's in a not-so-strong position."

"Oh, that's not snippy, Chief. That's my charm. And exactly what position do you seem to think I'm in?"

"Well, you caused all sorts of damage at the fraternity and now the fraternity, of course, is worried about their reputation, and they're threatening to sue if you start spreading false rumors about what happened last night."

O'Neil flicked a glance over her shoulder down the hall. "And it doesn't look like you can afford to be fighting off lawsuits right now. I mean, you're a grad student here on fellowship. Seems like you should be trying to make friends, not enemies."

She raised an eyebrow. "Is that what it seems like?"

"Yes, indeed. You don't want this to go to the courts."

"Actually, I do want this to go to the courts. The criminal courts. All of those boys should be charged with rape."

The chief winced again. "See, there you go throwing those heavy words around. You got to be careful when you say stuff like that. A charge like that, well, it could ruin a young boy's good reputation."

"And what about the young girls' reputations that you're just walking around here sullying all over the place?"

"Well, those girls shouldn't have been there. And those boys, they all come from good upstanding homes, and I think that really needs to be where the focus is. What's been done to the girls has been done, and they'll just have to live with it. But we don't need to take it any further and make life more difficult for the boys."

Nola smiled. "In my experience, it *is* necessary to make life more difficult for boys like that."

"We seem to have gotten off the point here. Now, your heart might have been in the right place, but your actions, well, those could spell quite a bit of trouble for you, but I'm sure if you just apologize—"

Nola nearly choked. "You want me to apologize to them? That's not going to happen. They should be charged."

"Well, Indiana University has its own police force, and we have decided not to pursue the case further."

Nola wanted to be shocked by his statement, but she wasn't. "Guess that means no investigation."

The chief's mouth dropped open, and then he shut it, his lips a thin line. "There will be an investigation. I'm just saying what the most likely outcome will be. I just thought I'd give you a friendly little piece of advice. It's up to you whether or not you want to take it."

"This is you being friendly?"

"Yes, it is, and you'd be well advised to remember that." He took a step back. "Now, welcome to the universi—"

A low growl cut off the end of his sentence.

His head whipped to the right as the gray pit bull appeared from around the side of the house. The dog's gaze focused on the chief as the hair on the back of her neck rose straight up.

The chief backed up a step. "That your dog?"

"Nope. Just a stray."

"Damn kids abandon these dogs when they move out." He stepped farther away from Nola, keeping his back to the road so he didn't turn his back on the dog and then made his way over to the jeep, giving the dog a wide berth.

The dog tracked him, her gaze never wavering as she watched him get into the car. Nola's focus was no less attuned.

The dog's growl didn't abate until the chief's door closed. Once he'd pulled out of the driveway, the dog looked over at Nola.

Nola met her gaze and nodded. "Yeah, I don't like him either."

Chapter Twenty

The girls from the attack the previous night lived on campus in a dorm just one building over from Jen's. It was quiet as Nola made her way through the campus at around ten a.m. Nola wasn't surprised. From what she could tell, most college kids were nocturnal. The few kids she did see looked as if they were stumbling home from wherever they had fallen down the night before.

The student at the desk in the dormitory glanced up at Nola but then looked back down at her magazine. Nola wasn't sure if the students she'd seen sitting at that desk were actually supposed to be there or were just using it as a place to sit.

Nola turned to the hall on the left and made her way down to room 124. She paused outside the door listening and could hear voices talking quietly. She knocked on the door.

The voices cut off. And then someone said loudly, "Who is it?"

"My name's Nola James. I was the one who was there last night."

The door wrenched open. A girl who couldn't be any older than eighteen looked up at Nola. "I saw you. Outside the house. I'm the one who went in the ambulance with them. Come in, come in. I was hoping we could find you. I'm Megan."

The room was actually a suite with a set of two bedrooms on either side and a living room in the middle. The living room was empty, but one girl was in the kitchen.

As soon as Nola stepped in, the girl from the kitchen moved into the living room and stood in front of one of the doors as if to protect it.

"Ashley, it's okay. This is the woman I was telling you about. She's the one who got them out of there," Megan said.

Ashley's shoulders dropped, and she gave a nod after a quick glance at the door and a tilt of her head, indicating she was listening for any sound coming from inside. "Thanks for helping."

Nola slipped in the door before Megan closed it. "I just wanted to check and see how they were doing. I was going to go by the hospital and then I learned that they'd been discharged."

A frown appeared on Ashley's face, and she practically snarled. "Yeah, *discharged*."

"Was there something wrong with the discharge this morning?" Nola asked.

Megan gestured to a chair as she collapsed onto the couch, and Ashley sat next to her. "Take a seat."

"There's something wrong with all of this," Ashley said before slamming her mouth shut.

Megan reached over and took her hand, giving it a

squeeze before she turned to Nola, who'd taken the seat Megan indicated. "Chief O'Neil picked them up at the hospital this morning and brought them home. Ashley and I were in the waiting room to take them, but he insisted that he be the one to drive them home. He said it was 'policy.'"

"That's not policy," Nola said.

"Yeah, we know that now. But who expected the guy to straight up lie to us?" Megan said, taking a breath. She shook her head. "Sorry. I know you're not the one responsible for this, but God, that guy just made me so mad."

"What happened?" Nola asked.

Ashley blew out a breath, pulling her hand from Megan's and rolling her fingers into fists. "Apparently when he got the two of them in the car, he scared the hell out of them. They're refusing to press charges. O'Neil told them that if they did that, in all likelihood they would get kicked out of school, and no one would believe them anyway."

"Can you believe that?" Megan cut in, her tone incredulous.

Ashley didn't wait for Nola to reply. "Well, he definitely said it. He also said the only thing they would be doing was ruining their own lives."

"Oh, he did, did he?" Nola asked, her own temper being encouraged by the obvious rage of the two women in front of her.

Ashley nodded, her eyes glittering with anger. "He scared the hell out of them. They've been through enough. And that jerk made it sound like those guys had every right to do what they did."

Nola leaned forward. "They didn't. And the girls can go ahead and fill out a report at a different police station. They don't have to go through O'Neil."

"He said they did."

Nola shook her head. "No, that's not true. Colleges try to act as if they are the last arbiter when it comes to sexual assault, but they're not. They can fill a report somewhere else."

Megan and Ashley exchanged a glance before Megan spoke. "I don't know if they'll do that. It's just their word against those jerks."

"Not entirely. There might have been a camera setup that caught at least part of what happened in the basement. I have it on good authority that that video will be making its way into the hands of the district attorney later today."

"Really?" Megan said.

"Really," Nola replied. "Can you guys tell me what happened? Beforehand? How the two girls came to be there?"

Megan looked like she wanted to spit. "It was all Travis's idea. He invited Michelle and told her to bring a friend, said that they were going to cook them this romantic dinner, him and his roommate. And when they got there, there were four guys there. Michelle and Amy wanted to leave, but Travis swore that he'd spent all day cooking and that it wasn't a big deal. The other guys would leave them alone."

Ashely jumped in. "And Michelle didn't want to make a big deal about it. She really liked Travis, so she agreed to stay. But the big dinner turned out to be frozen pizza. They were given drinks, like fruit juice or something. But Anna said that she started to feel dizzy almost immediately."

"Travis told her to have a bite to eat and she'd probably feel better," Megan said. "So she did. But she only felt worse. And she doesn't remember anything after that. She blacked out. She woke up in the hospital room."

"They don't know what to say," said Ashley. "They don't know what happened to them. I mean, it could have been just the guys in the basement or it could have been . . ." Ashley's words cut off, and she shook her head.

"It was wrong what happened to them," Nola said. "And they're going to need help to get through this. Is there someone on campus that can help them?"

Ashley nodded. "I already called the counseling center. They're going to send somebody over later this afternoon when the girls are awake."

"That's a good first start," Nola said.

Ashley leaned closer. "I heard that Travis has a broken jaw and that the guys each spent longer in the hospital than the girls did."

Megan's eyes glittered. "I'm glad you did that. But I wish you had done more."

"So do I," Nola said, picturing the young men in the basement. "So do I."

Chapter Twenty-One

Located in the middle of Genovese Street on a three-acre lot, the Briggs Auto Dealership was packed. Smiling and nodding, Tommy Briggs walked through the crowd in the parking lot toward the front door.

"Hey, Tommy!" a man called.

"Hey, buddy, how you doing?" A big grin on his face, Tommy waved at the man, not recognizing him. He didn't stop, though; he kept moving through the crowd.

Up ahead, two of his salespeople caught sight of him and quickly opened the door. He walked underneath the blue, gold, and white balloon arch into the showroom. The showroom was quieter. The public wasn't allowed in just yet. Tommy was shooting one of his commercials today.

More balloons, all in IUR's blue, white, and gold were arranged in multiple locations along the back walls. And strung across them was an enormous banner. Tommy grinned from each end of it with his go-to motto in between: *The best deals start and end with Tommy.*

The cars glistened in the large open space. He smiled at

the giant Hummer that sat in the place of honor in the middle of the room. It was his pride and joy.

That baby was going to make him a lot of money.

He drove one of the first that had rolled off the plant's lot. It was a bright yellow one, souped up with all the bells and whistles. At six foot two inches and weighing just over 240, Tommy needed a big car to go with his big personality.

He caught a glimpse of himself in the mirror over by the doors that led to the garage. His large tan ten-gallon hat sat on his head, allowing only a little of his dark-brown hair to show. His white shirt and tan blazer—his core outfit for commercials—looked good. He ran a hand self-consciously along his stomach, which had definitely grown a little bit in the last few years, but hey, just more to love. His bolero tie was silver with a little topaz, and he smiled at the reflection. He could still get the girls, and that was all that counted.

Tommy owned twelve car dealerships in western Indiana. He'd started out at his uncle's used car lot but had managed to furlough his small high school and college football career into a moneymaker. Now he brought in seven figures annually, creeping quickly toward eight, and he had a vacation home in the Virgin Islands and a weekend retreat at the lake.

He was by far the richest man in town, and that was exactly how he liked it. A big fish in a small pond. But he had plans to remain a big fish while getting himself a bigger pond.

A few years back he'd become a booster for Indiana University's football team. His name had gone out, connections had increased, and now he was opening up two more dealerships within the next year. That football team and the connections that came with it were the key to him having dealerships across the Midwest. He'd be making money hand over a foot. Football teams didn't have to be the most successful to bring its players the most cash. But they did have to keep those players in line.

And so far, Indiana had done that. His guys didn't have a mark against them. And they were all interchangeable. Four years in, four years out, Tommy didn't care what happened to them before or after. All he cared about was that they performed when they were at the university and therefore made him money.

"Did you see the team's coverage this weekend?" asked Billy Hoskins, his commercial director, as he walked up. They'd played ball together back in the day.

Tommy inclined his head, a big grin once again on his face. "Sure did. Boys are looking good, mighty good."

"Think they've got a chance this year?"

"Well, they've got Hartigan, don't they? That boy is a quarterback, tight end and running back all rolled into one. He's a shoo-in for the Heisman."

One of the lighting guys walked over, and the director nodded at Tommy. "Excuse me for a minute."

The door behind him opened, and six young women in tight white outfits with blue-and-gold appliques stepped in, ushered by a production assistant. Tommy smiled at the sight of them. "Well, you girls certainly class up the place."

A few of the girls giggled. One in the back rolled her eyes, and Tommy frowned. He'd have to make sure she didn't get hired for any more of these commercials.

"I'm just going to take them for a quick touch-up, and then they'll be ready," the assistant said.

"Well, they look perfect to me, but you're the expert." Tommy stepped to the side and waved the girls away. As they passed, he slapped the ass of the one who rolled her eyes.

She whirled around, narrowing her eyes, but he just grinned at her. "Looking good, sweetheart."

He chuckled to himself as the girl walked off. Ah, these little fish just needed to know their place. His phone rang, and he looked at it, frowning for a second. He stepped to the side of the showroom and into his office, closing the door behind him. "John? Everything all right?"

John O'Neil's voice was heavy. "We've got a problem."

"What problem? I'm having a good day, Johnny boy. I don't need anything ruining my mood right before I'm shooting a commercial."

"I know, I know. Sorry about that. We had a little incident at one of the fraternities last night."

"What kind of problem?"

"Oh, you know how it is. Girls had a little too much to drink, got a little caught up in the moment."

Tommy grunted. "So what's the problem?"

"Well, there's a recording and, well, it doesn't look good."

Tommy didn't need to ask for more details. If John was calling it was because he knew that the recording could affect how the school was viewed. And that could affect the money. And nothing was allowed to affect the money. "Who's got the recording?"

"The district attorney's office."

Tommy's smile returned. The DA and him were good friends. "Peter? Well, that's no problem. I'll give him a call."

"No, it's that new one. The New York DA, the special crimes one."

Well, that wasn't as good. Tommy grunted. "Okay, I'll give Peter a call, make sure he warns that lady DA not to let that recording get to the public. He'll be able to bury it. And I'll contact our media people, make sure they know there's money for anyone who buries the recording. All right? Let's just keep this thing from hitting the media until after the season. After that, we'll have months to turn everyone's minds to something else."

"Okay. Will do."

Disconnecting the call, Tommy tapped his phone against his chin, contemplating what this could mean. He wasn't about to let some stupid misunderstanding ruin his football season. He'd keep an eye on the girls, make sure they weren't going to be a problem. The boys would definitely want to keep things on the down low. A quick call to the DA and his media contacts, and things should run smoothly.

He quickly sent a text to the DA and then slid his phone back into his pocket. Contacting the media hounds could wait until after he shot his commercial. He straightened his bolero and plastered a smile on his face. Nothing was going to spoil his day.

Chapter Twenty-Two

Nola spent the rest of the weekend looking for something that would lead her to Cindy's attacker. But she had nothing. Bishop couldn't even find anything in the university's files.

But she was learning a lot about the college infrastructure. Apparently, the professors hadn't gotten a raise in five years, although they had added online teaching to all of their teaching loads. During that time, they had also added twelve new vice presidents, complete with staffs. Nola had no idea what half of these people would do. One was titled the Vice President of Admission Retention. Did they really need a full staff for that?

Meanwhile, it looked like the university was expanding, and instead of adding new tenure track positions, they chose to take the cheaper alternative: adjunct professors. They were not entitled to health care, job security, or even an office. They were paid $4,000 per course, which might sound pretty good until you broke down the time each class took including grading tests, prepping lectures, meeting with students, committee responsibilities, and so on. A full-time professor, a person with an actual PhD could earn less than $30,000 for a full year of teaching. It was insane.

But the university wasn't cheap in all their expenses. They had just renovated the sky boxes in the football stadium and repainted the entire structure. In addition, a retreat was financed for all administrators. And where else could it be held but Hawaii?

Nola's jaw nearly hit the floor at the amount of money being spent and how little seemed to be going to the critical function of the university: educating students.

By the time Monday rolled around, she was annoyed at the whole enterprise. It was needlessly expensive. Kids went into hock to get here and then couldn't get a job that would cover both rent and their student loans. The whole system seemed rigged.

And nowhere was that more clear than for the athletes, mainly the football and male basketball players. They got the nicest dorms, the best buses and training equipment. It was disgusting.

As annoyed as she was, she now had a target to direct that suppressed rage at. Bishop had sent the video to Leticia Brown, the sex crimes district attorney. She'd already arranged to speak with the girls tomorrow. Nola hoped the girls were strong enough for what was heading there way. Bishop knew that the frat had dug in and was already pressuring the DA to drop the investigation. And two of the boys now had high-priced attorneys working on their behalf.

After leaving more food for the dog, Nola locked the front door and headed to her truck. This morning, she'd go to campus and track down some of Cindy's other friends, starting with the ones at the party that night. Maybe they'd seen or heard something that might be useful.

She'd just started the engine when her phone buzzed. Her eyebrows raised when she saw the message there. *Or maybe I won't have to do any of that.*

Jen Winfrey had sent her a text. She wanted to talk.

Chapter Twenty-Three

The desk in the foyer was now unmanned as Nola entered Harriman Hall once again. She'd spied two security guards loitering nearby. She made sure they didn't see her as she made her way into the dorm.

The building was a hub of activity. Students were coming and going. Squeals of happiness occasionally rose over the din as students reconnected. On Jen's floor, it was still pretty quiet. Music came from behind a few of the doors, but that was about the only signs of life. She supposed it was too pretty a day to stay inside. If people were awake, they were no doubt taking advantage of the sunshine.

She reached room 212 and knocked. Shuffling sounded from behind the door before it opened, revealing a girl with dark eyes and black hair. The roommate.

"Hi. I'm looking for Jen Winfrey."

The girl called over her shoulder. "Hey, Jen, it's for you. I've got to go meet Scott. Catch you later?"

"Yeah, see you later," said the voice from inside the room.

The girl stepped past, gesturing for Nola to go in.

As Nola did, Jen, who'd been working at her laptop, turned from the desk. "Hey, um, sorry about before."

"That's okay. I get that this isn't easy to talk about. What made you text me?"

Jen took a deep breath. "I heard about . . . about the TAS house. I heard you helped them. You did, didn't you?"

Nola nodded. "Yes. It looks like I got there just in time."

"I wish you could have been here last March." Jen gave her a watery smile, taking a stuttering breath.

"Would it be okay if I closed the door? I think this conversation isn't really for anyone else's ears," Nola said.

Jen nodded mutely.

Closing, the door Nola pulled out the chair from the desk on the opposite side of the room. She took a seat, keeping her body language unthreatening. She slumped back in the chair, her feet crossed at the ankles.

Jen didn't speak right away. Nola gave her a moment to compose herself. She was about to speak when the young woman did. "It's just, you saw security. They've been like that. I'm pretty sure they're even reading my email."

Nola frowned. "What makes you think that?"

"Right after everything, I kept seeing these emails marked as read, but I knew I hadn't opened them yet. Cindy had the same thing happening to her. It was just . . . it was really messed up."

"It sounds like it."

"You start to feel paranoid. But it's not paranoia if someone's really after you, right?" Jen asked.

Nola smiled. "No, I think that's healthy. And I get that you're scared, but let me tell you a little something about why I'm here. Cindy's family asked that I look into what happened to her."

Jen's mouth parted a little bit, her already pale face growing even paler. "I-I don't really know what to say to that."

"Did you ever meet Cindy's uncle Jack?" Nola asked.

A ghost of a smile slitted across Jen's face. "Yeah. He came up for every one of her games. Cindy said he even made most of the away games, which was something because the team traveled all over the place. Whenever Jack came up, he would take me and Cindy out to dinner after, no matter what, win or lose."

"Well, I used to work with her uncle."

Jen's eyes widened in surprise. "Cindy, she never really knew what her uncle did, just that he worked for the government and that he couldn't tell her what he did. She always got the feeling it was a little bit dangerous."

That was about right, Nola thought. Out loud, she said, "At times. But his family was always the most important thing to him."

"Yeah, I get that. He's a really nice guy. I mean, I guess he still is a really nice guy."

"Jack told me you made it home for Cindy's funeral. That meant a lot to him and the family."

Jen let out a shaky breath and nodded. "She was my best friend."

Nola leaned forward. "Then you know we can't let someone get away with this."

Before Nola had finished speaking, Jen was shaking her head, her face collapsing into despair. "Cindy's gone now. What does it matter?" She looked up at Nola with eyes full of pain.

Knowing she needed to tread carefully, Nola kept her

voice soft. But leaned forward, her gaze focused on the young woman across from her. "Of course it matters. The scumbag who hurt her got away with it. Cindy didn't deserve what happened to her. It matters because he should be made to pay for what he did, and we need to keep him from doing it again."

Wiping away a tear that rolled down her cheek, Jen shook her head. "That's never going to happen. I told you, Cindy tried. She went through the college's process. She told people what happened over and over again. But it made no difference. They didn't believe her. He didn't believe her, and he's all that matters."

Frowning, Nola asked, "Who's he?"

As she rolled her hands into fists, Jen's mouth became a thin line. "That security chief. He told Cindy that she should have come to him right away. Told her that she was ruining a man with a huge future ahead of him with her accusations. She's sitting there crying her eyes out, and he's lecturing her. *Lecturing* her."

Jen bounded out of the chair, pacing across the room. "Bastard. She just . . . she wasn't the same after that. I mean, she left school, and I called her and even went to go see her, but she just pulled away. I couldn't get her on the phone for the last three weeks before, and then . . . and then it was too late."

She collapsed back into her chair, and her voice dropped until it was barely more than a whisper. "I should have tried harder."

The girl looked miserable, guilt ridden, and powerless. That was the problem with these types of crimes: the ones who should feel guilty rarely did, and the ones who weren't guilty at all felt like there must have been more they could do.

Waiting until Jen looked up, Nola leaned forward. "Don't take that on, Jen. Cindy, she was crushed by what happened to her. But you're not the one who crushed her. You're the one who kept her going for so long. The one who did this to her, the guy who did this to her, he's the one who should be feeling guilt. He's the one who should be feeling pain, not you."

Grabbing a tissue from the box on her desk, Jen let out a bitter laugh. "Yeah, well that's never going to happen. He's living his best life. I don't think that guy has even a shred of a conscience."

Speaking slowly, Nola said, "Cindy never told her family who it was. But you know. Can you tell me?"

Jen flicked a tear-stained gaze toward Nola. "It won't make any difference. You can't get to him. No one can get to him."

"You called me back, Jen. You *want* him to be punished for what he did. Why don't you tell me who he is and let me see what I can do?"

Jen met Nola's gaze for a long moment. Then she expelled a breath. "It was Chris Hartigan."

The name hit like a bomb. Even Nola, who knew zero about college football, knew the name Chris Hartigan. His name was splashed across magazines and news coverage of college football. He was rumored to be the number one draft pick. On campus, she'd seen his face emblazoned across the side of the stadium when she drove through on that first day.

Nola sat back, nodding her head. "That makes sense."

Surprise flashed across Jen's face. "That makes sense? Aren't you going to tell me that it can't be? Aren't you going to tell me that someone like him would never do anything like that? Because that's what everybody on the committee basically said. He's so handsome and so good looking and girls are flocking to him all the time that he has no need to rape anybody."

Nola had no doubt that was what had been said. But most people didn't understand what rape was about. It wasn't about attraction or sex necessarily. It was about power. It was about control. It was about inflicting your will on someone else and completely dominating them. Rape victims ran the gamut from young children to bedridden geriatrics. Attraction or emotions had very little to do with the act.

"I think you and I know better than that," Nola said. "Guys like Chris Hartigan, the world seems to fall at their feet, and they start to take and take and take when it comes to just about everything. That doesn't stop when it comes to women."

Nola let her words fall into the silence for a moment. She spoke again only after Jen raised her eyes and nodded. "So how did Cindy end up with him?"

Sniffing, Jen grabbed another tissue and dabbed at her eyes and nose. "It happened at a party one night. The football team was having one. We went with a bunch of other girls. We normally didn't do those kinds of parties. Me and Cindy, we weren't really big party people. But I'd just won my match earlier in the day, and Cindy had just found out that the US team was looking at her. So we felt like celebrating, you know?"

Nola nodded.

Jen let out a breath. "The party was a total crush. There was barely any room to move. Cindy and I were together with four of our friends for most of the night, and then I started to feel sick. One of our friends Susan, she took me home, and I didn't even see Cindy before I left. I mean, I just felt so out of it."

Nola narrowed her eyes. "Out of it how?"

"I was just so tired. It was like all of a sudden, I could barely keep my eyes open. I mean, I was lucky. I was with Susan because she wasn't drinking. She had a big chem test on Monday, and so she was going to study all day Sunday, but she agreed to go out with us anyway. Anyway, Susan brought me home, and she said I passed out on the way there. She had to get someone else to help carry me to my room."

Jen shook her head. "And it was weird. I didn't think I drank that much. I mean, I'm not really a drinker so I can't really say how much is too much. I guess I was just really dehydrated from the match earlier."

Her mind spinning, Nola spoke softly. "I don't think you drank too much."

"What do you mean?" Jen frowned.

"I think you were very lucky your friend got you out of there. I'm betting you were drugged."

Jen's mouth fell open as the gears shifted in her head and the horror of what could have happened to her finally hit her. She sat back heavily against the chair. "Oh my God."

Nola gave Jen a few moments to collect herself. She stared, looking at nothing, her trembling hand up at her mouth. After a few minutes had passed Nola spoke quietly. "And Cindy? Was she much of a drinker?"

Looking over at Nola as if shocked to see her there, the young woman's eyes blinked rapidly a few times. "Uh, yeah, um, I mean no, she wasn't much of a drinker either. Like I said, I lost her at some point. She told me later that she hadn't been feeling well and she went to go lay down in one of the rooms after she went to the bathroom. When she woke up, he was there, and he was inside of her."

Jen blew out a breath. "She blacked out again, and when she woke up, she was completely naked. He was asleep next to her. She scrambled around the room and came home. Her clothes were all messy, and tears just kept rolling down her cheeks. I mean, she wouldn't even talk. She just went straight into the shower, and she stayed in there for a really long time. It took her a full day to tell me what happened."

"But you knew."

With a nod, Jen said, "I figured it was something along those lines. The football parties, they have a reputation. I never should have left her there."

"You didn't have a choice."

More tears rolled down Jen's cheeks. She pulled her knees up to her chest, wrapping her arms around them. "None of it matters. What they did to Cindy. What they did to me. He's never going to pay. The university is going to protect their golden boy. They're going to make sure that nobody sullies his reputation. He's worth millions to them, and Cindy, she wasn't worth anything."

"That's where you're wrong. Cindy is worth more than a million Chris Hartigans, and he will be brought to justice."

The dubious expression on Jen's face made it clear what she thought of Nola's statement. But that was all right. The girl had a right to her doubts. After all she'd been through and what she was no doubt going to go through now that she knew that she herself had escaped the same fate as Cindy, she was allowed to doubt.

Nola, though, had no doubt that she would make this

kid pay no matter how many obstacles were put in her way. Because Jen was wrong about something else: Chris Hartigan might be the golden boy to the university, but to her, he was the golden calf.

And Nola was going to slaughter him on the altar of public opinion.

Chapter Twenty-Four

After talking with Jen, Nola went and spoke to the other girls who had been there that night. None of them could offer any more details, and Cindy hadn't told any of them who had raped her. That was all she had time for because she needed to get out to Claremont to see Melanie Price.

Melanie had a PhD in criminology with a specialization in victimization. All of her research was on sexual assault, in particular focusing on victimization trends and patterns. Melanie had moved to a nonprofit that was about an hour away from the campus. Nola looked for any research that Melanie had done on the campus itself, but nothing appeared to be published, although there was a national research project she'd conducted that had gotten some serious awards.

But Melanie was a prolific social media person and was often posting clips about making sure that people believed victims and that the benefit of the doubt should always go to the victims. In fact, she had a blog that she wrote every two weeks that talked about the process of victims getting legal, psychological, and medical help if they had been attacked.

Nola flipped back to Melanie's picture. She was in her late fifties with hair that had a large gray stripe along the front. Instead of making her look older however it made her look more badass. A bit like Rogue from the X-Men.

Speaking with Melanie Price the night before, she hadn't been surprised to find that Melanie was hesitant to meet with her until she understood that Nola wanted to speak with her about Cindy. After that, Melanie agreed quickly. She was working most of the morning at Planned Parenthood but said she would be available in the afternoon.

Nola decided to head over to the family-planning clinic and be there when Melanie finished her volunteer shift.

The drive out to Claremont was quiet. In fact, it was boring. The land was simply flat, with nothing to really break up the one-hour trip, which gave Nola more than enough time to think about how this case was different from her other ones.

In her normal cases, she was in and out quickly. She knew who the target was, and it was relatively easy to figure out how to bring them to justice. All of them had fears that could be played upon and enough of a trail of misdeeds to follow. None of them had a national spotlight.

Chris Hartigan, however, garnered that kind of attention.

She'd contacted Bishop and asked her to do a deep dive on Hartigan. Before she set off for Claremont, Nola did a quick search and got the broad strokes: handsome kid from a wealthy family, star football player from high school on. Lots of endorsement deals and NFL potential.

She could do something as simple as break his leg, and

that would destroy his football career. But it would also make him an object of pity, especially once his people finished spinning it. And with the media spotlight already focused on him, she had no doubt that he would be lauded in the press for his ability to overcome such a debilitating injury. She had no interest in helping Chris Hartigan shine a little brighter. Plus, it would increase the spotlight on finding out who had harmed the poor little football player.

That wouldn't do either.

What she needed was to find others who would testify against him or create an opening that would force him to admit what he had done.

But getting him to admit to raping Cindy, or any of the other girls that she suspected, would not be easy either. He wasn't the brightest bulb, but he also wasn't stupid. And the truth was, even if he did confess, or even with multiple testimonies against him, with the right lawyers, he could still do little to no jail time. Time and time again, the courts had demonstrated how difficult it was to get a conviction against someone accused of rape, even when there were multiple accounts.

That seemed to be especially true when the perpetrator was famous. Nola's thoughts turned to Bill Cosby or Donald Trump or those connected to the famous like Harvey Weinstein.

So, the bigger problem with Chris was all of the support backing him. She had to get to the money. She had to make Chris a losing bet so that the money backed away.

Even then, it wouldn't be enough, at least not for justice to be done. These people had backed Chris, covered for him, knowing the type of predator he was. If they backed away from Chris, they'd simply turn their attention to the next rising star. That next star might not have Chris's ability, but it would still gain them money. They would still be propping up the football team at the expense of other people's lives, other young women's lives. They were as responsible, if not more so.

Which meant she had to break the system as well.

Doubts flooded Nola's mind. Taking all of them down was a much bigger proposition. She needed to see who the biggest support beacon was and take that person out as well. Once that support was out, the house should fall.

She sighed, shifting in her seat. It would not be easy. And it might take a while. She was probably going to need help. Which, a few months ago, would have been impossible for her to admit.

At the same time, she wasn't sure exactly what kind of help she needed. Bishop was already running the background checks on all of the boosters for the athletic department and doing a deep dive on the security chief. She'd thought about confronting him, but she wanted to know everything about the man before she did so.

But she wasn't sure how much more help Bishop could provide in person. Avad was always good for some muscle and strategy, but she didn't think that this case was going to require that kind of help.

As much as she hated to even think it, she might be slightly out of her depth on this one.

Nola let her mind go blank as she stared out at the open fields. She pictured Cindy's face, and then Jen's face. The young woman hadn't been a victim of rape, but that had been luck. In her gut, Nola knew there were others out there. She just needed to find a way in.

There was always a way. It was usually something small, something overlooked. She just had to find that one thread and pull, and the whole thing would unravel.

Her GPS beeped, indicating she needed to turn. The exit for downtown Claremont was coming up on the right. She eased over to the right-hand lane and took the exit. Following the directions on Waze, she hit the outskirts of downtown Claremont. As she reached the ramp, her phone beeped with a text from Bishop: *no obvious trail for Hartigan. I'll keep digging.*

Nola sighed, placing the phone back down. Of course it wouldn't be that easy.

Fresh air rolled in through her open window, and she breathed in deep. But the shouts in the distance did nothing to increase her calm.

She put on her blinker, pulling into the medical complex, seeing the crowd with signs at the other end of the lot. Taking a parking spot at the back of the lot, she turned off the engine, staring at the demonstration.

"Choose life!"

"Hell is waiting for you!"

"Defund Planned Parenthood"

"Baby killer!"

"Babies are more important than woman's bodies!"

Nola didn't think the bearded guy in the American flag tank top realized exactly how that one was coming across.

There were twenty protesters. The shouting increased at the sight of a young woman who stepped out of the medical building escorted by an older woman. The older woman placed a protective arm around the younger woman's shoulder, keeping herself between the young woman and the crowd.

The crowd surged forward, their yells increasing. Melanie Price flicked a glance at them through the corner of her eyes. If looks could kill . . .

Nola stepped out of the car and headed across the

parking lot as Melanie reached the edge of the medical building's property. The moment they stepped into the parking lot, the protesters swarmed her. Melanie quickly took the young girl's head and tucked it into her shoulder, keeping one hand out, trying to keep the protesters at bay.

One large man wore a T-shirt with the arms cut off, and his stomach straining against the material stepped in front of her yelling. Even from where Nola was, she could see the spittle flying from the man's mouth.

Oh hell no.

Nola picked up her pace. She slipped through the crowd and then slammed her boot into the back of the man's knees, grabbing him by the back of his ugly T-shirt. She yanked, pulling him toward the ground.

The man let out a cry as he fell. Nola slipped to the side, watching with satisfaction as he fell into two other protesters. Another three had to back up. One reached out and snatched Nola's arm.

She grabbed the offender's hand and contorted it, forcing their elbow up to the air as the person dropped to the ground trying to release the pressure. She pushed the offender toward the other protesters, glaring at the others. "I would stay back if I were you."

Nola quickly slipped to the other side of the young woman. She gave Melanie a nod. "Let's go."

With the girl sandwiched between them she and Melanie escorted the woman to a small Honda sedan sitting in the corner of the parking lot. Nola released the girl and stood in front of the car. Arms crossed, legs braced, she stared down the protesters, daring any of them to come near the girl.

As the car engine started behind her, Nola stepped off

to the side, allowing the car to escape. The protesters glared at her, but none made a move toward her.

"Thanks for your help," Melanie said as she walked up to Nola.

"I wish I could do more."

"Don't we all. I'm guessing you're Nola."

Nola nodded. "Yes. I got here a little early. I thought I'd see what was going on."

Melanie gestured to the protesters who'd taken up their chanting again. "Well, this is normal. I volunteer here three times a week. These protesters are here every Saturday, and occasionally during the week as well, like today. They bark, harass and intimidate every single woman who went through Planned Parenthood's doors. They call everyone a baby killer and a monster and a murderer."

Melanie gestured to the car that had disappeared. "That young woman is going to be married in six months. They discovered a cyst on her ovary that had grown incredibly large. Unless it's taken care of, she'll never have children. She was here trying to ensure that she *could* have children, and these people called her a baby killer."

Nola knew that was unfortunately the reality of most women who took advantage of Planned Parenthood services. Abortions accounted for only three percent of all procedures. Most women went to the clinic for birth control, regular gynecological visits, and treatment for serious gynecological problems. Yet the protesters were out in droves, yelling and intimidating these women who were mainly showing up for their annual breast cancer screening or regular pap smears.

Melanie blew out a breath, running a hand through her salt-and-pepper hair. "Think you could give me about fifteen minutes? I just need to sign out and grab my things."

Nola eyed the woman, seeing the dark circles under her eyes. Melanie was a warrior, but a tired one. "I'll wait for you here. Make sure you don't have any problems getting to your car. Is there a place where we can maybe grab a bite to eat?"

"I know a diner not too far away that makes a great egg salad. I go there sometimes with some of the clients if they're having a bad time."

Nola wasn't a fan of egg salad, but she was becoming a fan of Melanie. "Sounds great."

Chapter Twenty-Five

Gripping the coffee mug, Melanie took a sip while closing her eyes. She let out a deep sigh, placing the mug on the table. "Nectar of the gods."

Nola couldn't help but smile as she sat across from Melanie. The woman definitely liked her coffee. The two of them had already ordered, and the waiter had disappeared after dropping off their drinks.

After a few more sips, Melanie seemed to revive. She'd obviously been drained by her work. As a clinic escort, what Nola had witnessed was no doubt only one of the interactions with the protesters that Melanie had to deal with today. So Nola stayed quiet and let the woman decide when she was ready to talk.

Half a mug of coffee later, Melanie looked across the table at Nola, her gaze straightforward. "So, you want to talk about my work at the university."

Nola nodded. "Yes. Cindy's family has asked me to look into her situation. And I know that you were one of the individuals she spoke with."

Sadness slipped over Melanie's face as she shook her head. "That poor girl. She struggled so much. I was thrilled that she managed to complete the semester. I wasn't sure if she would even be able to do that. Then to learn that she took her life . . ." Melanie let out another sigh, staring out the window, her chin trembling.

The silence stretched between them, and Nola knew she needed to give Melanie a little more time. Her work, all of it, was an emotional grinder. It took an amazing amount of strength to wake up each day and face it knowing how hard it was going to be.

After Nola thought enough time had passed, she asked, "Why don't we start with why you left the university?"

Turning her gaze back to Nola, Melanie nodded. "Cindy's case was the final straw for me. In the university setting, they require that students charging another student with sexual assault go through a mediation process. They have to go through the college system first. They can press charges, but John O'Neil likes to pressure them into going straight into mediation, saying it will be easier on them than the criminal justice system will be. "

"But it's not," Nola said.

Melanie shook her head again. "No, it's most definitely not. It *is* easier on the accused, however. The committee." Melanie's mouth curled up in distaste. "God, that committee. Students who've been through the trauma of a sexual assault have to speak with the campus's Sexual Misconduct Committee. It consists of two administrators, John O'Neil, myself, and one student representative. The students have to present their case to us, and then we decide whether or not to continue to the college version of a trial and then sentencing."

"How many cases have reached the trial stage?"

"In my ten years at the university? Five."

"Convictions?" Nola asked.

"Zero."

Nola wasn't surprised.

Melanie continued. "The system's rigged from the beginning. It's truly designed so that a victim is discouraged at every stage from even reaching the trial stage. With the two administrators and O'Neil on the committee, they always are able to outvote myself and the student representative. Even when cases have substantial damages, even when there's video or the perpetrator admits it through an email or some other means, the committee will still often vote to not bring the individual to a trial."

"Why is that?" Nola asked, having her own suspicions but wanting to hear Melanie's view.

"They're more worried about the reputation of the university than the impact this will have on the victim. And the victims are so emotionally destroyed and demoralized by the process that they don't even want to think of going on to bringing formal charges. And even if they did . . ." Melanie shrugged, her gaze cutting away.

"It would probably end in the same result," Nola finished for her.

Melanie nodded. "Almost all the victims end up dropping out of the university within a year or two."

"And I take it the college knows that?"

"I did a whole research project on it. It won national awards. And they ignored the findings. The college is more worried about their reputation. O'Neil in particular is more worried about the impact it could have on the perpetrator's future. Apparently the victim's future isn't much of a concern."

"Is that why you left?"

Shifting in her seat, Melanie sighed. "Partly. When I started at the university, I thought that I could really do some good. I was the first director for the sexual assault center. I thought that the university was moving in the right direction. I thought that I would be the one to help these young women get some sort of closure, help them move forward, knowing that what they went through should never have happened and that the perpetrators would be punished.

"But I was blocked at every turn. I was the director, yes, but I had one staff member for the first five years. And they made up all these rules of what could be classified as a sexual assault. The biggest one, of course, being that the college had to identify it as a such an incident. And it was that same five-person committee that had to give the stamp of approval.

"So, in my ten years, nothing was labeled a sexual assault. But I kept plugging away, thinking I could make a difference. Eventually I would be able to make these people see the damage that had been done. Eventually I would be able to help these girls." Melina's voice drifted off, and she turned to the window again. "But that never happened. Eventually never came."

"Did Cindy tell you who raped her?"

"Yes, but I'm afraid I can't reveal that."

"I know it was Chris Hartigan," Nola said softly.

Melanie's mouth fell open. "How?"

"Jen. She's really struggling."

"She's a good girl, a good friend."

Nola hesitated for a moment. "I think she may have been drugged that night as well. A friend took her home before anything could happen."

Melanie was shaking her head before Nola finished

speaking. "I'd like to say I'm surprised or shocked. But I'm not."

"And Chris Hartigan? What can you tell me about him?"

"Chris Hartigan." Melanie all but spit out the name. "Bastard."

"Not a sports fan?" Nola asked with a raised eyebrow.

"No, not with what I know."

"Care to share? I've been looking into Chris, and there's nothing on his record that indicates any sort of problems. No disciplinary actions of any kind whatsoever."

Melanie scoffed. "Of course there isn't. He's their golden boy. Or I guess it's more accurate to say the goose that laid the golden egg. When Chris first came to the campus, *Sports Illustrated* came with him. The president was over the moon, as were all of the board members. And it became clear that keeping Chris happy and at the university was priority number one. But Chris Hartigan, despite his all-American good looks, is the devil incarnate."

"There have been other victims," Nola said. It wasn't a question.

"Yes. Six that I know of. But I'm sure there are more. And in each case, the committee decided that there wasn't enough evidence. It didn't matter that each case was practically identical to the case before it. They simply said there wasn't enough evidence to move the case forward."

Her mouth turning into a tight line, Melanie gripped the table. "He ruined those girls' lives. Each of them struggled to stay in school. In two cases, their scholarships magically disappeared. In another case, she was harassed by members of the football team. Wherever she went, a football player would show up, watching her. Eventually she just left, even though she'd tried harder than the others to get justice.

"I mean, each of them just . . ." Melanie sighed. "Each of them just finally broke. Chris was the one who raped them. He did the initial attack, but the rest of them, they are the ones who completed the job. And now Cindy..." Melanie's hand flew to her mouth, tears springing to her eyes.

The college had closed ranks, protecting their most prized possession. And they didn't give a damn about the lives of the women that had been wrecked. Victims of sexual assault often spent a lifetime trying to get past their assault. In the short term, the effects ran the gamut from denial, guilt, and shame to forgetting the assault entirely.

For all, there was a sense of betrayal and an increase in mistrust. In the long term, survivors could experience a host of negative effects ranging from the physical—headaches, pain, insomnia—to the emotional—panic attacks, flashbacks, severe anxiety. Some even experienced post-traumatic stress disorder.

"I don't know what you can do to help now. I was there for ten years, and I couldn't change a damn thing. And now Cindy's gone. There's no helping her."

"There's no helping her, that's true," Nola said. "But that doesn't mean that Chris Hartigan gets to get away with this. He deserves to be punished. He deserves to be publicly flogged for what he's done."

"I agree. And I will be the first one standing in the town square with the whip. But that's not going to happen. He's got way too many people covering for him, supporting him."

Nola's anger rolled at the thought of all of those girls

and the wall of resistance that had been put up when they should have been offered support. Those bastards. "Then I guess I'm just going to have to rip all those supports out from under him."

Chapter Twenty-Six

As Nola walked Melanie to her car, the older woman offered one piece of cryptic information: "If you want to find out what kind of guy Chris Hartigan is, look up Jorge Fielding."

Nola frowned. "Who's that?"

"He was an IUR football player until Chris Hartigan came along." She climbed behind the steering wheel. "Check him out. Then you'll know what you're up against trying to bring Hartigan to justice."

The ride back to Richmond was much faster than the ride to Claremont. Partly because Nola's rage was building. She entertained herself with fantasies about how she would destroy Chris Hartigan.

Because there was no doubt in her mind that he needed to be destroyed.

And not just physically. She needed to pull everything out from under him. She needed to leave him desperate and alone, the way he'd left all of his victims. Her anger hadn't abated by the time she reached her rental house. She slammed the car door closed behind her as she stormed up the stairs.

The dog wasn't on the porch or in the backyard, and Nola was glad. Her current mood would only scare the poor thing away. Still, she dropped the takeout she'd picked up for her on the back porch and refilled her water bowl.

Back inside, Nola quickly made her way to the computer in the kitchen and booted it up. She hadn't contacted Bishop yet for backgrounds on either Hartigan or Jorge because she had a feeling she'd be able to find plenty on her own for now.

And she wasn't wrong, especially about Hartigan. Thousands of articles had been written on the guy. He was the star quarterback for the Falcons. He was a senior this year, and they believed he was going to be the Heisman trophy winner. NFL scouts were already talking about him.

Standing at six foot six, he weighed in at 280. With blond hair and blue eyes, he already had endorsement deals. The fact that he came from an incredibly wealthy family only added to the belief that he was heir to the football throne at IUR.

Nola sat at her kitchen table, scrolling through article after article on the guy. He'd been a student at Cushing Academy in Massachusetts. It was a top boarding school known for putting out not only incredible students but a significant number of professional athletes.

He'd made a name for himself in high school football and had been scouted by all of the big teams before he finally decided on IUR. There'd been some rumors about performance-enhancing drugs, but reading between the lines, Nola could tell that his family had shut down those questions quickly.

His behavior record at the university was clean. In fact,

the case brought against him by Cindy wasn't reported anywhere, nor was there a hint of any other sexual impropriety. Apparently, the university was making sure that their golden boy wasn't tarnished now or in the past.

Which meant Nola needed to find a way to speak with someone who wasn't going to toe the line. Obviously the security outside Jen's room meant they were keeping tabs on her, and she couldn't be the only one.

Nola worked her way through the last few years of Chris's life at the school and then checked the school roster to see if there was anyone that she could go to, when she came across the video involving Jorge Fielding. It was from tryouts last year, a tackle by Chris that had apparently went viral. She cued it up and then pressed play.

But instead of watching Jorge, Nola found herself watching Chris because he was the quarterback and seemed to be the focus of the cameraperson. She didn't know much about football, but she was pretty sure quarterbacks didn't tackle very often.

Yet, Chris held the ball and started to run. A guy got in his way, and Chris dove low, slamming right into the guy's knee.

Wincing, Nola all but heard the crack.

The guy hit the ground hard, holding his knee as his back arched. Chris leaned over him and looked as if he was saying something in the guy's ear before the medics pushed him to the side to get to the downed player.

Two other players helped Chris to his feet, and they backed away. Attention was directed on Jorge on the ground, who obviously was in pain.

But Nola zoomed in to keep an eye on Hartigan. He pulled off his helmet as he walked away with the other two players. But then he did a quick glance over his shoulder.

He was smiling.

Nola froze the image on the screen. Hartigan wasn't upset about what he had done. He was proud of it.

Quickly, Nola ran a search on Jorge. He'd been a freshman from Texas and had been the first in his family to go to college. He'd been given a full scholarship, and it looked as if the future in football was very bright for Mr. Fielding.

Until Chris Hartigan destroyed that future.

He'd dislocated Jorge's kneecap. He was out for the rest of the season, and the rehab had been extensive. When the prognosis went badly, the school had dropped his scholarship. Now he worked outside Dallas as a mechanic. But before that, he'd started getting a lot of buzz. The last article about him had been titled: A FALLEN STAR.

Returning her gaze back at Hartigan's smiling face, she murmured, "Got a little jealous, didn't you, Chris? Someone was stealing your spotlight."

Closing the laptop, Nola picked up her phone.

Avad answered quickly. "Nola?"

"I need to go to Texas."

Chapter Twenty-Seven

Manny's Auto Collision and Repair was a big operation. It sat on the outskirts of Dallas but took up three full warehouses.

Nola pulled into the parking lot and just watched as cars pulled in for oil changes in a few bays, for tire rotations or fixes in another, and then longer-stay vehicles were brought to the third. Whoever had set this up was a highly organized individual. Jorge had worked with them for the last year. He was putting in fifty-hour weeks, making fifteen dollars an hour. But it was nothing compared to what he would have made if he'd continued on his football trajectory.

Nola made her way inside and was directed by the guy behind the counter to the third warehouse.

Heading back out, Nola crossed the parking lot. The hot Texas sun beat down on her. She leaned her face up at it and breathed in. It was nice to feel the warmth on her skin. She'd left her leather jacket in the car.

And she liked the feel of the sun on her shoulders. She walked across the parking lot as a whistle broke out from two guys sitting at a car having their lunch. "Hey, mama. Why don't you come have a little talk with me?"

Walking over to the man, Nola stood in front of him with her hands on her hips. "And what do you think you have to say to me?"

The guy tripped over his own tongue. "I was just, I was going to say that, you know, you look good."

Nola leaned forward. "Women don't like when men do that. Cut it out."

He reached out to run a hand along her arm. "You ladies know you—"

He let out a scream as Nola grabbed his wrist and turned it ninety degrees. He bent over his knees, crashing into the asphalt. "And we especially don't like when people try to touch us."

His friend stood up. "Hey, let him go."

Nola stared him down. "You don't want to be part of this."

The guy held up his hands and took a step back. "Yeah, you're on your own, Scott." He grabbed his lunch and high-tailed it back into the building.

Nola looked down at Scott. "Now, as I was saying, women don't like when men try to talk to us when we're just going about our day. We don't like when random men yell at us. And we certainly don't like when they try to touch us." She twisted his wrist more for emphasis.

He cried out. "Okay, okay."

"Now, are we going to be respectful of women in the future, or are we hoping that some other woman does exactly this to you again?"

"Respectful, I will be respectful."

Nola released his wrist, and he stumbled back, falling on

his butt and cradling his hand to his chest. "You broke my wrist."

She smiled. "No, I sprained it. But if you'd like, I could break it for you."

Scott scrambled back to his feet. "You're crazy, man." He rushed back to the building, casting a nervous glance over his shoulder at her.

Nola watched him go and then turned toward the third warehouse with a smile. That was fun. She doubted it would change his future behavior overly much, but it might make him pause for a moment before he decided to do the same to someone else.

The third warehouse had five large garage doors that were open. Nola walked along them until she spied her target.

Jorge was at the third bay, walking around the front of a large Hummer as Nola stopped at the end of the bay door. He walked toward the driver's door with a slight limp. He was still muscular, with close-cropped hair.

"Jorge Fielding?"

The young man's head jolted up, and he caught sight of Nola. A frown crossed his face. "Yeah, that's me. Can I help you?"

Nola walked toward him, waiting until she was close enough so no one else could overhear her. "I was hoping I could speak with you for a few minutes."

He flicked a glance around. "Uh, I'm kind of working right now."

"Can you take a break?"

He shrugged. "I really need to get this done before—"

"It's about Chris Hartigan. I'm looking to cause him some trouble."

s face hardened. He looked over his shoulder. "Frank, I'm taking my fifteen."

Chapter Twenty-Eight

Out behind the warehouse was a shaded area where the workers could have their lunch or take a break. Jorge led Nola out there and into a back corner. There were two guys sitting closer to the door, but they would be too far away to overhear Nola and Jorge's conversation. On the walk there, Nola noticed that his limp was much more pronounced. He pulled out a white plastic chair and took a seat, relief covering his face for a moment at the pressure being off his leg.

Nola sat across from him.

He eyed her. "Are you a reporter?"

Nola shook her head. "No, more of a private eye."

"You're not lying to me are you? Maybe working for him and trying to see what I'll say about the guy?"

"Oh, I'm most definitely not working with him."

Jorge's shoulders relaxed. "That guy ruined my future."

"I saw the video."

"Yeah, *everybody* saw the video. He went right for the knee. He didn't even try to go anywhere else. I had six surgeries. And this was the best they could do." He pointed to his leg. "I was one of the few people that actually had a shot at the NFL. Do you know what a difference that would have made for me, for my family?"

Nola did indeed. On the plane here, she'd researched Jorge fully. His family was struggling, there was no way around it. They had to have been over the moon at Jorge's acceptance to the university. It would have been truly life-changing for all of them.

"You think he did it on purpose?"

Jorge scoffed. "Of course he did. God forbid anybody take any shine away from the golden boy."

"And were you taking shine away from him?" Nola asked.

Shifting in his chair with a wince, Jorge propped his leg up on a crate. He shrugged. "A little bit. I mean, *Sports Illustrated* had contacted me about doing an interview. You know, kind of a 'one to watch in college football' kind of thing? I was really excited. It was the first time anything like that had ever happened to me. I mentioned it to one of the guys in the locker room one day. That afternoon, Chris and two of his guys, they cornered me after practice. Reminded me that I wasn't the captain, and that Chris was in charge."

Jorge shook his head. "I mean, what the hell? It was one interview. Everybody knows Chris is a shoo-in for the Heisman. Everybody knows he's going to the pros. I don't see how my one interview was going to change any of that."

But Nola understood the type. They needed all of the light to shine only on them. Any light shining anywhere else was a threat to their existence. In their mind, it was someone stealing from them.

He was quiet for a moment. "Did he do something to somebody else?" He asked softly.

Nola nodded slowly. "A girl, maybe a few."

Jorge winced. "I wasn't there very long. It was like six weeks, and I was in the hospital. But I heard them talking in the locker room. I'm not surprised."

"You think Chris would be capable of raping someone?"

"I think Chris and his goons would be capable of just about anything. Especially with the money behind them."

"What do you mean?"

With a glance at the two guys sitting close to the door, Jorge lowered his voice, leaning forward a little bit. "When I was laid up in the hospital, I got a visit. It was a representative of one of the boosters. He offered me some money to keep quiet."

Nola frowned. "Keep quiet? What do you mean?"

"I was pissed. I mean, Chris did that on purpose. He destroyed my career *on purpose*. So yeah, I was angry. And I was going to talk to the press. The booster came in and offered me thirty thousand dollars if I stayed silent."

Thirty thousand dollars would be a lot to Jorge and his family. "You took the money?"

"Hell no. Don't get me wrong, it was tempting, but pretty boys like that, they get everything handed to them. The rest of us, we scrape, we scrabble to get by. People like that have life handed to them on a silver platter, and nobody does anything to stop them. Nobody says boo. And I wasn't going to be one of those people. I was going to stand up."

"What happened?"

Gripping the chair, his jaw tightened. "My mom started getting some calls. People threatening her. And then someone broke into the house. Just tore it apart. No one was home, thank God, but my mom was terrified. It happened when she was coming to pick me up from the hospital to

175

bring me home. We opened the door, and everything was destroyed."

"You're sure it was the same people?"

"Yeah. Because in my room there was a new gift. A flag had been pinned up to the wall from the university. The only thing that was still in good shape. So I got the message. Next time somebody called, I told them I wouldn't say anything. The calls stopped."

Jorge took a breath. "Look, whatever you think Chris is capable of, he is. But he's not the big problem. I mean, that guy honestly, he's not that bright. But the money and the connections behind him know he will lead to more money and more connections.. And his reputation is wrapped up in the university's reputation. If he goes down, they all go down. And the big pockets aren't going to let that happen."

Nola nodded.

"I need to get back." Standing up, Jorge glanced toward the door but made no move for it. "This girl, what happened to her? She still at the school?"

Nola shook her head. "No. She killed herself."

Jorge closed his eyes, letting out a breath, and then he opened them again. "Look, I can't let my mom get hurt, but if there's anything I can do to help, let me know, okay?"

Nola nodded, watching Jorge head back to the shop.

For most people, hearing Jorge's story would probably make them turn tail and run.

It had the opposite effect on Nola. More than anything, she knew she was taking this guy down. And she was going to take him down hard.

Chapter Twenty-Nine

Weather caused a delay in her return flight, and she didn't make it back until early the next morning. After dropping her stuff off at the house, she went for a bruising seven-mile run. There were a lot of hills around the campus, and she needed to feel that muscle strain to lose some of the kinks that were still hanging on from the plane ride, and she let her mind wander.

Jorge had confirmed her view on the type of person Chris Hartigan was. But he'd also confirmed that Hartigan had some people who were willing to do some serious damage in order to protect the golden boy's reputation. Bribery followed by threats, a standard protection racket. For the girls involved, it was probably just threats. No wonder no one had come forward before. And Nola was convinced there was someone before Cindy. Guys like Hartigan expected the world to fall at their feet. And so far, it looked like it had.

Getting justice for Cindy wouldn't be as easy as getting a

confession. She'd need more than that. But she just wasn't sure how to do that.

By the time she reached the rental house, her thighs were practically useless. Nola almost had trouble climbing the three porch steps.

She took a scalding hot shower, washing away the sweat and the anger, and then scrambled up some eggs. After a moment's pause, she scrambled up another four. After a quick glance at the back porch, she headed to the front door. As she walked out onto the front porch, the dog looked up at her, wagging her tail.

Nola walked slowly over with the plate and placed it down in front of her. "Morning, girl."

The dog waited until Nola had backed away and then stood up and started to eat.

Nola headed back inside, taking a seat at the chair in the kitchen. First she flipped to a local news site and scanned it to see if there was anything about the assault on Frat Row. She couldn't find a thing. She frowned and ran a Google search, but nothing came up.

That was strange. Apparently O'Neil had made good on his threat to bury the story. She sat back, thinking for a moment. She set up a Google Alert to let her know if anything popped up. If nothing appeared in another day or two, she'd have Bishop look into it and see what was going on. If O'Neil was trying to bury it, she'd leak the video and the names of the perpetrators to the media.

Satisfied she had at least a plan for the Frat Row douches, she did a quick search for any new information on Julie Blevins. She hadn't had any social media activity since she'd disappeared, and her parents from their social media pages were still looking for her. Nola switched over to the financial program Bishop had set up on her computer. She ran a check and saw that Julie hadn't accessed any of her accounts since she'd gone missing.

A rock settled in Nola's gut. That wasn't good. Someone could step away from social media for a little while. In fact, Nola thought more people should. But it was almost impossible for people to step away from their finances. It was possible Julie had gone to stay with friends, but that seemed unlikely.

Nola stared at her screen, wondering what she should do. Then she gave herself a shake. Cindy was the priority right now. If and when it became necessary, she'd look into Julie. So she turned her attention and focused on the files that Bishop had sent over on Hartigan, the football staff, the key players in the administration, and the boosters. It took hours to comb through everything, and when she was done, she felt nauseated. It was all so incestuous. There were so many links between all of them, with one hand washing the other.

But she knew what her first step was: It was time to lay eyes on Chris Hartigan. She flipped over to Instagram and did a search. Sure enough, Hartigan had posted. He was at a place called Poor Richards. Nola had seen the place. It was right next to campus.

Despite the eggs, her stomach grumbled. *Looks like I'm going out for lunch.*

Chapter Thirty

Poor Richards was a bar set up just off campus, next to a gas station. From the outside, it didn't look like much. In fact, it looked like an old garage. It seemed all they'd done was change the sign to turn it into a restaurant.

But Nola was pleasantly surprised when she stepped inside. An array of round tables sat in front of her with barrel chairs around them. To the right was a long counter where three individuals stood making steamed sandwiches. Over to the left was a large doorway that led into a more spacious bar area. Nola cut through the tables to a large rectangular bar in the center of the room. Around the edges was a raised platform that held more tables, most of them a good size.

A quick internet search before she left showed that at night, this place was full of college kids. It seemed to be one of the most popular hangouts for the college crowd. But during the day, professors, staff, and students all stopped by for food. It was one of those rare bars that actually had good food as well.

Today, only one occupant was not an obvious college student. A professor with gray hair and glasses sat at one of the tables with a stack of papers in front of him. He smiled at a waitress who placed his sandwich and drink next to him. The other occupants of the room weren't quite as academic in their pursuits.

Chris Hartigan stood at the far end of the room near a long table with six other large individuals who had to be also from the football team, based on their size alone. Another four females sat at the table with them. The football star looked like he was holding court standing up at the middle of the table, one foot on a chair, a beer glass clutched in his hand as he expounded on some story that had the others laughing.

A smaller group of four sat at the table adjacent to Chris's. They were also big guys, but they didn't seem to be in the middle of Chris's sphere of influence.

Nola made her way to a table in the corner of the room. It would allow her to keep an eye on the entrance as well as Chris's table. She'd just sat down when the waitress hustled over. She was young, probably about college age herself. She had long brown hair pulled back into a tight ponytail. A white apron was wrapped around her waist over her jeans and blue Poor Richard's T-shirt. She gave Nola a quick smile. "Hi. I'm Cassie. Can I get you something to drink?" she asked as she placed a menu on the table.

"Just a sweet tea if you've got it."

"Coming right up." She headed back to the front room, casting a glance at the loud table in the corner.

Nola pulled out her phone, scrolling through without looking at it while keeping an eye on the corner table. She took pictures of the group and the table next to it, sending them to Avad to do facial recognition. She didn't want to waste Bishop's time with something like this.

She continued to hold her phone, knowing it would look suspicious if she was just sitting there staring at them. She couldn't help but note the dynamic. Chris was like the king in the middle, with all his loyal subjects surrounding him. He seemed to be doing most of the talking, with only an occasional comment from the adoring crowd surrounding him.

Every once in a while, Chris would glance over at the other table to make sure that they, too, were paying attention to what he was saying. The table of four was definitely less enthusiastic about Chris's one-man show, but they didn't interrupt and gave him the attention, if not the enthusiasm, that Chris was looking for. Nola had no doubt that was why they had been banished to the second table rather than getting a spot at the main one.

In fact, at the main table, all of the guys were grinning, all their attention directly focused on Chris. The girls were appropriately simpering, which made Nola roll her eyes. She'd never been that girl. She didn't really understand that girl. Why would you bequeath all your power to some egotistical blowhard just because he could what . . . catch or throw a football?

She knew that people viewed football as modern-day gladiator battles. But Nola knew very well that those gladiators were more muscles than brain. And it was the combination of muscle and brain that made for a formidable opponent.

Those were the true warriors.

An image of Rafe slipped into her mind, causing her to jolt. She shoved the image away. She knew that she was attracted to him. She could acknowledge that much. But she also knew that any interaction with him was complicated, not the least of which because he lived on the estate. And because of Sophia and Enzo. They were in a tenuous position psychologically. They'd been enrolled in school and were doing well. In fact, Enzo was even starting to talk a little bit more. And Nola didn't want to do anything that would interfere with that.

But Nola was never one to hide behind excuses. A large part of her was just scared. Scared that if something happened with Rafe, that something would go wrong. And then the quiet home base she had created would be shattered.

And she simply couldn't do that. It had taken her a long time to finally start feeling more comfortable back at the estate. And she didn't want to risk that.

She *couldn't* risk that. And the longer she stayed away from Rafe, the easier it was to put him into a category in her mind as an itch that needed to be scratched. Even though she knew in her gut that he was much more than a one-night stand.

But Nola didn't do commitments, not anymore.

The waitress hurried back in with Nola's drink on a tray. She placed the large tumbler in front of Nola and then slipped the tray underneath her arm, pulling out her notepad. "Can I take your order?"

Flicking a glance at the menu, Nola nodded. "How are the steamed sandwiches?"

That question elicited a perfunctory smile. "They are so good. Honestly, I get one every day I come to work."

"What's your favorite?" Nola asked.

"Whole wheat with turkey, Swiss, spicy mustard, and mayo. Steamed, of course."

Nola handed her the menu. "Sounds good."

"Chips okay on the side?"

"Yes."

After scribbling a notation down on her pad, she headed back for the main room.

"Oh serving wench!" Chris's loud voice boomed across the room.

The waitress's shoulders rose with a wince that Nola could imagine even though she couldn't see her face. Slowly, Cassie turned and headed over to the table, her steps wooden.

Holding up an empty pitcher, Chris grinned. "You're getting slow."

Cassie stopped six feet from the table, her gaze flicking over the faces at the table, her expression wooden. "Another pitcher?"

Chris smiled. "As quick as your pretty little butt can get us one."

With a nod, she turned on her heel and all but fled to the front room.

The interaction was not a surprise. But Nola was surprised by the reaction of one of the guys from the other table. His eyes narrowed with concern as he watched Cassie disappear into the other room.

Nola's phone beeped, and she glanced down at it. It was a message from Avad. As Nola suspected, all of the guys were from the football team. She rapidly flipped through their names, looking for the one from the other table.

Dean Wallace. Nola ran a quick search through Google to get Dean's background information. Surprise filtered through her when she realized that Dean had gone to the same high school as Cindy.

A flip through the online yearbook showed that the two

of them were in more than a few pictures together. Had they dated? At the very least, they had been friends.

Nola hesitated for a moment and then sent a quick note to Jen. "Did Dean Wallace and Cindy date?"

The three bubbles appeared on her screen, showing that Jen had read the text and was responding, but she didn't send something back right away. It took over a minute for her message to come through. "Casually in college. But it was no big deal. Dean's a good guy."

She frowned at the response, wondering why Jen had hesitated in responding. It was entirely possible she was just busy with something else, but Nola wasn't sure.

Cassie reappeared this time with a pitcher on her tray. She walked carefully over to Chris's table. She started to place the pitcher down on the far side of the table, but Chris waved her closer. "Why don't you put that right over here, sweetheart?"

Dean stood up from the other table and quickly made his way over. He took the pitcher from Cassie. "It's okay, Cassie. I got it."

She gave him a relieved smile and then hurried away. Dean placed the pitcher in the middle of the table right in front of Chris.

"Oh, it looks like the little choir boy is back at work," Chris said.

Dean rolled his eyes. "Nope, just looking to get a beer." He grabbed one of the mugs from the table and poured himself a drink from the pitcher before heading back to the other table.

Chris watched him go with narrowed eyes. Apparently, there was a little bit of tension between those two. Probably because Dean wasn't nearly as subservient as the other groupies.

Over the next two hours, Nola watched as Chris held court with a group that seemed to only grow bigger as time went on. The professor who'd been grading papers in the corner left as the room started to fill up. More and more young people headed in, and the bartenders appeared in the middle of the large bar.

And while most of the groups seemed to be intent on getting drunk, Nola noted that Dean was sipping his beer and handing it over to the other guys at his table before replacing it with another one that he continued to sip.

Each time Cassie came in to replace the pitcher, Dean made sure he was nearby to run interference. And Chris was obviously getting more and more annoyed with that.

Now his group had swelled to about twenty individuals, half of them females. But Chris kept focusing on Cassie, even though it was obvious the girl wanted nothing to do with him.

She was a pretty girl, it was true. But Nola didn't think that was why Chris was focused on her. She wasn't falling all over herself to get his attention. The other girls, and the ones who'd shown up since, all seemed to be practically falling over trying to get his attention.

Nola had to keep herself from walking over and yelling at them to have a little respect for themselves.

At the same time, she knew it wasn't entirely their fault. Society had told them that their worth was wrapped up in how they looked. So was it really a surprise that when they were out on their own for the first time, they made sure that they looked as good as possible to attract someone like Chris? After all, that was what they were told their priority in life should be.

In a lot of ways, she felt bad for the girls. They didn't

seem to know that they were so much more than what was reflected back at them through a mirror.

As the night went on, Dean stepped out of the room, heading for the restrooms. Cassie walked into the back room at almost the same time, dropping off a pitcher at a table next to Chris's.

Chris waved her over. Once again, she stood six feet away from him, out of grabbing distance, Nola noted, and nodded at whatever Chris was telling her before she headed to the bar. It was too loud now for Nola to make it out.

The bartender quickly filled two pitchers and placed them on the bar top. Cassie grabbed them and headed back to the table. She flicked a glance at Dean's table and stumbled a little bit when she realized he wasn't there. Straightening her shoulders, she headed toward Chris's table.

Nola stood up, leaving some money on the table, acting as if she was heading to the restroom. She'd just reached the bar when Dean emerged from the restrooms.

At the table, Chris waved Cassie over to his side. Cassie walked around the group and then leaned over to place the pitchers on the table.

The quarterback reached down and grabbed her ass. She whirled around, but Chris just grabbed her around the waist and pulled her in tight toward him.

None of the other people at the table did a thing, although a few of the girls looked annoyed. Cassie pushed back against Chris to get him to let go, but he just smiled down at her.

Dean bolted toward the table and yanked Cassie out of Chris's arms.

"Go." He told her, his eyes intent as he glared at Chris.

Chris looked over at Dean, his face screwing up in rage. He swung at him. Dean ducked and landed his own punch in Chris's ribs. Two of the guys at the table grabbed Dean and yanked him back as two others stepped up to Chris and held him back.

"What the hell is wrong with you, man?" Chris demanded.

"You're drunk, Chris. You can't touch women like that. You need to cool off."

Chris glared at him. "I don't need to cool off. Maybe you should get yourself a girl. Oh wait, you don't roll that way, right?"

"Chris, man, don't go there," the guy holding Chris warned.

"Whatever." He sneered at Dean. "Get out of here."

Dean shrugged off the two guys that held him. "I'm going."

One of the guys reached for him, but Dean put up a hand, keeping him at a distance before storming from the room.

Nola slipped from her table to follow him. But he didn't go far. In the front room, Dean stopped by Cassie, who was leaning against the wall, her arms around her waist.

"You okay, Cassie?" Dean asked quietly.

Cassie wiped at her eyes. "Yeah. Thanks, Dean."

"Look, get someone else to handle his table."

Taking a deep breath, Cassie nodded. "I will."

"You need to tell your boss about him."

She gave a bitter laugh. "Yeah, if the choice comes between me and having Chris Hartigan in his bar, who do you think's going to win?"

Dean sighed. "He's such an asshole."

"Yeah, he is. But it'll be okay. I only have fifteen minutes on my shift left. I'll have John finish up with him. He already said he'd take care of it." She gestured toward a taller older man who stood behind the counter, watching Cassie with worried eyes.

Dean nodded toward the door. "You want me to wait and walk you out later?"

Cassie pushed off from the wall, shook her head, and placed a hand on Dean's forearm. "No, that's okay. I'll be fine. One of the guys will walk me out. Thanks, though. I really appreciate it, Dean." She headed back into the main room.

Dean watched her go, his brow furrowed in concern before he headed to the front doors. He flicked a glance over at John, who gave him a nod.

As Nola watched the interaction, she wondered what exactly the relationship was between Cassie and Dean. She wasn't getting any sort of romantic vibe, but she was definitely getting a friend vibe. She stepped outside of Poor Richards only a few seconds after Dean exited the restaurant. He turned to the right and started walking down the street.

Nola had gotten all of the football players addresses and knew that he had an apartment down this way.

She debated for a moment whether or not to follow him and then decided to go stay with Hartigan. She had a feeling she might get more information watching him, but she put Dean on the to-be-talked-to list before heading back into the restaurant.

Chapter Thirty-One

The university was set on over 300 acres. A good fifty of those acres were designated as a nature preserve. But walking trails had been carved out amongst the wilderness.

Nola ran along the trail, happy to see that she was alone.

She needed a little time with her thoughts. Last night, she'd stayed at Poor Richards almost until closing. Then she'd followed Hartigan's group back to a house, where they kept the party going until dawn. Hartigan has stayed and not stumbled out until ten a.m. Nola followed him back to his own apartment, which was in a luxury apartment building downtown.

She left him then, knowing that he was going to sleep for a few hours. She turned to her home to do the same. She'd spent hours watching the guy, and all she had to show for it was a sore back. He was a total jerk, but everyone flocked to him. Back at the house, she'd managed to find a spot in the woods outside that gave her a good view. The group had continued drinking, and Hartigan had disappeared into the bedroom with one of the females, but she looked more than willing.

All in all, it was a complete bust. She would have been better served speaking with his teammate Dean. She planned to do that later today, but right now they were all at practice. Nola felt a little achy and had a scratch in her throat. She hoped she wasn't coming down with something. She didn't get sick very often. Hopefully the run would burn the illness out of her.

The loop she was doing would take her seven miles from start to finish. She was already on mile six and hadn't yet figured out what exactly her next steps were going to be. She still hadn't found a way to tie Hartigan to Cindy's rape. And she had a feeling that she wasn't going to.

Somebody had been cleaning up for the guy, just like they had for the frat boys. There'd been no mention of the assault again today. Nola had sent Bishop a note, telling her to find a way to leak the tape anonymously along with the perpetrators' names.

That would at least bring some heat down on those guys, but she didn't have much to go on when it came to Hartigan. There were no mentions of Cindy's assault on any of the university's databases. Bishop hadn't even found mention of disciplinary infractions against him in the university's computers. Nola's trip to the athletic office had also failed to yield any helpful information.

But the information had to be somewhere. She had to figure out a way to tie him to all of it. She just didn't know how she was going to do it.

The weight of that settled on her shoulders, and she dragged it with her as she ran. Cindy deserved justice or at least the shadow of justice. Some crimes, in fact, *most* crimes could never be fully adjudicated. Once that ugliness touched a person, they were changed forever, their families were changed forever, and in this case, Cindy was gone forever. There was no making that right.

There was just vengeance.

Nola's feet pushed down against the ground as she picked up her pace. She sprinted the last 200 yards, shutting out all her thoughts, letting her legs pound the packed dirt of the trail. And then she reached the end of the path. Her breath came out in pants, and she felt lightheaded. She embraced the feeling. These types of exertions fed her soul, especially when she was running into roadblock after road-block with a case.

She headed back to her car, which she'd parked behind the stadium. The path was only a few hundred yards from the stadium.

As she walked toward it, her mind once again returned to Cindy, and then her roommate. Jen was scared, and from what Nola could tell, she had every right to be. Those guys had a lot of power over people's futures. And they were more than willing to use that power.

Not quite ready to head to home yet, she turned to walk around the stadium. The facility had been built six years ago and had cost hundreds of millions of dollars, paid for by the city, and they even gave the stadium huge tax breaks on top of it.

But people wanted their sports.

The stadium before this had been actually in pretty good shape, but they'd wanted to update it with all the bells and whistles. They had wanted it to be the largest stadium college football in the United States.

They ended up just shy of reaching that goal. But the Tommy Briggs Stadium was the second largest in the nation, just behind Michigan's. It could hold just over 107,000 attendees.

And yet it had never hosted a bowl game. The football team was decent, maybe even pretty good, but the reason it made money hand over fist were the television rights. Richmond football appeared on channel nine every Saturday during football season. The college took in a ton of money for the well-watched sport, and its advertisers did as well.

The kids on the football team didn't fare quite as well. So far, only one in the last twenty years had made it to the NFL. The rest had usually gone on to low-level jobs, despite each of them coming out of the university with a degree. The students were pushed through academically, keeping them in easier majors, having other people take tests and write papers for them—at least, that was what Nola assumed.

It was a racket designed to benefit the rich and keep the kids who were struggling in the limelight for a few years while they were useful and then make them go away.

Hartigan, however, was a different story. Unlike any of the previous players, he had a shot at not just the NFL but at incredible advertising deals. He was a good-looking kid and knew how to talk to the media. He was going to be a huge star in the not-too-distant future, and the university knew it.

In the bookstore, she'd seen posters and folders and bumper stickers with Hartigan's name or face on them. She shook her head, imagining what that kind of attention did to an already inflated ego.

It must make him feel invincible, like a god. And like a god, he didn't care about the mere mortals he stepped on while feeding his wants.

She had no doubt that Cindy was one of those who had

been stepped on and discarded. Just the same way she had no doubt that Cindy was only one of many.

People like Hartigan didn't simply assault one individual and then move on. He was a predator, and there was undeniably a trail of victims in his wake. Nola had heard a few stories before people clammed up, but no names. Not that she would know that from any of the official reports on the guy.

She rolled her shoulder, anger burning through her. She contemplated doing another seven-mile run for a minute. No, that wasn't wise. Exhausting herself wasn't going to help anything, especially when she was already feeling a little run down. She rounded the back of the stadium and spied her car toward the back of the lot. This part of the stadium had tall chain-link fencing blocking the less-attractive aspects of the stadium.

The gate to the loading area was unlocked. She frowned, staring at it. A muffled shout reached her ears. The hairs on the back of her neck rose, and she slowly made her way over. At the sound of a cry of pain, she picked up her pace and slipped through the gate. Walking forward cautiously, she stayed in the shadows, listening.

"I got a C!"

Nola frowned as she moved forward. The voice was raised in anger.

"I can't have a C. I already got an F on the first paper. You should have written a better one!"

"The paper was perfect," a small voice replied. "You were the one who had to reproduce it in class. It's whatever you remembered that went into it. That's not my fault."

"Well, it is now." The anger was now barely contained rage.

A crash sounded, followed by a thud, and Nola knew

that sound very well. A body just hit the floor. She sprinted around the corner and came face-to-face with three guys. One had been leaning back against the wall, watching his friend kick some poor kid on the ground. He tapped his buddy's arm, and the guy looked up.

"Walk away," he growled at Nola.

The guy was big and all muscle, muscle too large to be naturally created. His friend was a good size too, although not quite as large. Maybe he'd just started his steroid habit.

Cold fury rolled over Nola as she looked at the kid on the floor. He was maybe five six and 120 pounds soaking wet. These guys, their legs were heavier than him. "Get away from him."

The bigger monster nodded to his friend, who walked toward Nola with a smirk and a swagger. "What are you going to do, sweetheart? Bat your eyelashes at us?"

Nola rolled her eyes as she stepped forward and slammed her foot into his groin. A puff of air escaped the guy as his hands dropped to his groin and his knees buckled. Nola grabbed onto his hair and slammed her knee into his face. He let out a cry as he fell to the side.

The bigger guy's nostrils flared, reminding Nola of a bull. He cracked his knuckles. "Bitch, you're going to regret that."

Nola just sighed. These big guys tended to rely on their muscles, but they did nothing to actually train in how to fight. They just assumed that no one would go against them, and if they did, their strength would win the day. And she had to admit that if she got hit by one of those meaty paws, she would be in a world of pain and hurt.

So she'd just have to make sure she didn't get hit.

The guy stomped forward and threw a straight punch to

Nola's head. But he telegraphed it from a mile away. Nola easily slipped the punch, shooting her own at his nose.

She didn't miss.

But the guy just shook it off like a dog shaking off water. He growled at her. "You're going to have to do better than that. What did you take, some sort of women's self-defense class?"

Nola smiled. "Something like that."

She stepped forward and launched her foot as if she was going to kick him in the groin, just like she had his friend. As expected, the guy dropped his hands, his head leaning forward. That was the reaction Nola was looking for. She splayed her fingers wide and plunged them into his eyes. He screamed, and she punched him in the throat. He gurgled as he stumbled, leaning against the wall. "I can't see!"

Nola slammed her boot into his face, and his head cracked into the metal beam of the bleachers up above.

The two of them were now down and out, one moaning not so softly. Right now, she could choose to leave the two meatheads here. But the other kid looked like he was in bad shape. She leaned down to check him out. He was unconscious. Blood dribbled from his nose, and she had no doubt that a few of his ribs were broken from those kicks. Damn it. She pulled out her phone and dialed quickly.

"9-1-1. What's your emergency?"

"I need the police and an ambulance at Briggs Stadium. We're around the back by the chain-link fence."

Chapter Thirty-Two

Another exchange with campus security was not what Nola wanted. Luckily, it was Rosario who showed up, and solo this time. He shook his head when he saw the two that Nola had restrained with rope she'd found under the bleachers.

"I take it you know them?" she asked.

"Unfortunately. This is not the first time they've had issues." He flicked a glance at the kid who was being loaded onto the stretcher. "But it may be the last."

"Do you know the victim?"

"Yeah, his name's Shawn Finnigan. Good kid. He's here on scholarship. He's worked in a couple of different college offices as part of his financial aid. I don't know what he's doing with these two."

Nola could explain it, but she didn't want to get Shawn in any trouble. He was having a bad enough time of it. "Any chance I could make a quick statement?"

Rosario pulled out his pad. "What, you're not having fun dealing with security multiple times in just a few days?"

"Well, some officers I'm growing to like," she replied with a shrug.

Rosario grinned. "Good. Go ahead. I'll write it up and send you a copy later."

She quickly and succinctly told him what she'd seen and heard, and he wrote it all down. When a second security car pulled up, Dobson inside, Nola quickly got into her truck.

He gave her a heavy glare as she drove by. Nola wiggled her fingers in his direction.

Instead of heading home, Nola followed the ambulance to the hospital. The parking garage was quiet as she pulled into a spot next to a beat-up Ford Escort. Cutting down the sidewalk, she walked around a young woman being pushed in a wheelchair by an orderly. She made her way to the emergency room behind a woman and four kids. They all moved to the admittance desk. The woman, holding a one-year-old on her hip, leaned forward over the desk. "My husband. I was told my husband was here."

The attendant turned to her computer. "Name?"

While she was distracted, Nola snuck into the back and found the young man from the stadium lying on a hospital bed. He was alone. The curtains were pulled between him and some kid in the bed next to him, who looked like he had a broken arm.

Nola slipped into the curtained area. "Hey."

The young man's eyes flew open. "Hey. Um, hi."

"I'm the woman from the stadium. I'm the one who found you. My name's Nola."

The young man frowned. "But the EMT, he said that someone beat up the guys . . . That was you?"

Nola nodded.

The man's eyes blinked hard. "Wow. Thanks, um, seriously thanks."

"You're welcome." Nola closed the curtain on the other side and then took a seat in the chair next to the bed. "Think you could explain to me what that was all about?"

Not meeting her gaze, Shawn shook his head. "Nothing. It was nothing."

"You're in a hospital. I think it was something."

Footsteps sounded down the tile floor, moving toward them, and then the curtain was pulled back. Dean Wallace stood there. "Shawn, are you okay?"

He stopped still when he caught sight of Nola sitting next to the bed. "Uh, hi."

Nola stood. "Hi. I'm Nola."

Dean stepped inside, flicking a glance at the bed. "Uh, hi. What are you doing here? Are you with the cops?"

"She's the one who helped me out," Shawn said.

A nurse bustled in, looking surprised at Nola and Dean before turning to Shawn. "We need to take you up for X-rays now. You two will have to step outside. You can wait for him in the waiting room."

At Dean's concerned look, Shawn nodded. "It's okay. I'll be fine."

Dean nodded and then flicked a glance at Nola. She nodded toward the curtain. "Why don't we go outside for a little chat?"

With a stiff nod, he slipped through the curtain and then headed down the hall. Nola was right beside him. The two of them didn't say anything as they cut through the waiting room and stepped out into the cool afternoon air.

They walked to the little park across the street from the hospital. Dean took a seat on one of the wooden benches and looked up at Nola. "What happened?"

She gave him a brief rundown of the scene that she came across. Dean closed his eyes, throwing his head back.

"I told him he needed to stop working with those jerks. The steroids have just wrecked their brains."

Nola didn't comment. She had no doubt that Dean was correct, and she also had no doubt that Shawn needed the money. He was on scholarship, and it was a symbiotic relationship: He was smart, his attackers weren't. He did the work so that they could stay in the sports program. It was a win-win for both of them, except for today, when it was a definite loss for Shawn.

Opening his eyes, Dean studied Nola. "I've seen you twice in a week, and both times you seemed to be helping people out."

"Twice?" Nola asked with a frown.

Dean nodded. "I was down on Frat Row when you helped those two girls at the TAS house."

Nola grunted. She hadn't seen him, but there had been a lot of people around. "That's what I do. In fact, I was sent here to help somebody else out."

"Who?"

"Cindy Smith."

Shock splashed across Dean's face as his eyes widened and his mouth parted. Then he shook his head. "You're too late. Cindy can't be helped now."

Nola shook her head. "No, that's where you're wrong. Bringing the guy who raped her to justice will help her and her family."

Dean winced at the word but didn't argue against it.

"You know what happened to Cindy."

Letting out a slow breath, Dean nodded. "She was such an awesome girl. I mean, she was just one of those people that was always kind of happy, you know? Being around her energy was kind of addicting, even if you weren't talking or doing anything. We've gone to school together ever since junior high and became good friends senior year. We didn't hang out as much in college. We each kind of had different classes, groups. You know how it is."

"Were you ever more than friends?"

Dean shook his head. "No. We were strictly in the friend zone. Besides, she's not my type, if you know what I mean."

Nola had thought as much. "You know she killed herself because of what he did?"

"Yeah," he said softly.

"Yeah? That's it?"

Dean ran a hand through his hair. "I don't know what to say. I tried to help her afterwards. I mean, you know, I just tried to be there for her."

"How about testifying on her behalf?"

Dean winced again. "She asked me that too. I couldn't do it at first. I mean, I didn't really know anything. It was just guys talking in the locker room, and my scholarship . . ." He ran a hand through his hair again and stood up, his frame filled with anxiety as he started to pace. "I'm one of five kids, and I'm the only one who managed to get to college."

"And football let you do that."

He nodded. "And it's the only thing keeping me here. My grades are really good, but my parents, they had no money to send any of us kids, and I don't want to be up to my eyeballs in debt. If I don't follow the rules, then I have to repay them for every year I'm here. They've got this clause in my contract, and so if I testified against him, I'd have lost everything."

"Does that include a shot at the pros?"

"I'm never going pro. I never *wanted* to go pro. Football is a means to an end. But I just got into med school, early admittance. That's what I'm going to do when I get out of here. That's what I've wanted to do since I was a kid. I just have to get through this last year, and then I can get to my real life."

"Football is not your real life?"

He scoffed. "Yeah, I'm a gay biracial kid on a Midwest football team. No, it's not my real life. I mean, most of the guys are fine, but Hartigan, he's such an ass, and everybody knows he's an ass. But he throws really well, so the university and its boosters keep puffing up his ego."

"Have you heard about any other girls?"

Dean shrugged. "Rumors. I'm not trying to keep you from finding stuff out, but I'm not really in that circle. I go to the games, I do my job, I go do the things I have to do to go, but I don't spend time with these people. They're not my friends, not like Cindy was."

He took a seat again, dropping his head into his hands. For a moment, he didn't say anything. Then he looked up. "You know, in the end, even though I knew what I would lose, I offered to go testify when she was going before that stupid committee. She told me no, that she'd changed her mind. She said I didn't have any facts to back her up, and so I'd be risking my scholarship for nothing."

He was quiet for a moment. "And I felt relief. I felt relief that *I* didn't have to risk my future. How selfish is that?"

"It's not selfish. It's human nature."

"But maybe if I had said something. Maybe if I had been willing to speak on her behalf, to tell them she's not a liar, then things would have been different. Maybe the committee would have come to a different decision, or maybe she wouldn't have felt so alone."

Nola waited until Dean met her gaze. "Do you honestly think it would have changed anything?"

"No. No, it wouldn't have changed anything at all.

They're protecting him from on high. I mean, you should see the press that is trying to get to him before every game and the amount of money they have rolled into him. It's just insane. It's completely messed up. There's one guy on the team who didn't even have enough money to eat outside of football season. Like he's legit going to food pantries, and yet Hartigan, who was born with a silver spoon in his mouth, they're throwing money at him that he doesn't even need. The boosters gave him a car. He already had one. The system's just so completely messed up."

"What if I asked you to testify now? Would you do it?"

Dean shook his head, staring at the hospital as the doors opened, and a hospital worker in scrubs stepped outside and leaned against the building, talking on their phone. "What's the point? Cindy's gone, and Chris Hartigan, he can't be touched. All I'll do is destroy my chance at a future."

"What if I could protect you from that?"

"You can't. There are people in this world who just get away with stuff, and Chris Hartigan is one of them. Thank you for helping out Shawn. I really appreciate it, and if there's anything else I can do to help that doesn't involve me testifying, then I'll do it. But I can't risk my future for a long shot that maybe Chris will get what he's owed. I just can't do it."

Dean walked back across the street, his head down, his shoulders hunched.

Nola let him go. There was no point in talking further with him. He probably knew more than he realized, and just providing the names of other victims could help build a case. But he was right that Hartigan was being protected from on high, and until Nola was able to get rid of some of those protections, no one would be willing to come forward.

She could slip into Chris's apartment and beat the hell

out of him. But that would be temporary, and then she'd have everybody coming after her, and he would still be there, untouched and martyred in the public eye. She needed to find a way to make the public turn against him. She needed to find a way to make the public see who he really was.

And for once, she had no idea how to do that.

Chapter Thirty-Three

TOMMY

The showroom buzzed with excitement. Gold, white, and blue balloon arches draped the entryways once again. Streamers hung down from the ceiling along with more balloons. The giant banner with Tommy's face had been replaced with an even larger one. "Sweet Home Alabama" played over the speakers.

Tommy found his gait lining up with the beat. It might be the wrong state, but the song spoke to the American in everyone.

"How you all doing this morning?" Tommy slapped the back of a man standing with his wife talking to Chip Dickerson, one of his newer salespeople. Young, muscular, and good looking, the kid was a natural. He had the good looks that the women liked and the raw masculinity that the men hoped they also had. He also had an ambition that resonated with Tommy. Chip was going to be one of his best salespeople in short order. Tommy was sure of it. "Everything going all right here?"

The man stared at Tommy, his eyes bugging out of his head, looking a little starstruck. "Yeah, going great."

Tommy nodded toward his sales clerk. "Chip here is good people. He'll take care of you." This time he clapped Chip on the back before he headed across the showroom.

"Yes, sir, Mr. Briggs," Chip said with a confident grin.

The showroom looked good. The ground was spotless, the newest models gleamed. Tommy puffed out his chest. This was going to be a good day. Tingles of excitement rolled along Tommy's skin. He loved this time of year. The new line of F-150s had just come in, and people were excited. He smiled as a familiar face strode through the door. "Clive, you old son of a gun. Good to see you."

The silver-haired man with the deeply tanned face smiled back at Tommy, his hand extended. Dressed in dark slacks and an IUR fleece, Clive Hafner looked like most other customers except for the confidence. Plus, if you knew what you were looking for, you could pick out the $10,000 watch and the expensive Italian leather boots. "Tommy. Looks like it's that time of year again."

Tommy chuckled good-naturedly. "Yes, it is, and we've got a beaut set aside for you." He looked over his shoulder.

Maria Snopes, another one of his salespeople, who exclusively worked with their VIP customers, or at least their male ones, hurried toward the two of them, a smile on her face. And what a face: she was a former beauty queen who had maintained herself very well.

"Maria here will show you to the truck we've got squirreled away in the back for you. When you're done checking her out, you and I will sit down and talk about what we can do for that business of yours as well."

She extended her arm. "This way, Mr. Hafner."

Clive smiled as he looked Maria over from head to toe. He chuckled as he grinned at Tommy. "You sure do know how to do customer service, Tommy."

"That I do. See you in a few. Take your time." He watched as Maria escorted Clive to the back room, where they had set aside a completely souped-up Hummer. Clive would buy it within the hour.

But that wasn't the reason Clive got special treatment. No, that SUV was for Clive's personal use. It was the business acquisitions that Tommy would see to himself after he got his one-on-one tour from Maria.

If all went well—and Tommy intended to make sure it did—Clive would only leave after he signed a contract for twenty F-150s. Those F-150s wouldn't be the top of the line like his personal vehicle, but each would cost a pretty penny and would be used for his construction company, which did business across the state.

Every two years, Clive came in like clockwork and upgraded his own personal SUV and signed a contract for new pickup trucks for his business. The newer business pickups weren't for the construction workers but for the managers and office individuals for when they went out to visit a site. Clive knew it looked better if they were driving a pickup than some Mercedes when going to a construction site.

Tommy grinned as he turned back to his office. Today he was going to make a lot of money.

His phone rang as he headed down the hall. He pulled it from his pocket, flicking a glance at the screen, and frowned. He slid his finger across the screen. "Hold on a sec. Let me get to my office."

On the other end of the call, John O'Neil stayed quiet,

knowing that their business was not something that needed to be publicly broadcasted.

Tommy made his way down the hall and closed his office door behind him. His office had a wall of windows on one side that overlooked the parking lot, which was filled with brand-new gleaming cars. A dozen people wandered through, looking at different models with another half a dozen salespeople strewn throughout the lot, some walking with them, some giving them time and waiting to move in to make the sale.

Tommy took off his hat and hung it on the coat rack by his door before he settled in behind his desk. He pulled his phone back up. "Okay, O'Neil, this better be good. I've got a busy day ahead of me."

"It looks like we might have a little problem," O'Neil said.

Tommy sighed. "That's what I pay you the big bucks for. Is it those frat boys again?"

"Well, yeah, the video somehow made it online."

"What? I thought you were handling that."

"I was. I locked down all our copies. But the woman who made the recording, she's been a bit of a problem."

"Look, the frat boys are a nuisance. But none of them are related to the football team. It should be easy to separate them. Cast them out, make them pariahs. We'll have the school expel them and make a statement. No problem. So why are you calling me? You know how this works. You're supposed to make all my little problems go away."

"Yeah, well, this little problem is becoming a big one. That woman from the frat house? She's been speaking with Cindy Smith's roommate and her other friends who were there that night. If she hasn't linked Hartigan's name to it, she will soon. She even beat up two 'roid heads at the stadium the other day."

His eyes narrowing, Tommy went still. "Who is this woman?"

"A graduate student. Her focus is sexual assault. She's doing some research, and I guess the questioning is part of that. But I don't really like it. I think it's cutting a little too close for comfort."

Tommy swung around in his chair, staring out the window. He'd been protecting Hartigan for years now. The kid was an incredible football player, but he was also a predator. Tommy didn't really mind that so much, except if it got in the way of his money, and so far it hadn't been a problem. The university didn't want a scandal attached to their good name, so they'd swept everything under the rug. But if this grad student was digging into things, it was possible that she might stir up some dust that could cost him and the university some money.

And Tommy didn't like anything getting in the way of his money.

"Get some guys. Have them send her a message that she can do all the research she wants. She just needs to keep Hartigan's name out of it."

There was a pause on the other end of the phone. "How strong a message do you want to send?"

Outside the window, all his cars stood shining in the sun in uniform rows. He'd built all of this up over decades of hard work, and like hell he was going to let some grad student come along and rip it all out from underneath him. Because if she started digging into Hartigan, and then someone started digging into his past, they'd find the links to Tommy, and they'd drag him through the mud. He'd probably survive the scandal, but his business would take a hit for a little while, that was for sure.

"Make it strong. I don't want her asking any more questions."

"Ever?"

Considering it, Tommy paused for a moment and then shook his head. "No. That'll bring too much heat. She's a grad student. Just scare her away. It shouldn't be that hard."

Chapter Thirty-Four

NOLA

The rest of Nola's day didn't get any better. She tracked down everyone on campus and off that might have seen something at the party that night with Cindy, as well as the women that Melanie had suggested she speak with. But no one was willing to speak up. As soon as she brought up Hartigan's name, people's mouths slammed shut.

She was walking down the sidewalk toward the stadium when a voice called out behind her. "Nola, wait up."

Leslie jogged down the path toward her. She fell in step with Nola, flicking a glance around. "So I hear you've been asking a lot of questions."

"Where'd you hear that?"

Leslie rolled her eyes. "Everywhere. The word came down from on high that no one is supposed to talk to you. I don't know that they know exactly who you are yet, but people are getting suspicious. It helps that your graduate work is on sexual assault, but still you're making people nervous."

Normally Nola was fine with making people nervous. In fact, it was a reaction she generally encouraged. But in this case, it definitely wasn't working in her favor. "Everyone's clamming up. No one wants to talk about the golden boy."

Grabbing Nola's arm, Leslie pulled her to a stop, her eyes wide. "It was Hartigan?"

Nola turned to face her. "You didn't know?"

Leslie shook her head. "No. I mean I've heard rumors about Hartigan and women, but it's all been so vague. It's impossible to tell the difference between truth and just locker room talk."

Nola was really beginning to hate phrase.

The trainer continued. "But I never thought he was the one . . . not with Cindy. I mean, Cindy just . . . she wasn't the type of girl he would go for."

Nola grunted. "Yeah, well, I'm getting the impression that Hartigan's type of girl is pretty much any girl."

Leslie narrowed her eyes. "Did someone say something?"

"Not specifically. But the way people are dancing around his name, I can tell that people know something. They're just not sure what to say without getting themselves in trouble. But there're dozens of them. If they all spoke up together, then it could have an impact. But right now, everybody feels like they're cast adrift on their own, and so no one is willing to be the first one to step forward."

"Because they figure all they'll end up doing is hurting themselves."

Nola nodded. She wanted to tell each person that it wouldn't be a waste. She wanted to tell them that change would happen because of their actions.

But she knew that wasn't the truth. It was entirely possible that even with dozens of people coming out to speak against Chris Hartigan, nothing would happen to the guy or it would end with a slap on the wrist, the accounts being watered down to the point of unimportance.

Media accounts of well-known individuals being accused of sexual assault bore that out. Harvey Weinstein being the most egregious individual whose assaultive behavior was apparently common knowledge in Hollywood circles. Bill Cosby had dozens of individuals come forward, and people still doubted the veracity of their claims, arguing that all the women knew each other and were somehow in it together. And he'd even been released early from his sentence. Donald Trump was another one, who had more than two dozen women come forward to make complaints about him, and yet he'd skated by unscathed. Men who were rich and powerful tended not to be held to account to the same standard as someone at a lower level.

In football, those reactions were even worse. Domestic violence seemed so high, it was endemic. There had been eighty-seven arrests amongst eighty players over fourteen years. The NFL got a lot of flak for only suspending players for a few games for domestic violence incidents—until Ray Rice.

But generally, they still could do more. It seemed that video evidence made public was the necessary catalyst for someone to be booted from the league. College was perhaps even worse. More than a few colleges and universities had been found guilty of covering up the sexual assaults of its players. Most recently, LSU had gotten in trouble for covering up incidents that went back years. In fact, college athletes were way overrepresented in sexual assault statistics.

While they made up only a small percent of college students, they accounted for 20% of the assaults.

But Nola couldn't allow Cindy to just be another statistic. She owed it to Jack, but she owed it to Cindy as well, to that adorable little girl who at one point was Nola's picture of Christmas.

Chapter Thirty-Five

Three hours later, after Nola pulled into the driveway of her rented house, she sat behind the wheel, too tired for a moment to reach over and open the door. Somewhere in the last three hours, she realized that she had caught whatever was going around on campus.

At first, she'd thought it was just the frustration of no one being willing to talk that got to her. The run hadn't helped the way it normally did. But after speaking with Leslie, she began to feel more and more drained. Now, as she sat staring through her windshield, she couldn't deny the reality: she was sick.

Sickness was never really much of an issue for Nola. She kept moving, kept healthy. Honestly, she wasn't around people long enough to get sick.

But this case was dragging on. Of course, she'd known when Jack asked her to look into it that it wouldn't be one of her in-and-out cases. She'd known that getting to the heart of Cindy's assault would take time. She hadn't expected illness to be another stumbling block to getting to the truth, though.

Reaching over to the passenger seat, she grabbed the bag of medicine she'd picked up at the pharmacy and the takeout of chicken noodle soup. She'd already swallowed down two aspirin, hoping that they might stave off or reduce the fever that had started an hour ago. She'd also swallowed some cold pills, not sure if they would help, but willing to try.

The front door seemed like it was miles away, even though she knew it was less than twenty feet. *Come on, Nola, you've got this.*

She couldn't remember the last time she'd gotten this sick. And then it came back to her: Molly's kindergarten year. A stomach bug/cold combo had been going around her school. Molly had come home with it, and it quickly spread to both Nola and David. Within twenty-four hours, they'd all been down for the count. Avad and Ileana had stopped in and stocked them up with food and meds. David, Molly, and Nola had stayed wrapped up together those first two days.

The third day, they'd all stopped throwing up and had a little more energy. Not going-out energy, but *moving to the living room for a Disney marathon* energy. It had turned into a great couple of days. A snowstorm had hit that second night, and they'd been snug, all cuddled up together. Strangely, it was one of her favorite family memories.

Staring at the sad little house out of her windshield, a feeling of loneliness rolled over her. There'd be no fully stocked fridge here for her. No David tucking the blankets around her feet to make sure they didn't get cold. No Molly holding her hand for hours. It would just be Nola.

Grabbing the handle, she shoved the door open and

stepped out. Her knees shook for a moment, and she thought she might go down. This sickness, whatever it was, really packed a punch.

Slamming the door behind her, she made her way to the front door, each of her limbs feeling like it had somehow magically gained ten pounds in the last day. By the time she reached the front porch, it felt like that weight had doubled.

She dragged herself up the short porch steps, and her breathing was ragged by the time she reached the door. She leaned against the house as she fumbled in her pocket for her keys. Finding the correct one, she inserted it into the lock and all but fell into the front foyer, shaking her head.

I need sleep.

Stumbling over to the table in the front hall, she dropped the medicine and soup container on its top. It could wait until she'd slept a little. Her keys slipped from her hand and dropped to the floor.

With a groan, she reached down to grab them. A thump sounded above her head.

She fell forward, reaching out a hand to the ground. A man stood above her, the bat he'd just swung at her head embedded in the plaster wall. What? She hadn't even heard them. Damn it.

Scrambling back like a crab down the hall, her gaze flicked to the doorway. She hadn't heard his friend either. They were both big, with wide, broad shoulders, but they were on the edge of fat. Both had the beginnings of a paunch, and the wrinkles around their eyes suggested that they were heading up there in years. Maybe they had once been athletes, but that had been long ago. Now they looked like the type that relied on muscle to get the job done.

Which, today, with her in her current shape, they probably could do. Who the hell were these guys?

"Where you going?" Meathead One demanded as he shoved the lamp off the table by the door. Her meds went flying, as did the soup.

Meathead Two gripped the bat tightly. "You need to stop asking questions."

Apparently someone was getting nervous. Any other day, she'd actually be happy at this turn of events. Two guys versus her—that didn't even count as exercise. But today, her reflexes were dull, her thoughts even duller.

Nola stopped backpedaling, having put enough distance between herself and the two men. Managing to get to her feet, the air swayed in front of her, but she managed to lock her legs. She didn't want to turn her back on them, and there was no way she was going to be able to get to one of her weapons in time.

Which meant she needed to take one of their weapons with the least amount of energy possible. Puffing out a breath, her chest felt tight. *I might be in trouble here*, she thought. So when in doubt, bluff. "And who sent you?" she demanded.

Meathead Two smiled. "A concerned citizen."

He swung the bat to accentuate the point.

Nola would have rolled her eyes, except it would have taken too much energy. Ignoring her weakness, she twirled into the man's chest, completing the swing, wrapping her arm around his. He let out a yell as his feet came up off the ground and he went flying into the living room. Nola held onto the bat but then had to grip the wall as dizziness overtook her.

Meathead One slipped a knife from his sheath. "You shouldn't have done that."

As the world swam before her eyes, Nola had to agree.

The man lunged for her. Nola darted to the side. The

edge of the bat struck the counter, pushing back against her grip. Unprepared, she lost her hold on the bat. It crashed to the floor and rolled toward the back door.

God, she was all sorts of out of it. She couldn't remember the last time she'd just let go of a weapon. This was not good.

The man continued forward, forcing Nola away from the back door as his friend stumbled to his feet in the hall.

Nola backed up, trying to keep her focus on the guy, even as the edges of her vision began to waver. Stupid meds. Weren't they supposed to have kicked in by now? Or maybe they had and that was why she was so dizzy.

The man jabbed the knife straight for her gut.

Slipping to the side, Nola placed her hand on his wrist and yanked him forward. He let out a cry as he lost his balance. Nola quickly shifted his wrist, turning the knife back toward him. As she twisted his wrist toward the ground, he let out a yell. Following him to the ground, she stabbed the knife into his shoulder. He screamed. Nola stumbled to the side, shaking her head. It felt twenty pounds heavier too.

Do not lean down, she warned herself, as that seemed to be what brought on the dizziness.

With a roar, his partner charged down the hallway and into the kitchen. Having collected his bat, he arched up for a swing.

Nola knew she wasn't going to be able to get out of the way in time. She was trapped, the wall on one side and the guy on the other. And her body was just moving so slow right now.

A growl erupted from down the hallway. A flash of gray fur appeared behind the man before the dog sunk its teeth into the man's calf. He let out a scream, shifting himself so that his swing landed on the side of the dog.

The dog didn't let go, holding on for all it was worth. The man brought the bat up again and landed his second shot.

Scrambling to her feet, Nola yanked the knife out of the second man's shoulder. He screamed, his hand flying to the wound to try to staunch the bleeding.

Gripping the cabinet, Nola pulled herself forward. As the man reared up to take a third hit at the dog, she plunged her knife into the man's back. He let out a cry, and his back arched. Ripping the bat from his hand, she slammed it into his face. She turned, and for good measure, slammed it into the side of the head of the guy still on the ground. Both of them let out grunts before they went unconscious.

Taking a trembling step, the dog collapsed with a cry. It whimpered as it tried to get to it's feet, but it's leg was injured. It cried out again and fell.

Nola dropped to the ground next to it. Casting a glance at the dog's underbelly, she spoke softly, "It's okay, girl. It's okay."

The dog let out another whimper. With a groan, Nola leaned back against the wall, stretching her legs out as she pulled out her phone. The dog inched closer to her and placed her head on Nola's thigh. Her vision wavering, Nola quickly dialed as she placed her other hand on the dog's chest.

"9-1-1. What's your emergency?"

Swallowing, even Nola could hear the weakness in her voice when she answered. "Two men just broke into my home. I need help."

Chapter Thirty-Six

A cop showed up ten minutes later. Luckily, he wasn't a university cop. By the time he arrived, the meds had started to kick in, and her world was a little less blurry. Explaining to him what had happened had taken a little time, time Nola really didn't have. She was worried about the dog, who growled when the cop went near her.

"Is she yours?" the cop asked.

Nola shook her head. "No, she's a stray. But she saved me."

"We'll call animal control and get someone out to take her."

"No," Nola said quickly.

The cop's eyebrows arched.

"She saved me, really. I'll take care of her."

The cop made her go over her statement again as they waited for the other patrol car to arrive to take Meathead Two. Both were handcuffed and finally coming around.

"Do you know them?" the cop asked.

Nola shook her head. "Never seen them before in my life."

"Any idea why they'd target you?"

"Single female living alone, I guess."

The cop looked like he wanted to press the point, but another patrol car showed up just then.

"Look, I really need to get her to the vet. Do you need me anymore?" she asked.

The cop shook his head. "No. Let me carry her to the car for you, and then we'll lock up so you can get going."

"Thanks," Nola said.

The dog growled as the officer leaned down to pick her up. The cop backed away. "Uh, yeah, we might need animal control."

Leaning down, Nola looked at the dog. "Let me help you, girl." She reached under her and carefully picked her up. "Can you open the back of my car?"

Walking in front of her, he scooped her keys off the floor. Outside, he unlocked the tailgate of Nola's truck and spread out the blanket back there.

After placing the dog gently down, Nola ran a hand over the dog's head before shutting the gate. The dog barely stirred. The cop gave her directions to the nearest vet and promised to call ahead to let them know she was coming.

Thanking him, she hopped into the driver's seat, urgency taking over her. She quickly put the car into gear and pressed down on the accelerator. "Hold on, baby. Hold on. We'll get you some help."

Less than ten minutes later, Nola pulled into the vet parking lot with a screech of tires. A tall African American vet assistant was already waiting outside. He hustled over to Nola's car as she opened the tailgate. He reached in and gently picked up the dog. The dog didn't make a sound.

Alarmed, Nola's gaze shot to the dog's chest, but it was moving up and down.

A second vet assistant stood at the door and held it open to allow the man and the dog through. They disappeared inside.

Nola closed the tailgate and stood staring at the vet door, trying to figure out her next move. *It's not your dog, Nola. You got it to the vet. That's the important thing.*

But she couldn't forget those deep-brown eyes staring up at her.

Reaching into her pocket, she downed two more aspirin, hoping she could keep off the worst of the effects of the illness for at least a little while longer. Squaring her shoulders, she headed into the vet's office. The dog had put its life on the line for her. The least she could do was make sure she was okay.

Forty-five minutes later, Nola found herself sitting in a small examination room. The receptionist had ushered her in just a few minutes ago, promising to bring the dog in in a moment.

Now the door opened, and the dog was laid gently on the table.

"She has a couple of busted ribs and a fractured back leg. We've got a cast on the leg, but there's not much we can do about the ribs. We've bandaged her up pretty tight, but she needs to not move much for at least two weeks. I can give you some sedatives to make sure she stays still. Oh, and we gave her a flea bath because she was in pretty bad shape." He glared at Nola.

She held up her hands. "Hey, she's not my dog. She's a stray."

"Oh, are you taking her, or should I call animal control?"

"No, I'll take her."

The guy looked around and then frowned. "Hold on a sec. I left her meds in the back room. Let me go grab them."

He disappeared out the door before Nola could say anything. The dog's eyes were closed. She lay silent on the metal table. Nola stared at her, trying to figure out what she was going to do. She certainly couldn't take care of a dog in the middle of everything. Even if it was healthy, she didn't exactly have a lifestyle that screamed for dog ownership.

The dog's eyes opened and looked straight into Nola's. She let out a little whimper and then started to move as if trying to get closer to her.

"No, no. Don't move." Nola quickly shifted so she could reach the dog. She lay her hand on the dog's head, gently running her hand over her fur. With a sigh, the dog closed her eyes. Nola shifted her hand and gently ran it over the dog's belly. It was obvious she'd had puppies, probably a lot of puppies over the years. She was a beautiful dog with a shiny gray coat, with just a little bit of white under the chest and between the eyes.

The dog's breaths evened out. Nola started to pull her hand away. The dog's eyes opened as it reached up with a paw. She placed her paw over Nola's hand, holding her in place.

Nola smiled at the dog. "Thank you. I would have been in a lot of trouble if you hadn't stepped in."

The dog let out another sigh. And Nola knew that no

matter the inconvenience, she had a debt to repay. And she intended to do just that.

Chapter Thirty-Seven

The vet said they could keep the dog overnight, but Nola decided to take her home. She figured she was recuperating anyway, so they might as well recuperate together. So the vet tech loaded the dog back in her car, along with a bag full of meds and three pages of instructions.

Nola pulled into the driveway at 7:30, feeling like it was three in the morning. The meds had started to wear off, and she was back to feeling dizzy. She sat for a few moments, trying to regain her strength, and then pushed open the door.

Opening up the back of the truck, the dog gave her a slow tail wag. "Okay, girl, I'm going to need a little help here."

Taking a breath, she slipped her arms under the dog and carefully pulled her to the edge of the gate and lowered her to the ground. Nearly losing her balance at the end, she let the dog down a little heavier than she would have liked. She winced. "Sorry."

The dog stood for a moment and then walked over to

the grass and did her business, while Nola held onto the edge of the leash she'd bought at the vet's office. Once the dog was done, she grabbed the dog's meds and shoved them in her pockets. Leading the dog over to the stairs, she stopped, staring up at them. *Okay, I've got this.*

Squatting down, she gathered the dog in her arms and carried her up the stairs. She walked to the front door and slid down it as she lowered the dog to the ground, more gently this time. Nola sat on the ground for a moment. The dog leaned toward her and licked her face.

Nola smiled, leaning toward the dog. "Thanks."

One hand on the wall, she stood up and fished her keys out of her pocket. Unlocking the door, she paused for a second in the doorway, but there was no noise coming from inside. The cops had grabbed her meds and placed them back on the table and even cleaned up the broken lamp and spilled soup.

The dog walked forward tentatively. Nola locked the door behind them. She made her way into the kitchen and filled a bowl with water for the dog and A glass for herself. She hadn't eaten in a while, but she wasn't hungry, and the dog wasn't supposed to eat until tomorrow.

Heading back down the hall, the dog stood in the same spot, looking uncertain. Nola placed the bowl against the wall. Even with one hand on the wall, it was an effort to get back up. She really needed to sleep. "Okay, baby. Drink up and get a good night's sleep."

She walked into the bedroom. Sitting on the edge of the bed, she kicked off her boots and pushed herself back, her whole body practically weeping with joy at the idea of being able to lie down.

In the hallway, she could hear the dog lapping up the water. Then her footsteps moved tentatively toward the bedroom. She walked around the bed a few times before leaning her head on the edge and letting out a whimper.

Nola cracked open an eyelid. The dog stared back at her, giving a hopeful wag of her tail. Not a single cell in Nola's body wanted to move. But she couldn't resist those big brown eyes. With a groan, she rolled off the other side of the bed and then walked around toward the dog.

The dog tensed, and Nola realized she'd unintentionally boxed her in. "I get it. You don't like being cornered. Me either. But let's just trust each other a little bit, okay?"

Not sure if the dog understood her and too tired to care, she carefully picked the dog up and placed her on the bed. Then Nola crawled into it, practically collapsing on the pillow.

The dog walked around for a moment and then moved closer to Nola. She turned in a half circle and then lowered herself to the bed, her back against Nola's chest. The dog's warmth spread into her.

Falling off to sleep, Nola placed a hand on the dog's back, a smile on her face. "Night, girl."

Chapter Thirty-Eight

For seven hours, Nola slept with the dog curled up next to her. She would have slept longer, but the dog's growl shook her awake. It was still dark out.

Opening her eyes, she squinted, her mouth feeling like cotton and her thoughts fuzzy. The dog's growl continued next to her as the hair along her scruff rose.

Nola slipped from the bed and grabbed her Beretta from the weapon's trunk. Shaking the cobwebs out of her head, she walked toward the front door as footsteps grew closer.

A knock sounded. "Nola?"

She let out a breath. She knew that voice. Lowering the gun, she undid the locks and then frowned at the man who stood framed by the doorway. "Rafe? What are you doing here?"

He flicked a glance at the gun in her hand and then frowned even deeper, taking her in. "We've been monitoring the police channels. We heard about the home invasion. And then you didn't answer your phone."

Crap. She hadn't taken her phone to the vet. She hadn't even checked it when she got back either. She waved generally toward the back of the house. "Yeah, I just, I just didn't have it on me."

Rafe stepped in, closing the door shut behind him. "Are you all right?"

She nodded, even as she swayed. "Yeah, I'm just a little under the weather. So I was just getting some sleep. You don't have to stay."

Her knees buckled, and she reached out to the wall. He took a step forward as if he was going to catch her. She held up a hand. "No, I'm fine. I don't need any help."

Rafe looked at her, and he clearly didn't believe her. She leaned against the wall, trying to make the move look casual and not like the wall was holding her up. He took a step closer to her. "Nola, you help all of these other people. Now let me help you."

She opened her mouth to argue, but the world spun around her, and she pitched forward.

Rafe grabbed her before she could fall. "Yeah, I don't think I'm going anywhere," he murmured.

Chapter Thirty-Nine

The smell of meat and herbs came from the kitchen, tickling Nola's nose. She sniffed, taking in the scent before she even managed to open her eyes. When she did, she recognized the rental bedroom.

The dog still lay on the bed next to her. But her eyes were open as well, and she thumped her tail as Nola looked over at her.

Reaching out, Nola scratched her behind the ears. The dog leaned her head into Nola's palm. Apparently, they had crossed the trust threshold. Nola couldn't help but smile.

"Good, you're both awake," Rafe said as he appeared in the doorway. Tall with a strong build, he leaned casually against the doorway, his jeans hugging his waist and his T-shirt showing off his perfectly chiseled chest. His thick dark hair was disheveled but in all the right ways, and his dark eyes sparkled as he smiled.

There were worse sights to wake up to.

The dog let out a low growl but still thumped her tail.

Rafe grinned down at the dog. "Still growling, I see. I swear, she's like the canine version of you."

"Uh, you're still here."

"I've been here for a full day. You've been really out of it."

"A full *day*?" That explained why Nola felt like she was covered in dried sweat and her mouth had a horrible taste in it. But her mind felt much clearer now. And while she still felt weak, she had the feeling that it was due more to a lack of food than anything else.

Careful to keep a healthy distance from the dog, Rafe walked around the other side of the bed. The dog continued to growl at him. "Think you could tell your friend here that I'm not the enemy? Every time I've taken her out to go to the bathroom, she's growled. Every time I've fed her, she's growled. Every time I've given her water, she's growled." He carefully placed a couple of pieces of hot dog in front of the dog. The dog snapped them up and then returned to her growling.

Rafe rolled his eyes. "I swear, I give the dog pain meds in hot dogs and still I get no love."

Nola stared at Rafe. He'd stayed. He'd taken care of both of them.

Walking to the other side of the room, Rafe leaned back against the wall. "So, where'd your friend come from?"

"She's a stray from the neighborhood. She helped when those two men we're waiting for me."

Rafe nodded. "I read the police report. Any idea who they were?"

Nola pictured the two men. "They're not important. Who's important is the one who sent them."

Chapter Forty

TOMMY

The tuxedo lay on the bed as Tommy stepped out of the bathroom, steam wafting into the room behind him. He smiled at the pitch-black ensemble on the bed. He'd bought the tuxedo two years ago and had gotten a lot of use out of it. Tonight, he'd wear it to the governor's fundraiser.

It would be an expensive night. Each plate was $1,000, and that was before the silent auction. Tommy had his eye on a fishing trip with Dan Marino. That would be worth just about any price.

Quickly donning the suit, he sat on the edge of the bed to tie his shoes. The shoes were the one part of this whole getup he could do without. The tux made him look like James Bond, but the shiny Italian shoes were damned uncomfortable.

His phone rang, and he pulled it out, puffing out a breath at the sight of John O'Neil's name. What had happened to the man? When he'd first met him, he was this tough ex-cop. He'd handled their affairs with barely a word. Now he practically needed Tommy to hold his hand.

"Yeah?" he answered as he stood up, wincing at the tightness of his shoes. Maybe he should just wear his cowboy boots. Who looked at feet anyway?

"Hey, it's John."

"I know, John. I'm getting ready to head out. What's going on?" Tommy leaned toward the mirror, peering at his face. Was that a wrinkle?

"We have a problem."

"You seem to be having a lot of problems lately. What is it this time?"

"Uh, two of the guys, we've used them before. Normally, they don't have any problems. Well, they went to deliver the message to that grad student, and they got arrested."

Straightening, Tommy turned away from the mirror. "What do you mean they got arrested? Where?"

"Uh, at that grad student's home."

Tommy's mouth fell open and then slammed shut. "What the hell kind of two-bit operation are you running? How the hell did that happen?"

"She, uh, had a dog."

"A dog? They couldn't handle a dog?" Tommy seethed. He was surrounded by idiots.

John was quiet for a moment. "So what do you want me to do?"

"Bail them out and send them somewhere. Get them out of town. I don't want anyone to be able to find them until this has all settled down."

"That's going to take some money."

Tommy's jaw was tight as he spoke. "Fine. Let me know

what you need and I'll arrange it. But this better not come back to me."

"It won't. And what do you want me to do about the grad student?"

"Did she get the message?"

"Yeah, she definitely got it. Both guys . . . yeah, she got the message."

Tommy took a breath. "Okay. The message was sent. She'll leave it alone if she knows what's good for her."

Chapter Forty-One

NOLA

The late morning was quiet. Most of the students in the surrounding houses were either sleeping or at class. Nola sat on the back porch sipping coffee as the dog sniffed around the backyard.

She couldn't believe that she'd slept for a full day. She had zero memory of any of that time. She'd been completely vulnerable. If more guys had come to finish the job, she would have been completely at their mercy.

But Rafe had stayed. She wasn't surprised by that, but she was surprised that he was here. Avad and Bishop had shown up before. That felt different. This, it was strange, but . . . nice.

Nola had taken a shower, which felt great, and then she'd eaten a little bit. And then she needed a nap. Apparently, she was a little overly optimistic about being back to normal.

When she woke up, Rafe had left a note saying he was running errands and would be back soon.

Nola booted up her computer and added some notes about the situation with the two men and then started to look through all her notes, hoping something would pop out at her. She'd only been at it for a short while when the dog started to get restless, and Nola knew she needed to go out, so she picked her up and carried her outside. She'd forgotten the leash. Part of her wondered if the dog would just wander off, but she seemed content to just sniff around the backyard, every once in a while glancing back as if to make sure Nola was still around.

As if hearing Nola's thoughts, the dog made her way over to her and very slowly climbed up the stairs. She walked over to the water bowl that Nola had refilled and then curled up next to Nola, her warm back leaning against Nola's hip.

Nola reached a hand down and ran her fingers through the dog's fur. It wasn't easy for her to admit she needed help, but twice in the last twenty-four hours, she'd needed it. First, she would have been in dire straits if the dog hadn't shown up, and then if Rafe hadn't come, she would have been here alone, sick and completely vulnerable.

And that got her thinking. She'd been doing this for so long, ever since David and Molly. Maybe she was getting too old for it at this point. But she didn't know what else she could do. She wasn't cut out for normal life anymore. She'd been too bruised, too battered.

In fact, she'd never had a normal job. She'd gone into government work right after high school. She doubted she was cut out for some sort of office work. Even the idea of needing a business wardrobe of suits made her skin itch.

"You could always work with Rafe back at the estate,"

Molly said as she sat down on the dog's other side and began to pet her head.

The dog lifted her head for a moment, tilting it as she stared at Molly and then lay her head back down with a contented sigh.

"I don't think that's in the cards for me, sweetheart."

"It could be. You can do anything. You could even go back to a normal life, maybe even have a family again."

The breath hitched in Nola's chest as she stared at Molly. "You're my family."

Molly gave her a sad smile. "I'll always be your family, Mama. But it's okay to have more than just me in your life. It's probably healthier."

Nola gave a little laugh. "Healthier? Are you reading self-help books wherever you are?"

Molly shrugged with a grin. "Sometimes we learn things."

A car backfired out on the street. On instinct, Nola's head jerked up, turning toward the drive. But there was no cause for concern. When she turned back, though, Molly was gone.

Once again, there was that sense of loss she always felt whenever Molly disappeared. She didn't think that would ever go away. Grief had set up shop in her chest and was her one constant in her vagabond life. But it felt a little different now, slightly less painful.

Grabbing her coffee mug, she clasped it in her hands and embraced the warmth, letting it seep through her palms. Something about this case was getting to her. She didn't realize at first what it was, thinking that it was just the injustice of it, but then she realized it was more than that. This case, this guy, all of it reminded her of Beth. Cindy and Beth didn't look anything alike, but with the impact of what had happened to them, she couldn't deny the simi-larities.

And she felt just as frustrated right now as she did back then about what happened. It was just so unfair. Cindy was gone and all these people were running around protecting that monster, and she knew in her gut that there were more Cindys out there. She just couldn't get any of them to talk to her.

A vision of Beth, her eyes filled with tears, rolled through her mind. The monsters, they never stopped coming, did they?

Chapter Forty-Two

NOLA
TWENTY-ONE YEARS AGO

After giving Jerry some well-deserved hits, Nola had been dragged down to the vice principal's office. He demanded that she explain why she had attacked Jerry in the middle of class. But Nola kept her mouth shut, her arms crossed over her chest. She wasn't going to say a thing about Beth. Beth would hate that.

Mr. Muskopf towered over the desk at her. He wasn't a tall man, topping out at maybe five foot eight. But when he got excited like this, he seemed taller. "You cannot behave like this, Nola. Beating up on a student in the middle of class? What on earth were you thinking?"

"That he had it coming," she replied.

Blowing out a breath, Mr. Muskopf sat back down. "I can't look the other way on this, Nola. There have to be repercussions."

Nola scoffed, then her words came bursting out. "Yeah, for me. What about repercussions for him?"

He narrowed his eyes. "What did Jerry do that was so bad?"

Nola stared up into his eyes. Mr. Muskopf was a decent guy, unlike the principal, who was an absolute jerk. Mr. Muskopf actually seemed to care. She knew he'd stuck his neck out a few times for students.

"You can tell me, Nola. Maybe I can help," he urged.

And that one word, *maybe*, removed any possibility of Nola confiding in him. "Maybe" was the word that people used when they wanted you to unburden yourself and simultaneously let them off the hook for actually helping you. So Nola just glared at him, not saying a word.

Mr. Muskopf shook his head. "Then you leave me no choice. You're suspended for three days. I'll call your dad and have him come pick you up." He reached for the phone.

Nola stood up. "Don't bother. You won't be able to reach him."

The vice principal's hand stilled before it reached the receiver. He placed it back on the desk in front of him. Mr. Muskopf knew Nola's home situation. Right now, her dad was no doubt in Murray's Bar hustling pool. Or working off his hangover with a new round of drinks.

"Nola, there are things we can do to help. There are people I can call—"

Nola shook her head as she headed for the door. "No. There's nothing you can do to help."

The same way there's nothing I can do to help Beth, she thought as she stormed out of the vice principal's office and through the school's main office.

The eyes of the receptionist followed her as she walked

out. Nola slid a glare at the woman, who quickly looked back down at her paperwork.

For a moment, she contemplated stopping by her locker to grab her things. But then she discarded the thought. There was nothing important there anyway. Without Beth here, none of this mattered.

Chapter Forty-Three

NOLA
PRESENT DAY

Lost in her thoughts of Beth, it wasn't until the dog lifted her head and emitted a little growl that Nola jerked herself away from the memories.

But the feeling of helplessness lingered. Beth had been so devastated. Everything had felt out of her control. And everything had been: Jerry had stolen her first sexual experience, and then he'd turned around and stolen her right to grieve that loss in private. He'd done everything he wanted, and Beth had just been bandied about like a cat with a toy, except she was the toy.

The slam of a car door told her Rafe was back from running errands. Shaking her head, she shoved the thoughts away, although it took effort. She had relegated the memories of Beth to the back corner of her mind. But those memories weren't willing to stay in the shadows as easily as they had before. This case was cutting a little too close to home.

"Nola?" Rafe called from inside.

"Out back," she said.

The screen door opened behind her, and Rafe stepped out onto the back porch. The dog let out another growl, although the hair on her neck stayed flat.

Apparently, she was getting a little more used to him.

Opening up the paper bag he was holding, he handed a wrapped sandwich to Nola. "Picked you up an egg-and-bacon sandwich."

Nola took it with a nod of thanks.

Reaching into the bag, he pulled out another one. Unwrapping it, he placed it on the ground in front of the dog slowly. The dog stopped growling as she chowed down on her sandwich. Rafe took a seat on Nola's other side. "What are you guys doing out here?"

"She needed to use the bathroom, and then we just kind of . . ." Nola shrugged, her words drifting off.

"It's a nice morning," Rafe said.

Nola didn't make any comment. She just stared out at the backyard, the ghost of Beth drifting over her thoughts.

"You feeling better?"

It took Nola a moment to nod. "Yeah, still a little weak, but better."

"I called Dr. Ahmed." Dr. Ahmed was Ileana's personal physician. "He said you should be fine by tomorrow. Apparently, it's working its way through the university."

That might be true, but the feeling of weakness was unsettling for Nola. Her limbs felt brittle, nearly hollow. When she'd walked outside, she felt dizzy. She didn't like this feeling. It made her feel vulnerable, and Nola did not do vulnerable. Even so, she found herself wrapping her arms around her legs as a slight wind kicked up.

Rafe studied her, a frown marring his handsome face. "What's wrong?"

Jolted, Nola focused on keeping her emotions locked down, all traces of vulnerability carefully tucked away. "What do you mean?"

He shook his head. "Something's off. You're not you. Is it this case?"

The denial was on the tip of her tongue, along with a quick brush-off to keep him at a distance. But for the first time in a long time, she stopped herself.

For years, she'd been going it alone, and it had worked for her. It had worked for the people she was trying to help. But now, it wasn't working at all. Because Rafe was right: something was off.

In fact, she'd felt off since this case began. Maybe it was because she kept picturing Cindy as a little girl. Or maybe it was because of Beth. But for whatever reason, she just felt not right. Even before the illness knocked her low, she'd felt vulnerable. Powerless.

But she didn't want to do this alone. She wanted someone to help her figure out her way through. She wanted someone to listen to her worries.

"I don't know about this one, Rafe. I don't know if I'm going to be able to get this guy. I mean, there are so many protections around him. I just don't think I'm going to be able to get through them and get Cindy the justice she deserves."

Rafe stared at her for a minute and then scoffed. "That's bullshit."

Nola jerked her head up, her eyes widening. "Excuse me?"

"You're Nola James. You don't let anything get in your way."

She shook her head. "But this case—"

He cut her off. "Is what? A bunch of rich guys in suits? You're going to tell me they're tougher than the gang members that were going after me and my kids from both the United States and Mexico? Or what about the child traffickers down in Georgia? Or the smugglers over in Kansas? How about that serial killer you took down in Nevada? You're going to tell me that those cases were easier than this one?"

His words resonated on one level, but still, she just couldn't see her way out. "They're closing ranks. I can't get anyone to break."

"Then break them," Rafe said, his voice steel. "Look, when I first met you, I thought you were tough. I thought you were strong. I thought you were beautiful. But I had no idea *how* tough, strong, and beautiful you really are. I know about the cases you've taken the last couple of months, and the ones before that. I know the odds were radically against you being successful in any of them. But you *were* successful. You got justice for all of those victims. This case, it's no harder than those. So what's really going on?"

Nola leaned back a little bit, letting his words roll through her mind. Objectively, she knew he was right. This case was no harder. These individuals were no more violent, despite the incident yesterday. And the truth was, if she hadn't been sick, yesterday would have been nothing. Honestly, it would have been fun. If she'd been in her normal physical shape, she would have wiped the floor with those guys—and she would have gotten them to turn on their boss.

But she hadn't been in her normal form. "You're right.

I'm off. This case, it's just, it's cutting a little too close to home."

He frowned. "How?"

Now it was Nola's turn to study Rafe. He was a good man. Actually, he was an exceptionally good man. As a cop down in Mexico, he'd risked everything to do the right thing. Then he'd put his life on the line time and time again to keep his kids safe, even being willing to walk away from them in order to do so.

Nola had kept a wall between the two of them since they'd met because she could tell that he wasn't someone that she would be able to easily lock out if she let him in, even just a little bit.

But right now she found herself wanting to lower that wall. She found herself wanting to confide in him and hear what he had to say in response. So she took a deep breath and began. "When I was a kid, I had this best friend. Her name was Beth."

Chapter Forty-Four

NOLA
TWENTY-ONE YEARS AGO

After leaving the vice principal's office, Nola headed for the main doors and walked home, thinking about Jerry's smug face the whole way. She should have at least knocked out a tooth. If she'd twisted her hip a little more, she might have even been able to break his jaw. That would have been good and the least the guy deserved.

The whole walk home, she envisioned different ways she could have enacted her revenge against Jerry, each one more creative than the last. In what felt like no time, she looked up, surprised to find that she was home. She hadn't even realized she'd been walking that long.

One house over, Nico was washing his car in the driveway. Sponge in hand, his eyes went wide at the sight of her. "Nola? What are you doing home?"

For a moment, she thought about ignoring him and heading inside without saying anything, but Nico deserved better than that, and besides, she wanted to talk to someone. She walked toward him. "There's something I need to talk to you about."

Twenty minutes later, Nola had told him the whole sordid deal over a grilled sandwich and a glass of milk.

Nico hadn't said anything, just sat there quietly as she unburdened herself. When she was finally done, she finished the last of the sandwich and pushed the plate away.

"That kid deserved worse than what you gave him," Nico growled.

His words were exactly what Nola needed to hear. Tears pressed against the back of her eyes, but she refused to let them fall. She'd felt so helpless this whole time. She'd known that Jerry was bad news. If she'd trusted her gut, she would have stopped Beth from going out with him. But she hadn't. Instead, she'd ignored the warnings running through her mind. The only time in this whole situation where she'd felt even the slightest amount of power was when she was punching Jerry's face.

"Yeah, but the school doesn't see it that way. They suspended me."

"Not surprised," Nico said as he stood up and went to the cupboard and pulled out a package of fudge-striped cookies. He placed them on the table. "The world has got two types of people, kid. The powerful and the powerless. Jerry, he's in the powerful group. He's not going to get punished for what happened to Beth. He's going to get away with it. And you, well, you know which group you're in."

Nola slumped lower in her chair. "That's just so wrong."

"Yes, it is. But that's how the system works. It doesn't always protect those who need it. Sometimes it protects those who deserve to be punished, and there's no legal way around that."

"What do you mean no legal way?" Nola tilted her head, studying him.

He crossed his arms over his chest. "Sometimes for justice to be done, it needs to fall outside of the system. Sometimes the guilty need a little push to help make sure that they get what they're due."

"What do you mean?" She asked.

He opened his mouth to answer, but then his eyes shifted, focused on the front windows.

Following his gaze, Nola saw Beth hurrying up the path to Nola's house. She bolted out of her chair. Flinging open Nico's front door, she hurried across the driveway.

Beth had just reached the front door was about to knock when Nola called out to her. "Beth?"

Looking over, her friend's eyes were bloodshot, and her cheeks were streaked red, at least the parts that weren't bruised. She looked pale and haggard. Her hair looked like it hadn't been brushed in days, and her clothes were obviously something she'd just thrown on in a rush to get out the door. She wrapped her arms around her stomach as if giving herself a hug. "I need to talk to you."

Anger laced Beth's words, making Nola frown. Why was Beth angry? Had Jerry done something else? She hurried forward and opened up the door. "Come on in. How are you?" she asked as Beth slipped in behind her.

Beth's back was ramrod straight as she walked past Nola. She stood with her back to the front door, her hands curled into fists.

Uncertain, Nola stood next to the door, not sure what to do or to say. "Beth? Are you okay?"

Hands in the air, Beth whirled around toward her. "Am I okay? How could I be okay after what you did?"

Rearing back, Nola's frown deepened. "After what I did? What are you talking about?"

"You beat up Jerry! You don't think people are wondering why?"

Nola stared at her in shock.

Her eyes wild, Beth took a step toward Nola. "Why did you do that? You shouldn't have done that!"

Her own anger growing, Nola clenched her hands into fists. "What did you expect me to do? Just stand by and let that jerk get away with it?"

Beth's face crumbled under Nola's words. She sank to the floor as if her strings had been cut. "Everybody will know," she sobbed. "Now everybody will know."

Frozen in place, Nola didn't move for a moment. Then she dashed across the short space to her friend and sank to the ground next to her. Wrapping her arms around Beth, Nola didn't have the heart to tell her the truth: they already did.

Chapter Forty-Five

NOLA
PRESENT DAY

Nola and Rafe spoke for two hours. Nola told him everything about Beth and Jerry and how hopeless she'd felt in that whole situation. After she finished, she felt like a weight had been taken off her chest. Her whole body felt lighter.

"What happened to Beth?" Rafe finally asked.

The old pain crested in her chest, breaking out of the box that she'd locked it in. "That day at my house was the last time I saw her. Her family sent her to her grandmother's to get away from everything, and while she was there, they sold the house and bought another house near her grandmother. I never saw her again."

"You must have looked her up."

The newer pain blended in with the old as Nola nodded. "I did, years later. I didn't know where they'd moved to. I didn't know what town they were in. I knew the grandmother was somewhere in Illinois, but that was all I had to go on. So I looked her up on and off, but there was never any information. Finally, I found a story about her mother. She'd become an advocate for suicide prevention amongst teenagers."

Rafe sucked in a breath. "Oh no. I'm so sorry."

With a nod, Nola accepted the compassion and realized it was the first time anyone had offered her any sort of condolences for the loss of Beth. Because she hadn't told anyone that Beth had died. Nico himself was already gone by the time she'd learned about Beth's suicide. He'd had a heart attack a year after Beth moved. Nola had found him the next morning.

Not looking at Rafe, she spoke softly. "She killed herself three years after the rape. She was found hanging from a tree in her parents' backyard. I can't help imagining how desperate she must have felt, how alone. Beth, there was such a light to her. For it to be snuffed out, her pain must have been immense."

And even now, when Nola knew there was nothing she could have done, she cursed herself up one side and down the other for not finding Beth sooner. For not reminding Beth that she still had people who cared about her. And that what Jerry had done hadn't defined her. It had only defined him.

His voice full of both compassion and conviction, Rafe said, "It wasn't your fault, you know. None of it was."

"No, it wasn't." She'd come to that realization a long time ago, but just like with the people around Cindy, knowing it and believing it were two entirely different beasts. The only person truly responsible for what had happened to Beth was Jerry.

"But that's not everything. Beth, she had a little girl. She gave her up for adoption the same day that she gave birth to her."

Nola felt the catch at the back of her throat. When they'd been younger, they'd both talked about what they were going to do when they grew up. Nola had been focused on a career in the military or law enforcement. Beth had talked about being a teacher, but her heart wasn't truly in it. The only thing she truly wanted was to be a mom, and she was born to be one. She was so caring and loving. That was her absolute dream.

But she wasn't ready to be one at age sixteen, and her family definitely wasn't ready for her to be one at that age.

The idea that Beth gave away her child was heartbreaking enough. But that revelation was nothing compared to the other one. It nearly broke Nola. There'd been complications during the birth, and Beth had bled profusely. They'd ended up doing an emergency hysterectomy. There'd been no other choice at the time.

Which meant, at the age of sixteen, Beth had finally realized her dream of becoming a mother and lost any chance of it at the same time.

Jerry had so many things to answer for, but that, in Nola's mind was the greatest injury he'd inflicted upon her. Beth would never be a mom to anyone but Jerry's child. She would never have that house full of kids that she'd dreamed of. Nola supposed that she could have adopted, and Beth probably would have if she'd been unable to have kids for any other reason.

But for the reason for her dream to have to be switched to be because of Jerry, to be because he felt he was entitled to take that which wasn't freely given, that was just a step too far for Beth. Nola knew her friend. Every time she thought about her future and having kids, she no doubt had to relive the past and the horror of her rape.

Without a doubt, she knew that was why Beth had finally stepped off that branch. Her future was inextricably tied to her past, and Beth couldn't see beyond it. During the pregnancy and after the birth, she'd been homeschooled, so she had very little interaction with other kids. She'd started at a community college, which she commuted to. It sounded like Beth's life was incredibly lonely.

And Nola wondered what she could have done to have made it easier for her. Perhaps there was nothing, but she couldn't let herself off that easily. She knew that there must have been something that she could have done to stop Beth from taking that last horrible step.

"And Jerry? What happened to him?" Rafe asked.

Nola stretched out her legs, rolling her shoulders, feeling the ache of sitting there for so long but not quite ready to get up yet. "He went to college and got a degree in business. He joined his father's accounting firm, and now he's doing seven consecutive twelve-to-twenty sentences in Folsom, a maximum-security prison."

"What's he in for?"

"A string of seven rapes."

"How'd that come about?" he asked.

Nola could feel Rafe's gaze on her. She looked him dead in the eye, wanting him to know exactly who she was. It was important that he knew *exactly* who she was.

"Someone broke into his apartment late at night and got him to confess all the names of the women that he'd assaulted over his life. They spent hours getting him to say every single name and exactly what he'd done to them and how he'd done it and where. By the time they were done, he was a blubbering mess on the floor. Every single bone in each of his hands was broken, and his cheekbone and jaw were shattered."

Rafe didn't look away from her. "But she left him alive to make sure he would face justice."

Nola nodded. "Yes, she did."

"Good."

His response shocked her. She'd expected that her confession would have disgusted him. "I thought you'd disapprove."

Rafe ran a hand through his hair as he sighed and looked over his shoulder at a slow-moving car in need of a muffler heading down the road. "Nola, I think that I am well aware of the limits of the criminal justice systems of this world. Whether it's here or back in Mexico, there's always someone who's able to hide behind power. But you make sure that the powerless have a defender. You make sure that the powerful that try to skirt around the law get the justice they deserve. Why would you think I'd disapprove of that?"

"Because my methods are violent?" She asked.

He kept his gaze locked on hers as he spoke. "Yes, they are. But I'm not so naive to think that you could just ask someone to admit to the horrible things they'd done and they would acquiesce. Sometimes a little pain is necessary to get to the truth, and you could have done a lot worse to Jerry. You and I both know that. And I am very sorry about your friend. She didn't deserve what happened to her. And neither did you. You and Beth deserved the chance to be friends for all your lives."

A sob crowded up Nola's throat. Friends with Beth for life. What would that have looked like? She could admit that losing Beth had closed Nola off even more. She barely spoke to anyone in high school for the remaining years. Nico had been her one confidante, and a heart attack had taken him away from her too soon.

But if Jerry had never happened? Would that all have been the same? She knew she would have still ended up in the CIA or some other law enforcement agency, but Beth, she would have been a bright spot in the darkness. A reminder of the good in the world, just like Molly had been.

"What you did," Rafe said, "it was the only way to get them all justice. I'm amazed at your strength to do what needs to be done, and I know all that it costs you, even though you act as if it doesn't cost a thing."

Nola stared into his deep-brown eyes. And she felt seen, truly seen and accepted for the first time in a very long time. It was such an unusual feeling.

"Thank you," Nola said. Suddenly her chest felt lighter and her head felt clearer. The burden, the fear, and the devastation that came with Beth's rape and suicide had been weighing on her for years. For the first time, she felt, well, not good, because that would be stretching it, but she felt better. She felt like she wasn't carrying the burden alone.

"I understand why this situation has got you spinning. It's very similar to Beth's."

Nola nodded. "Yeah, it is."

Rafe reached out and took her hand. "But you got justice for Beth. You're going to get it for Cindy, and I'll help you however I can."

"I don't know where to go from here, though. I don't know what the next step should be."

Standing, Rafe stretched his back. "Then I guess you need a fresh set of eyes. I picked up some supplies for lunch.

I'm going to go get that started, and you are going to get everything you have on this case. We'll work through it as I cook and we eat."

"What are you making?"

He grinned. "My famous enchiladas."

Despite the breakfast sandwich she'd just eaten, Nola's stomach grumbled in response. She'd had Rafe's enchiladas before at the estate, and they really should be famous. "The kids are going to be upset if they learn that you made them when they weren't around."

He winked at her. "Then I guess it'll be our little secret."

An idea popped into Nola's mind. "What day is it?"

"Tuesday. Why?"

Nola smiled.

Rafe raised an eyebrow. "I know that smile. It's good for us and bad for the bad guys. You've thought of something."

"A loose thread I can pull." She stood up.

"So no enchiladas?

"Oh, definitely enchiladas. And then I have some calls to make."

"So you're good?"

"Oh, I'm good. But some other people are about to be in a world of hurt."

"Well, you'll need a full stomach. Should be ready in about thirty minutes. Come in when you're ready to get to work."

He walked back into the house and the door shut quietly behind him.

A warm glow developed in her chest as Nola stared at the door. She normally liked to do these cases alone. It was just easier on so many levels. But Rafe being here felt right. She didn't want to look too deeply at that feeling or analyze it too much. Right now, she was just going to enjoy how it felt to have someone else around who was as focused as she was on what needed to be done.

Next to her, the dog rolled onto her side and then onto her back, exposing her belly.

Nola smiled as she leaned down and rubbed her stomach. "Well, girl, it looks like it's time to get back to work."

Chapter Forty-Six

The Blue Bell Motel sat on the outskirts of Richmond. If it had seen better days, Nola would have been shocked. It was a long white building with doors leading straight into the parking lot. Some places looked like they had always been in a state of disrepair. The white siding had long since turned to a dull gray. The blue bells on the sign by the road had flaked off, leaving only a vague outline of what they had once been.

Nola pulled into the parking lot and backed into a spot. The lot was quiet, which wasn't a surprise, given it was a Wednesday afternoon. There were only three cars in sight. One she recognized: John O'Neil's black Yukon sat in front of room 18.

Apparently, John made a weekly trip to the Blue Bell Motel, unknown to his ex-wife. Or perhaps known to his ex-wife, which was the reason she was an ex. John was behind in his child support payments but always seemed to have enough money for his extracurriculars.

A man had to have priorities she supposed.

There was no one in the parking lot as Nola stepped out of the car and closed the door softly behind her. She crossed the parking lot and paused outside room 18.

Muffled noises came from inside. She moved to the window and could see a figure lying prone on the bed: John O'Neil. Standing at the foot of the bed was Sasha, known on the internet as Mistress Sasha, bringer of pain. Her hands were on her wide hips, accentuating the leather ensemble that looked ready to burst at the seams. Mistress Sasha was not a small woman. And she was also John's regular "date" every Wednesday afternoon.

Nola crossed to the door and opened it, striding into the room.

"Someone's been a bad boy," Mistress Sasha said as the whip snapped loudly against John's milky white thighs.

"Well, this is an image that is now seared into my brain," Nola said.

John's eyes nearly bulged out of his head as they landed on Nola. But the gag in his mouth prevented him from talking. His cheeks reddened—whether from lust or anger, Nola couldn't tell. Probably a little of both. He strained against silver handcuffs that had him attached to the bed.

Grabbing her coat from the other bed, Sasha slipped it over her shoulders. She held out her hand, and Nola placed a roll of hundreds in it as she walked past.

"Thanks," Nola said.

Sasha gave her a nod. Without even a backward glance at John, she headed out the door, closing it behind her. After Nola explained to Sasha yesterday that John would be tied up with the criminal justice system for the foreseeable future, she had no problem handing him over to Nola.

For a price.

Nola strolled toward the bed. John wore only his boxers, white ones with red hearts. She shook her head. "John, John, John. I'd say this is such a disappointment, but really it's more of a cliché."

The muscles in his arms strained as he tried to pull his arms from the cuffs.

"I think you know that won't work. From what Sasha says, you like to have those keeping you tied down tight. She, of course, doesn't enjoy it as much, but apparently she's a pretty good actress."

John said something from behind the ball gag that Nola couldn't make out. She leaned forward. "What was that?"

He mumbled again, his face growing red from the effort.

With a sigh, Nola pulled a knife from the sheath at her waist. "Hold on a second."

John tried to rear back, but the headboard and the handcuffs kept him where he was.

Carefully Nola slid the knife between the restraints and his cheek, and then with a quick slice, it came undone.

Spitting the sex toy out, John worked his mouth around for a moment before he spoke. "Who are you? You're not just some grad student."

"Nope, I'm not."

"Well, you better let me out of these right now if you know what's good for you," he said, his eyes narrowed to slits.

Nola rolled her eyes. "Seriously, do you guys all get together and decide on the useless threats you're going to make? Maybe a little originality, something different next time?"

John glared daggers at her. "What do you want?"

Nola walked over to a picture of a beach that hung on the wall opposite the bed. Reaching up, she pulled it off the wall and removed a small recording device from it. She'd installed it yesterday after the enchiladas—after she'd rented the room and given Sasha a key. "What do I want? Well, I have everything I want right here."

His mouth falling open, John's face paled. "That, that's illegal."

A chuckle burst out of Nola as she held up the small camera. "This is illegal? And what you were doing in this room was all on the up and up?" She flicked a glance at his groin. "From what Sasha says, up and up is not really your thing."

His eyes narrowing further, John's mouth slammed shut. "Let me out of here."

"Oh, not quite yet. You and I are going to have a little chat."

"I'm not telling you anything. My lawyer will take care of all of this. It's all going to go away. No one will even know what happened."

Nola tsked. "Oh, John, John, John. Silly, silly John. You think I'm just going to hand this all over to the cops? Oh no, I'm giving this to the college newspaper. And the local news, and make sure it gets spread online. I'm sure there are some good angles that we could take from the video that would make great shots. Good luck keeping your job after that, or getting a new one."

"You wouldn't."

"I wouldn't? Why wouldn't I? Why on earth do you think I would protect you?"

"What do you want?" He demanded.

"I want to have a little chat about Chris Hartigan."

He was already shaking his head before Nola finished speaking. "I don't know anything about him."

Nola eyed him. "You're probably wondering if you can beat this rap. You're thinking, maybe after a little time, this will all blow over, and then you can come back again. After all, you have powerful friends that owe you, right?

"Well, let me tell you a little secret: Your powerful friends are going down. And you can either go with them or rise up above them. But they won't be in any position to help you."

He smirked at her. "Yeah, well, I think I'll be all right on my own."

Nola looked down at her fingernails. She really needed to trim them. "Oh, you mean because of the Cayman account? The 1.2 million dollars you've stashed away? Sorry to tell you, but I'm afraid that money's gone."

His face paled. "Gone? It can't be gone."

"Actually, it can. You're not very good with passwords, are you? Password123? Seriously?"

He gasped, which only made Nola smile more. "You used that password just twenty minutes ago and transferred all that money out. And now, poof, it's gone. Well, actually, that's not true. You split it up between some very worthy causes: Planned Parenthood, domestic violence shelters, legal aid. I have to say, I didn't realize you were such a philanthropist."

John's body began to shake. Once again, Nola wasn't sure what the cause was. She doubted it was lust, but rage and fear seemed good candidates. "Now, let's have a little chat about Chris Hartigan."

Teeth gritted, John shook his head. "I said I'm not telling you anything."

Nola walked over to the bed and yanked his head back.

She placed the tip of her knife at the edge of his chin. "Let me make this clear: I don't care about you. You're low-hanging fruit. I want Chris Hartigan. And if I have to go through you to get him, I will do that. The choice is up to you whether that process is painful or slightly less painful."

"You don't have the guts."

Nola smiled. "I guess we'll just see about that, won't we?"

Twenty minutes later, Nola stepped out of the hotel room. Shutting the door behind her, she pulled out her phone. After she texted the information to Bishop, she slid the phone back into her pocket, her hand shaking.

It wasn't what she'd done that was making her hand shake. It was trying to keep herself from going back into that room and continuing that was making her shake. John had spilled his guts, just as Nola had expected. It had taken surprisingly little pain to get him to do so. He was unconscious now, once again muzzled. Nola would leave him there until she was sure his information panned out.

Eventually she'd call the cops on him, but not anytime soon. It was the least the man deserved.

She headed for her car, his words running through her mind. None of the futures of the girls they'd thrown away and bowled over mattered to John and the people he worked for. But they mattered to their families. They mattered to their friends. And they mattered to Nola.

And Nola was going to make sure that the ones responsible paid. Because like she told John, he wasn't her target, not really. Just low-hanging fruit. And now it was time to go after the fruit at the top of the tree. But first, there was something she had to do. She pulled out her burner phone and dialed the police.

Her call was answered quickly. "Richmond PD. How may I direct your call?"

Nola took a breath, staring out over the parking lot. "I think I may know where you can find a body."

Chapter Forty-Seven

Middle Fork Reservoir was on the outskirts of Richmond, only about ten minutes away from the college. A dock had been erected, and Nola stood on it as the light rain hit the thatched roof above her.

On the opposite side of the lake, two dozen people milled about. Two cop cars stood blocking the way, yellow tape cordoning off the area. A couple of people stood behind the tape, trying to get a glimpse. A few of them held their camera phones up, recording as the tow truck tires spun before they found traction and started moving slowly up the embankment.

Nola shook her head at the lack of precaution taken with the witnesses. They really needed to be farther back. Where they stood right now, only about a hundred yards from the edge of the water, they'd have a bird's-eye view of what was about to be unearthed.

The tow truck slowly made its way up the grassy hill toward the yellow tape. Police officers stood on either side, inching closer to the edge of the lake as the car first appeared. First, the red hood appeared, followed by the windshield. The windows were open, and water poured out of them.

A step on the dock behind her caused Nola to turn. Rafe gave her a nod, handing her a coffee without a word. She took a sip, her gaze returning to the scene across the water. The car was fully clear of the surface now, resting on the bank. Without being able to read it, Nola knew that the license plate would match that of Julie Blevins. One of the officers walked over to the driver's door and peered in. He took a quick step back, his hand to his mouth.

Rafe nodded toward the car. "It's good they found her. She can rest now."

Nola shook her head. "She won't rest until those responsible are brought to justice."

Her gaze scanned the crowd, watching the macabre scene. A few people's hands went to their mouths. Some leaned closer, extending their phones to get a better view. Nola fixed her attention on a familiar girl with long brown hair, her gaze directed at the lake.

Moving next to her, Rafe's jacket sleeve rubbed up against Nola's. He spoke quietly. "You're not done yet, are you?"

Nola stared at the red car, her gaze going back to the young woman at the edge of the crowd. "No, I'm not done yet."

"Nola, they found the girl. They'll be able to get him with this."

Her mouth a thin line, Nola shook her head. "No, finding Julie won't change anything. They'll come up with a way to make sure it doesn't tie back to him. It's going to look like a suicide."

"What do you need to do?"

"I've got an idea about that. I think—" She cut off as a cry went up across the water. Amy and Mike Blevins burst through the tape, running for their daughter's car. Two police officers caught them before they could reach it, but the wail that went up from Julie's mother made it clear she'd seen there was a body in the driver's seat.

Nola closed her eyes, imagining what her daughter must look like right now and knowing no mother should ever see her child like that.

Chapter Forty-Eight

The local news anchor was trying to hide his excitement as he spoke. "Police have cordoned off parts of the Middle Fork Reservoir. Divers are in the water. Although they will not officially comment on their activities here, many believe that they are looking for the body of former IUR student Julie Blevins. Blevins went missing—"

Tommy muted the set, his whole body rigid. Damn it. How had they figured out where she was? He wiped his mouth, tugging at the skin. *Think, think.*

He sat back at his desk, taking a deep breath. Could this come back to him? O'Neil had arranged to have the body dumped. But he wouldn't turn. He wouldn't dare. He had too much at stake.

Despite the thought, he grabbed his phone and quickly dialed O'Neil. The phone rang and rang before finally going to voicemail. Tommy disconnected the call and slowly lowered the phone to the desk. *No.*

Taking a breath, he shook his head. He would be fine.

There was no way to tie it to any of this to him, or to Hartigan for that matter. O'Neil would have seen to that.

He leaned back against his chair. Yeah, it would fine. Just fine.

Chapter Forty-Nine

The hotel lobby was quiet as Nola sat on a maroon-colored loveseat, flipping through the news on her phone while keeping an eye on the doorway. The body had been taken to the morgue, and the Blevinses had been escorted to the police station. She and Rafe had waited outside the station for an hour while the Blevinses were inside.

When they finally reemerged, they looked as if they had aged dramatically. Amy Blevins held her husband's arm as if her legs were too weak to hold her upright. Nola wasn't sure if she'd make it to the car under her own steam. Her husband didn't look like he was doing much better. His eyes had a lost look, as if he'd somehow stumbled into a different world and couldn't quite figure out how.

And she supposed, they had. She knew it well.

When the couple finally pulled out from the parking lot, Nola and Rafe had been behind them and followed them to the hotel. The couple barely hit thirty miles per hour the entire ride. Nola was little worried they might get into an accident. Their minds weren't on the task of driving.

Finally, they safely pulled into the parking lot of the Hampton Inn.

That had been thirty minutes ago. The couple sat outside in their car, still talking quietly.

Nola was giving them their space. No doubt today had been a shock to them, first hearing that a girl's body had been dragged from the lake and now knowing it was their daughter's. As much as they had entertained the idea that something had happened to their daughter, a part of them had no doubt hoped and prayed that she was all right. That she'd just run away somewhere and was safe, still living and breathing and walking around.

Even Nola had gone through a stage like that, and she had seen Molly and David die. Yet part of her embraced the fantasy that she had been wrong and that they hadn't been killed. That both of them were living somewhere else, still happily breathing.

Molly climbed up onto the couch next to her. "You never really believed that, Mama."

Nola looked down at her little girl. Molly had changed in the last few months. When she had first started seeing her, she was so solid that she looked real. But over these last couple of months, each time she saw her, she'd become more and more transparent. Now she looked like all the other ghosts that Nola saw. It was clear that she was not part of the land of the living.

"No, baby, I never really believed that."

"They're hurting. They *did* believe it. They believed that they would see her again."

"Yes, they did."

"But now they know the truth. It's going to be hard for them, Mama. But you'll help them, won't you?"

"I'll do what I can."

The doors to the hotel lobby swished open, and Nola looked up to see the couple walk through.

Amy Blevins looked nothing like the smiling woman from her social media pages. The registered nurse's posts were always uplifting, highlighting charitable works people could do or donate to. Now, instead of a bright smile, her face was drawn. Her light-brown hair was pulled back in a disheveled ponytail. Her brown eyes, the same brown eyes as her daughter, were swollen and red.

She looked so fragile, hunched over, still clinging to her husband, as if he was all that was keeping her here. He wasn't in much better shape. His eyes were wild, and his hair looked like he'd been running his hands through it incessantly.

The two of them looked like they had just had the worst shock of their lives.

And the truth was that was exactly what had happened to them. Someone had told them about the car being pulled from the lake. They'd shown up, seen the car, and immediately knew that all their fears and late-night worries had been realized. The worst possible outcome for their daughter had come true.

Then the sheriff had had to bring out a sheet to cover the body. Nola hoped again that the parents hadn't gotten a good glimpse of their daughter. A body that had been in the water for that long—that definitely wasn't the last image anyone needed of their daughter.

The two of them were going through hell. But hell would be their temporary address for at least the next few months. There was no avoiding that. There would not be a good time to speak with them for a long, long time. So Nola stood and crossed the lobby. She stopped just a few feet away from them. "Mr. and Mrs. Blevins?"

Mike Blevins winced as if he'd been struck, but Amy didn't even seem to hear her. He turned his bloodshot eyes toward Nola and cleared his throat. "Yes?"

"I was hoping I could speak with you."

Mike was already shaking his head. "We have no comment for the media."

"I'm not with the media. I'm a private investigator."

Clearly confused, Mike frowned. "Are you here about Julie?"

Nola shook her head. "No, I'm here about a different girl who went to the university. But I'm trying to see if maybe what happened to her is also what happened to Julie."

"This isn't a good time." Mike started to usher his wife forward.

But Amy dug her feet into the ground and finally turned her gaze to Nola. "Another girl?"

Nola met her grief-stricken eyes with a nod. "Yes. Her name was Cindy Smith, and she's gone too. I was hoping maybe I could speak with you two for just a few moments."

"Amy, it's not the time," her husband said.

A tear rolled down Amy's cheek, and she wiped it away. "There's never going to be a good time."

Nola got them situated in a small conference room off to the side of the lobby. By the time they'd sat down, Rafe had returned with coffee and food. When he and Nola arrived at the hotel, he'd immediately left to go and get supplies, figuring that the parents hadn't eaten in hours.

When Rafe stepped into the room with his arms laden down with food and drinks, the couple looked up in surprise and then suspicion. But Rafe immediately put them at ease as he offered his condolences and spread out the food and drink, urging them to eat.

And for a moment, Nola caught a glimpse of the kind of cop he had once been. He was very good at putting people at ease. He was very good at getting them to trust him.

Taking a seat across from the couple and next to Nola, he handed her a coffee. She nodded her thanks, and he met her gaze. She read the hurt that he felt for the couple sitting across from them before he pulled over his own sandwich and took a bite, less because he was hungry, she knew, and more in order to encourage the couple to eat themselves.

Nola did the same, just letting herself eat a little bit. The couple took a few bites, and then Mike managed to finish his whole sandwich and reached for another. He was halfway through it before he shook his head. "I didn't realize how long it had been since we'd eaten. With everything going on, we just . . ." He shrugged as his words drifted off.

"It's understandable. You two have been through a lot these last couple of days," Rafe said.

More tears rolled down Amy's cheeks as she nodded. This time she didn't wipe them away. "I don't know how we're going to get through this."

"When was the last time you spoke with Julie?" Nola asked gently.

Amy took a shuddering breath. "The night she disappeared. She was going out to a party. It was a Friday night. She always called me before she went out. We'd talk about how her day went and what the plans were for the night. Every single time, we ended the conversation the same way: I told her that I loved her, and I told her to be careful. She always laughed and told me not to worry."

Her chin trembled, and she looked down at the table, the tears coming in earnest now.

Mike reached over and gripped her hand. "We didn't hear from her the next day, and that was strange. She always called, so we called her a bunch of times, but there was no answer. We tried to tell ourselves that she just got busy with something or that maybe her phone hadn't been charged. But we knew. We knew something was wrong."

"When did you realize she was missing?" Rafe asked.

"It was Sunday afternoon. Her roommate had just arrived. She was frantic. She said all of Julie's stuff was gone. That Julie had left a note saying that she was leaving college."

Mike ran a hand through his hair, causing it to stick up even more. "We couldn't understand what she was saying at first. It didn't make any sense. Julie wouldn't leave school, and she certainly wouldn't be able to pack up all her stuff and fit it into her little car, at least not on her own. She'd need help. Besides, she would talk to us about that kind of decision. She wouldn't just leave. But she was gone, and all her stuff was too."

Amy continued the tale. "We drove to the school right away. When we arrived, it was just like her roommate said. We spoke with everyone we could think of, but everyone told us the same thing: none of them had seen or heard from her."

"What about the police?" Rafe asked.

Mike rolled his hands into fists. "The police," he spat out the word. "We went first to the Richmond police, but they told us to speak with the university's police. So we went there, and all they said was Julie was an adult, and if she wanted to leave school, she was legally allowed to do so. They wouldn't even take a report."

Amy took a shuddering breath.

His eyes shiny with unshed tears and anger, Mike leaned

forward. "That police chief. He was so dismissive. Told us that girls did this sometimes. As if *he* knew our daughter better than we did."

"Mike." Amy placed her hand on her husband's forearm. Her touch dissolved his anger. Tears rolled down his cheeks as his chin trembled. "Our baby girl was missing, and they didn't help us. And now . . ."

Amy pulled him into a hug. Neither Nola or Rafe said anything as the couple murmured softly to one another. Nola wanted to give them their privacy, but she needed whatever information they might have. If they waited, they'd be caught up in funeral preparations, and grief would take over. She needed to speak with them now, so she could bring those responsible for Julie's death to justice.

Because Nola had no doubt that Julie had been helped into that lake.

Finally, when the couple across from them released one another, dabbed their eyes, and took a shaky drink, Nola spoke. "Was there anything that happened on campus that had Julie worried?"

Mike shook his head. "No, the opposite, in fact. She was pulling nearly all A's. She'd just decided that she was going to go for a graduate degree in psychology. She'd just stared prep work for the GREs. She was in a really good place."

"What about her friends? Did you speak with any of them?" Rafe asked.

Amy nodded, wiping at her fresh tears. "Yes. They all went to the party, but it had been so packed that they lost track of her. They hadn't seen her since eleven o'clock that night. The security footage shows her leaving the dorm around ten."

Nola frowned. "You saw the security footage?"

"One of the security officers, he was nice," Amy said.

"He scrolled back and looked at the footage, and we saw Julie leaving the dorm. She looked happy, excited. She was wearing her favorite red sweater."

Even from a distance, and despite the damage done by the water, Nola had seen that the body pulled from the lake had also been clothed in a dark sweater that could have easily been red.

"And what about seeing her return?" Rafe asked.

Mike shook his head. "The cameras went down that night afterwards. So there was no sign of her coming back. The last video we have of her was leaving with a bunch of friends for the party."

Convenient, Nola thought.

Amy pulled out her phone, her focus on the screen as she scrolled through. "But we did get some images from Julie's phone, which uploads to her cloud account automatically. They were taken the night she disappeared. It was her at the party with all of her friends. They're the last pictures on her phone. It's the last activity." She took a deep shaky breath. "Would you like to see them?"

Nola held out her hand. "Yes."

Amy handed over the phone, and Nola quickly swiped through the photos. There were six of them that had been taken that night. All had Julie in the center with a group of four girls. The first few were standard group shots, with a few people in the background behind them. Scanning each one, she swiped through to the fourth when her hand stilled as she noted a familiar face in the background.

Nola sucked in a breath. Chris Hartigan stood against a wall, surrounded by another group, but his gaze was focused on Julie.

Rafe, who'd been leaning into Nola to see the photos,

met her gaze. He nodded, turning back to the couple. "Was Julie dating anyone?"

Mike shook his head. "No, no, nothing like that."

Amy cut in. "She'd been dating a boy from back home, but they broke up about two months ago at the beginning of the summer. She hadn't been interested in anyone since then. I think she was hoping that she and Gavin would get back together."

"What about Chris Hartigan? Has Julie ever mentioned him?" Nola asked as she placed the phone back on the table after sending the photos to Bishop.

Surprise splashed across both parents' faces. "The football player?" Mike asked. "No, I mean, *we've* mentioned him in relation to school, but I don't think she even met him."

"Why are you asking about him?" Amy asked.

"Because he might have something to do with Cindy, the other girl," Nola said.

Amy's jaw dropped. "What?"

"We have some information that links him to our case, and I'm hoping you could give us the names of Julie's friends who were with her at the party. It would help."

Amy stared at Nola and then grabbed her phone and quickly dialed. "I can do better than that."

She put the call on FaceTime, and a young blonde girl appeared on the screen. Her eyes were red, and she sniffed as she answered. "Oh, Mrs. Blevins. Oh my God. I just heard. I wanted to reach out, but . . ." Her voice broke off as a sob cut through the room.

Sucking in a breath, Amy's chin trembled. "Thank you, Luanne. But I was hoping we could ask you some questions." Amy barely got through the sentence before her face dissolved as well.

Rafe reached out a hand. "Mrs. Blevins, let me."

Her shoulders shook as she handed over the phone. Rafe tilted the phone so both he and Nola could see the young woman.

Nola leaned forward. "Luanne, my name's Nola, and this is Rafe. We wanted to ask you some questions about the party you were at that last night you saw Julie. Do you think you could answer them?"

"I'll . . . I'll try," Luanne stammered, taking a deep breath and trying to pull her emotions back.

"That's good, Luanne. You went to the party with Julie, correct?" Nola asked.

The young woman nodded. "Yes. We all went down to Frat Row. The Tau Sigma house was having a big blowout. It wasn't our usual scene, but it sounded like fun. I mean, it was the beginning of the semester, and we all said we'd try to go out more this year, not be so serious, you know?"

"Of course. You just wanted to let loose a little bit," Rafe said.

Luanne nodded again. "Exactly."

"What happened when you got to the party? Did you guys split up or stay together?" Nola asked.

"There was a group of us. Me, Julie, Michelle, Shayna, Miko, and Michonne. We were all kind of hanging out together for like the first little bit, and then Michonne and Shayna went to go dance and . . ." Luanne frowned. "Then I think Michelle, Miko, and I went to go find a bathroom, and when we came back, we couldn't find Julie."

"You left her by herself?" Rafe asked.

"No, she was talking with a girl from her English class."

"Did you look for her?" Nola asked.

"Yeah. I found the girl from her class, and she said Julie went to go find us. We searched everywhere, asked everybody. We have a rule: No one goes off alone. Finally, one of the football guys he said that she'd left."

Nola leaned forward. "Which football guy said that?"

"I think his name is Billy or something? We don't really follow football."

"Did you talk to any other football players that night?" Rafe asked.

Luanne paused, biting her lip.

"Whatever happened, it's really important that we know," Rafe said.

Luanne expelled a breath. "Well, Chris Hartigan was there. He's kind of, oh, he was being a douche. He kept trying to get Julie to dance with him, and she just wasn't interested. I mean, he's good looking and all, but he's just really full of himself, and Julie, she was not at all interested. Honestly, we kind of thought that might have been why she left early, that she just kind of wanted to get away from him."

Nola met Rafe's gaze, and a thrill of excitement rolled through her. Finally. Something.

Rafe nodded toward the screen. "Thank you, Luanne. That's very helpful."

"Can you tell Mr. and Mrs. Blevins that if they need anything that I'm here? We're all here. We all want to do something. We just we don't know what to do."

His voice full of compassion, Rafe nodded. "They're right here. They know. Take care of yourself, Luanne, okay?"

The young woman nodded mutely, tears rolling down her cheeks as she disconnected the call.

Rafe slid the phone back across the table toward Amy. Mike looked between the two of them. "You think Hartigan has something to do with this?"

The tone in Mike's voice made it clear that he was looking for someone to focus his rage on, and while Nola believed in her gut that Hartigan was part of this, she also knew that she couldn't direct Mike toward him. Not to protect Hartigan, but to protect Mike. So she kept her tone even when she spoke. "We're not sure yet. It's possible. We need to do a little more research."

Mike deflated almost immediately. "Oh."

"Thank you for speaking with us. We know it's a difficult time." Nola pulled a card from her back pocket and handed it over. "If you think of anything else, or if you need anything, if the police are giving you the runaround, give us a call. We can help."

Julie's dad took the card and stared at it. He glanced up at her with a frown. "You don't put your name on your business cards?"

Nola shook her head. "No, I don't."

Chapter Fifty

Speaking with the Blevinses had been draining. The devastated couple's emotions seemed to cover every aspect of that room. Even now, Nola could feel their grief as if it was another layer of skin covering her. She turned off the highway and headed into the small neighborhood that held her rental home.

"You okay?" Rafe asked.

She started to nod out of habit, then shook her head instead. "No. They're going to go through a lot in these next few months, maybe years."

"Yes, but they have one another. That's more than you or I ever had when we went through our grief."

Nola looked over at him in surprise. That was a commonality between the two of them that she hadn't really thought about before. Nola had been on her own because David and Molly were gone. But Rafe had been on his own because he'd lost his wife and then his country. Plus, he'd had to stow that grief away to take care of his two children and keep them safe. Nola had been on her own as well because she had pushed the people in her life away, too broken inside to accept their help. But Rafe, he hadn't had anyone to help him. She'd never really thought about it that way. The two of them had both gone through their grief solo.

She pulled onto the street where her house was and parked in the drive, noting as she did the individual sitting in the car across the street.

"You saw him?" Rafe asked quietly.

"Yeah. I know him. It's all right."

Rafe nodded before he stepped out of the car, stretching as he got a better look at the man sitting in the car. Then he headed for the house. But Nola got out of the car, closed the door, then leaned against it and waited.

It didn't take long. Dean stepped out of the old Jeep Cherokee. He walked across the street, his hands shoved into the pockets of his jeans. He came to a stop at the end of the driveway and looked around nervously.

"Hey, Dean. How you doing?" Nola asked.

"Uh, hi. I was hoping I could maybe talk to you."

Nola gestured toward the porch. "Why don't we go speak up there?"

Dean nodded and followed quietly behind Nola. She took a seat in one of the plastic Adirondack chairs, and after a moment's hesitation, Dean sat in the other one. She didn't say anything, just waited to hear what had brought Dean to her doorstep.

For a moment, Dean seemed content to watch the street. But Nola knew he wasn't relaxed. His whole body was tense, so she gave him time to gather his nerve. Finally, he spoke. "I heard they found a body in the reservoir. The rumor around campus is that it's Julie Blevins."

Nola waited until he looked up and met her gaze, then she nodded. "It is."

He sucked in a breath, his face paling as he gripped the armrest of the chair and leaned back. "Oh my God."

Nola gave him another moment before she spoke. "You knew her?"

"A little. She was in my philosophy class last semester, and we saw each other here and there. One of those people you just kind of say hi to as you pass or make small talk with when you stand outside a classroom, you know?"

Nola didn't have that experience, but she understood it. "Yes. I was just speaking with her parents. They're pretty devastated."

Dean nodded mutely, his face haggard.

"Why are you here, Dean?"

His knuckles turned white as he gripped the chair. "Because I feel like a jerk. Cindy's dead, and I'm what, worried about my future? I mean, I'm already in med school. Even if I get kicked off the football team, I can still figure out a way to pay for my tuition for one last year, and if I have to go into debt, if they want me to pay back the last couple of years, well, that's okay too. So I guess what I'm saying is if you need me to testify, I can testify. I'm not sure how helpful I can be, but I'm willing to talk to anybody you need me to talk to."

Nola leaned forward. "Did somebody say something about Julie? Is that what spurred this on?"

Dean swallowed hard. "When Julie disappeared, I thought like everybody else that she just, you know, decided college wasn't for her. It seemed out of character, but you never really know what's going on inside someone's head, do you?"

Dean wasn't looking for an answer, so Nola didn't give him one.

"I heard some of the guys, they made comments in passing. I can't even remember what they said now. But they were about Julie, and I just, I didn't like how they talked about her. At the time, though, I didn't think anything of it. I just thought they were talking."

He took a deep breath, his gaze going back to the street, but Nola knew he wasn't really seeing what was there. "But now they found Julie. It . . . I just . . . I don't know. I don't know what to think. But I do know that some of the guys on the team, they're not good people. Julie, she was good people. Cindy was good people."

He ran a hand through his hair, reminding her of Mike Blevins. "Not all the guys on the football team are jerks. Some of them, they're just kind of like me, using football to pay for college. But Chris and his crew, they're a totally different story, and I'm done helping protect them. We all sit there quietly because he's the big star and the whole university revolves around him. Hell, the universe practically revolves around him the way people treat him. This is just too much.

"Yeah, I need football to pay for college, but I'm not willing to sell my soul to pay for it. That's where I am right now. That if I keep my mouth shut, I'm selling my soul. So I guess it's time to start talking."

Determination lined Dean's face, and the nervous tension that had covered his frame had slowly dissipated the more he talked. She didn't doubt that he was ready. "Good. And I have just the person for you to talk to."

Chapter Fifty-One

The special prosecutor for Wayne County was situated in City Hall in downtown Richmond. The building was built in 1971, and it definitely looked it. It was tall, thin, with tiny windows and that tan-brown combination that a lot of buildings from that era sported. There was nothing appealing about it whatsoever.

The interior wasn't much better. Dark-brown paneling against white tiles flecked with brown and chrome lighting. Did all the buildings built in the seventies get issued the same tile floors? Was there a massive special?

Nola paced along those tiles outside the conference room where Dean was speaking with Assistant DA Leticia Brown.

Nola didn't know Leticia. But she'd done her research after Bishop had mentioned her. She had come down from New York to take over the division in Richmond. She'd successfully prosecuted a string of high-profile cases back in New York, and she was bringing that same no-nonsense approach to the department here. According to the scuttlebutt, though, her take no prisoners approach wasn't going over well with some of the good old boys, but Leticia hadn't backed down.

But this case would be an absolute powder keg. That was, if they had enough to even make a case.

Shifting in the leather chair of the waiting room, Nola tried to get a little more comfortable. Dean had been talking with Leticia for over two hours now. Nola hoped that was a good sign. The waiting room was a small alcove with three chairs in it and two side tables, each with five out-of-date magazines. The hallway had several doors, two on each side with a fifth leading out of this section of the district attorney's office. This section was dedicated to sex crimes and special crimes, a term given to cases that might engender a great deal of publicity.

This case, therefore, deserved to be here for both reasons.

The door to the conference room opened. Leticia stepped out, closing the door behind her. With ebony skin and dark-brown eyes, she was a tall woman who had to at least be 5'10"before the heels. She wore a bright-pink blouse with dark-gray slacks and heels that Nola would never be caught in in because it was a neon sign screaming *look at me*. But Leticia walked confidently down the hall toward her and gave her a nod. "Why don't we go into my office?"

The question wasn't really a question.

Nola smiled as she followed her. She approved of the tactic.

Leticia stepped into her office and made her way around a big wooden desk. Nola closed the door behind her and took a seat in one of the leather chairs in front of the desk.

Sitting back with her hands clasped across her stomach,

Leticia studied Nola. "This is quite a case you've dropped in my lap."

"Yes, it is. Are you willing to take it on?"

Leticia shook her head. "Actually, I misspoke. It's not a case. It's conjecture."

Nola took her time responding. "I think we both know that the university has been covering for this kid for years, and I'm sure you've heard rumors, little snippets of information about Chris Hartigan. A predator like him doesn't go unnoticed."

"Oh, there have been rumors, all right. What there hasn't been is anyone willing to sit down and swear out a complaint."

Pausing, Nola considered Leticia's words. "But if you could get all of them to do so, how many are we talking?"

"That I've heard of? Four."

In Nola's mind, she doubled that number, knowing that there had to be more out there. If they could just get half of those women to come forward, the rest would come out of the woodwork. "What about what Dean told you?"

Leticia sighed. "Conjecture, hearsay. He's given me a lot of strings to pull but not a lot of actionable information. Certainly not enough to make an arrest."

"But you have to be able to pull on some of those strings. I have to think some of those other kids have gotten themselves into trouble, and you can hold that over their heads."

"I know how to do my job, but I'm a little curious about your job." Leticia raised an eyebrow.

"How so?" Nola asked, sinking comfortably back into her seat.

"I had my people run a background check on you.

Apparently, you're a grad student studying sexual assault on college campuses."

"Apparently, I am."

The attorney leaned forward. "I've never met a graduate student like you."

Nola shrugged. "Thank you. I like to think I'm unique."

"I also read about the incidents on campus that you seem to have been involved in: the frat house, and then those two steroid junkies at the stadium. You're pretty tough for a grad student."

"Academia is a brutal world at times."

A soft laugh preceded Leticia's response. "You should try the legal world."

"Are you willing to go down this road? It's going to bring a lot of heat," Nola said.

Leticia smiled back at her, the smile of a predator. "Oh, I like the heat."

And Nola knew that was true. Leticia had been on the front lines taking down the head of a Fortune 500 company who had been assaulting the women who worked for his company for years. Every obstacle imaginable had been thrown in her path, and she'd bulldozed through them. She'd finally gotten him locked up for twenty-five years to life for four consecutive sentences. It was a death sentence. He would languish in prison and not be eligible for parole until he was 112.

The heat that had come down on her for that case must have been huge. Nola had read about death threats and also about the pressure that had been placed upon her by the DA in New York, who'd been up for reelection at the time.

But Leticia hadn't wavered.

Nola nodded. "Good. Let me give you another string to pull."

Pulling over a legal pad, Leticia grabbed a pen. "Okay, who?"

"His name is John O'Neil."

Chapter Fifty-Two

TOMMY

Sunlight glinted off the new cars in Tommy's parking lot. He smiled at the sight. He always came in through the north entrance and drove down the aisle of his cars. He loved looking at them in the early morning light. Everything was brand spanking new and pristine, all in their orderly rows. He got such a thrill out of it. He'd built all of this from scratch, and now he had dealerships throughout the state. Later this week, he was meeting with the bank to discuss expanding to two other states. This time next year, he would be absolutely rolling in money.

He smiled at the Indiana University at Richmond football sign strewn across the bay of the garage as he pulled around the back of the dealership. Football had gotten him here. Oh, he'd made lots of money before he became a booster for the team, but his sales had skyrocketed once he linked up with the university. His name and likeness were emblazoned across a football stadium that was beamed into millions of people's homes every weekend during football season.

The amount of money he'd made from those ads was insane. People stopped him on the street because of his commercials. Football had raised him to this level, and now it would take him even farther.

He pulled into his spot and stepped out of his car, breathing in deep. Yes, this was going to be a great day. Closing the door of his brand-new F-150, he strode toward the showroom.

One of the gals from the front desk was washing the glass of the front door. She caught sight of him and quickly moved to open the door for him.

"Thank you, darling," he drawled as he passed. He strode inside and made his way to his office.

The sound of heels coming down the hallway behind him meant that Rochelle was on the job this morning.

He hung his suit jacket up behind his chair as Rochelle bustled in, placing his coffee and breakfast sandwich on the desk in front of him.

"Anything important for the day?" he asked as he settled behind the desk.

Rochelle flipped over her tablet and quickly brought up his schedule. "Some preliminary conversations with the Realtors out in Ohio about potential dealership sites. Mac wants to bend your ear for a minute about a new promo he came up with, but other than that, it looks like it's just more of the regular. I sent your schedule to your phone."

His phone beeped in response. He flicked a glance over the events of the day and nodded. "Okay. Have them send me the specs on the possible locations, and, uh, tell you what, why don't you go grab me a bear claw? I'm feeling the need for a little bit more sugar this morning."

Rochelle nodded. "Sure thing. Back in five."

She disappeared down the hallway, and Tommy watched her go, his eyes glued to her butt. He smiled. It was good to be the boss.

Propping his iPad up on the desk, he scrolled through the morning news as he ate his breakfast sandwich—eggs, cheese, bacon,, and some home fries all piled on a Kaiser roll. Delicious.

The headline today was the discovery at the lake. The body had been dragged from it yesterday and was the main topic of the local news. A quick Google search showed that it had even been picked up as a short mention on some national news sites.

A vague sense of unease of what that could mean for him rolled through him, but he'd been assured that there was absolutely nothing that could tie the body to him. That was most likely true. He'd certainly never met the girl, and O'Neil had assured him that there was nothing linking the body to Hartigan either.

He still remembered the frantic phone call from O'Neil. One of Hartigan's buddies had called him to tell him about the girl. Hartigan had killed her and was passed out drunk in the bed next to her. Tommy had ordered O'Neil to get rid of the body and make sure there was no link to Hartigan. The last thing he needed was the star of the team linked to a murder. Because if Hartigan was, then by association, Tommy would be. And that just wouldn't do.

It had been a shame what had happened to the girl. But apparently she'd been long dead by the time O'Neil got to her. Hartigan had gotten a little carried away. There was no saving the girl at that point, and so the best thing was to just make the girl disappear. And that was what they had done. Right until she popped back up from that lake.

Tommy cursed inwardly. O'Neil needed to find better people. First those two clowns botched the warning to the grad student, and now the body had reappeared way too quickly. Of course, he still hadn't talked to O'Neil. He was probably just lying low. Or at least, that better be the reason he couldn't reach him.

But O'Neil was only a small part of the problem. Hartigan was the bigger one.

He frowned as he thought of the football star marring his otherwise good mood. That kid was an absolute disaster. True, he'd helped bring in the money and the fans. The take from the merchandising with his likeness on it was insane. But Tommy would be glad to see the back of him. He was becoming more of a headache now than a help.

He just needed to keep the kid under control for the next couple of months until he became the NFL's problem. And he had no doubt that he would be. But better them than him.

Rochelle returned with the bear claw and placed it on the desk. He smiled his thanks, his attention returning to the news as he flipped over to the sports coverage. The university team wasn't doing so hot, but they still had a shot at a few of the bowl games. That would bring in the money. He really needed to look into expanding into more hotels. That could definitely help boost his coffers.

He sat back and was munching on the bear claw, mulling over the possibilities, when his cell phone rang.

A quick glance at the screen had him sitting up straight. He swallowed the piece of donut and took a sip of coffee to remove any leftover pieces from his mouth. Then he answered the phone. "Pete. How you doing this morning?"

Pete Davis, the district attorney of Richmond, gave a

deep chuckle. "I'm doing pretty well. Life is a blessing, isn't it, Tommy?"

"That it is, that it is. I was just thinking the same thing this morning. Have you seen how beautiful it is out there today? It is going to be a gorgeous day in Richmond."

"Well, if I'm lucky, I'll see it at lunch," Pete said. "But I'm afraid I'm not calling to talk to you about the weather. It seems you might have a little bit of a problem on your hands."

"Oh?"

"Scuttlebutt around the office is that my new sex crimes prosecutor is gathering some information against one of your football guys."

Tommy leaned forward in his chair, his elbows on his desk as he forced his tone to stay casual. "Well, I'm sure it's nothing. My guys are good guys, you know that."

"Well, when Leticia focuses in on a target, she's very rarely wrong."

Gripping the phone tighter, Tommy tried to figure out which one of his guys Pete was talking about, although he had a sinking feeling he knew. "You know who they're looking at?"

"No. Leticia's playing that one pretty close to the vest. But I did manage to pull up some footage of one of your guys leaving her office. It was Dean Wallace."

Tommy frowned. He didn't know much about Dean. He was the backup quarterback. Reliable. Played a few games here and there whenever Chris needed a bit of a break. But he really wasn't much of a team player in that sense. Tommy had absolutely no knowledge of him going to any of the parties or taking advantage of any of the perks that he and the other boosters had provided to the teams.

"Is that so?" Tommy murmured.

"That it is. Just thought you might want to know. Hey, any chance I could get some tickets for the next game? My brother-in-law is coming to town, and I think it'd be fun if we managed to get down on the fifty-yard line."

His mouth tight, Tommy smiled. "Of course, of course. I'll send them by your office."

"Better send them by the house. Don't want anybody thinking anything, now do we?"

Tommy chuckled good-naturedly. "You're right, of course. I'll send them by the house. I'll get them to you this afternoon."

"That would be great. Now you go on and enjoy this beautiful day." Pete disconnected the call.

Tommy stared around the office, his mind whirling. *God damn it.*

Chapter Fifty-Three

NOLA

Nola woke up feeling better than she had in days. After a quick run and then breakfast, she called Leticia. It sounded like she was making some headway, especially after her people picked up O'Neil. They had him hidden away with some cops she trusted, and he was singing.

Finally, things were falling into place. Julie had been found. O'Neil had even given the DA some names of other women that Hartigan had assaulted. She had her people already speaking with the women to see if they would be willing to come forward. She was going to ask if they could reveal what had happened to them to the other victims. Not names or anything, but just their existence could hopefully convince someone to talk.

Nola had no doubt Leticia would get them to finally file a complaint. Everything seemed to be moving in the right direction. She stepped out onto the back porch to let the dog out and flicked a glance at her watch. She wanted to check in with Dean and see how he was feeling. But he had a big test sometime today. She didn't want to pull his mind away from his work. She'd try him later in the afternoon.

Her phone ringing cut off her thoughts. Nola pulled it out with a frown. She didn't recognize the number, and very few people had this number. "Hello?"

"Nola, thank God. I didn't know who else to call. It's . . . it's Shawn, from the stadium."

"Shawn, hi. Everything okay?"

"No, no, everything's definitely not. I called the cops, but they said he hadn't been gone long enough."

"Slow down. What's going on?"

"It's Dean. He didn't show up for our biology exam this morning. And we were supposed to study for our calculus test this afternoon, but he didn't show up for that either. I've tried to call him, but I can't reach him."

A knot forming in her gut, Nola's mind swam. Dean was out of reach?

"I went by his room, but he wasn't there. Dean, um, said you're some kind of private eye. I mean, I don't have any money, but is there anything you could do? The cops seem to think it's no big deal, but it is. *Something* has to be wrong. That exam this morning was a third of our grade. No way he'd miss that."

Shawn sounded like he was on the verge of hysteria, so Nola kept her tone even. "Did you speak with anyone? Has anyone seen him this morning?" she asked.

The young man exhaled hard, and she could picture him pacing nervously on the other end of the phone. "Yeah, one of his hallmates said that he saw him leave."

"What time would that have been?" She asked.

Rafe joined her on the porch, giving her a concerned look.

300

"Uh, maybe ten a.m.? He would have been heading to the campus at that time. But he never showed." Shawn took a deep breath. "Look, I know it's probably . . . no, it's not nothing. I know I sound crazy right now, but there's no way he would miss this exam. We were studying for it late last night.

"I texted him before the exam started, and then I ran back to his room after. But he wasn't there. And he did get up this morning. He sent me a text saying he was heading to campus early just to chill a little before the test."

"Did anyone see him on campus?" Nola asked.

"No, I asked around. But the weird thing was, after Dean went with you to the DA, he said that if anything happened to him that I should call you. So I'm calling."

"Okay, you're going to go to his dorm. Ask around see if anybody saw him. I'll call you when I find out something."

Disconnecting the call, Nola quickly sent a text to Bishop. *I need you to trace Dean Wallace's phone. Get me a location.*

"What's going on?" Rafe asked when she was done.

"I think the big fish just made his move."

Chapter Fifty-Four

TOMMY

The lake glistened in the bright sunlight as a raft of ducks swam lazily away from the shore of Tommy Briggs's private lakefront. From his enormous all-seasons room, Tommy took a puff of his cigar and blew the smoke against the twenty-foot-tall wall of windows that overlooked the pristine water.

He loved it out here. He'd had the place built five years ago. He'd brought up all the crappy little houses that had been here before, having to twist the arm of the last hold-out, a little old woman who'd lived in the same little trailer for the past forty years. But finally, she'd seen reason and signed the papers.

He'd had the bulldozer rip that place apart that very afternoon.

And all so that he could build his dream home.

As a kid, he'd never imagined that he would have a home like this. He'd always wanted more, but he never really knew what more was, not until he went to college. Before that, he'd grown up in Florida. Not on the coast near the ocean, which would have been pretty nice, but smack dab in the middle with no water nearby, just brutally hot and humid summers that offered no relief.

For college, he'd gone to the University of Alabama. Sophomore year, he went home for spring break to a friend's house. They had a house right on the water over on Galveston Island in Texas.

Tommy had never seen anything like it. Water as far as the eye could see. Waking up to that view with ATVs, Ski-Doos, and a jet boat at their disposal, it had been life-changing. It had been such a great week, and it had really opened his eyes to what he wanted for his life.

That house, the one he had once been so impressed with, could now fit in a small corner of his current 8,000-square-foot home.

Yes, he really had reached beyond even his early hopes.

And now that stupid Hartigan boy was risking all of it. He'd known the kid was arrogant, but honestly, he kind of respected that. You didn't get anywhere in this world without a little bit of an ego, and as far as he was concerned, the more ego you had, the farther people let you get in the world.

He knew about Hartigan's problem with women, but he was a football player. Of course he was going to play around and be a little rough in the bedroom. People paid to watch that boy get rough, and Tommy felt certain allowances should be made.

But the kid had been worth it. Tommy had been making money hand over fist ever since the kid joined the university.

Now, however, it looked like that golden goose was

about to steal all the riches from him. The call from the DA was the last straw. The body of that girl had been found, that grad student was poking around, and now one of his football players was talking to the DA. He'd left things up to O'Neil to handle, and he'd completely botched it. And now, even O'Neil had gone MIA. He was done letting other people handle it. As far as he could see, they were steering them all right into a jail cell. No, it was time for Tommy to take the reins.

He knew it wouldn't be long before Chris was brought in for questioning or even arrested. He couldn't let that happen. The kid was so stupid, he would no doubt reveal everything or at least enough to allow the DA to dig further. Or maybe they'd hit up one of Chris's buds. There were a thousand different ways to get to Chris. Which meant Chris needed to be taken out of the equation.

"Yo, Tommy, where are you at?" Chris's voice called out from the long hall leading into the great room.

Tommy turned from the window as Chris stepped into the massive room. Chris ran an unimpressed eye over the tall thirty-foot ceiling with dark wooden beams reaching up to its peak. He barely glanced at the multi-million-dollar view out of the floor-to ceiling windows.

The high-end furnishings meant nothing to him. Chris was nothing like Tommy in their upbringing. He'd grown up with wealth. He'd had the world handed to him on a silver platter. The stench of entitlement rolled off of him, which meant he had absolutely zero respect for anyone else's material wealth. After all, he'd seen it all before.

Chris nodded at Tommy as he headed over to the bar. Without asking, he reached over and grabbed a decanter of scotch, pouring himself a healthy serving into a tumbler. He took a sip and let out a sigh. "The good stuff. Haven't had this in a while. The crap they sell at the bars around campus is practically gasoline."

Tommy narrowed his eyes. "Glad you like it."

His gaze scanning the room again, Chris nodded. "Don't think I've been out here before, have I?"

"No, you haven't."

"Nice little place you've got here. Reminds me of my grandpa's."

The kid was insufferable.

"Now what am I doing here? I'm missing practice. And I don't like to miss practice." Chris glared at Tommy.

Tommy met his gaze, his anger only rising at the arrogance of the spoiled little prick. "You're getting yourself into a little bit of trouble, Chris. The DA has your name associated with a criminal case."

Although Chris's eyebrows rose, he didn't look at all alarmed. And he should be. "Okay. So what? I haven't done anything." He shrugged.

"There's a rape claim, maybe more than one."

Chris scoffed. "Oh, please. I've never raped anybody."

"Now we have a problem, Chris."

"I don't have a problem. I'm doing great. If you have a problem, that's on you."

"No, this is a problem for both of us. They found Julie."

Chris stared at him. "Who?"

"Julie Blevins."

Shaking his head, Chris took a sip of his drink before he spoke. "I have no idea who that is."

Tommy gritted his teeth. "The girl you strangled and killed."

Chris's glass stopped halfway to his mouth. He stared over its rim at Tommy. For a brief second, fear slashed across his face before it was immediately replaced by anger. "You said you took care of that."

"And we did. But it's not so easy to hide a body."

Chris's glass finished its journey to his mouth, and then he slammed it down on the counter. "Well, so what? They can't prove anything. I mean, she's been dead for a while now. There's probably not even anything left that can tie me to her. Besides, she got what she wanted."

Tommy stared at the powerful young man. He was a force of nature on the football field. And he had been given every single opportunity in life. And yet despite all of those advances, the boy was as dumb as a rock. "She wanted to get dead?"

Chris shrugged again. "Things happen. She liked it rough. Not my fault. She should have remembered the safe word." He chuckled to himself.

Tommy rolled his hand around his cigar, imagining plunging it into Chris's eye. The stupid little meathead was going to ruin everything, and he wasn't even smart enough to know it.

Draining the last of his drink, Chris placed the tumbler back on the bar top. "Is that everything? Because I really need to get back to practice."

"You need to take this seriously."

Chris laughed. "No, I don't. That's what I've got you for. Do what you've always done and just clean it up." He turned to the door, but Tommy snapped his fingers.

Two of his men stepped inside, blocking Chris's exit. Both men towered over Chris and had a few pounds on him as well. Plus, their guns were clearly in view in the holsters at their waists.

As he turned to look back at Tommy, Chris frowned. "What the hell is this?"

A yell came from the side hall leading to the guest rooms. Two more men dragged in Dean and threw him on the floor.

Blood was dried on the right side of his face, and he had a large cut across his scalp.

Staring at Dean, Chris took a step forward, his mouth falling open. He looked back at Tommy. "What the hell are you doing to Dean?"

Tommy smiled. "Oh, I'm not doing anything to Dean. Dean's doing something to you."

Chapter Fifty-Five

NOLA

Bishop traced Dean's phone out to Eagle Lake. She couldn't get an exact bead on it, but since Tommy Briggs, one of the biggest boosters of the football team, had a place out here, there had to be a connection. Plus, O'Neil had mentioned Briggs when he and Nola had their little chat. Briggs was in this up to his eyeballs.

"Why'd they leave Dean's phone on? Anyone who's watched a cop show knows to turn it off," Rafe said as Nola pulled over to the side of the road at the edge of Tommy's property. His lake house sat on ten acres. Only about two acres had cameras. The other eight were unsecured.

"I don't know. Maybe they're just serious amateurs. Tommy left all the dirty work to O'Neil. This might be his first time dipping his toes in himself," Nola said. She stepped out and surveyed the area. It was quiet. They hadn't passed another car for the last five minutes.

She was a little worried about the fact that they'd traced Dean's phone so easily as well.

Getting out of the car, Rafe made his way to the back and pulled open the tailgate. Nola reached in and grabbed her weapons, carefully placing the magazines into her vest and checking to make sure that a round was chambered in her Beretta. Then she reached over and grabbed the large silver case, pulling it forward.

Rafe gave it a quizzical look. "What's that?"

"A little gift from Bishop." She flicked open the lock and then opened the lid. Grabbing the earpiece, she tapped it once it was in place. And then she tapped the mic at her throat. "Bishop, you there?"

"I'm here. Little birdie ready to go?"

"Hold on a sec."

Nola grabbed the drone and then walked to the middle of the road to place it on the ground. She stepped back and then tapped her mic again. "You're good. Send her up."

The drone whirled to life and then slowly began to ascend.

"Is Bishop driving that thing?" Rafe asked.

"Yep. She should be able to give us a little more intel. There's no other way to see what's going on inside there right now."

"Hey, uh, some new info," Bishop said.

"What is it?" Nola asked.

"I wanted to check where Chris Hartigan was during all this, so I traced his phone. He's somewhere around there too."

Nola frowned. Hartigan was here? What the hell was that about?

O'Neil was currently trussed up with the cops, hopefully spilling his guts about every underhanded deal and action he and Tommy had been involved in. If all went well, O'Neil's testimony would put Tommy away for a good long time, along with everybody else involved in this mess.

But O'Neil's testimony wouldn't come in time to help Dean. Nola knew in her gut that Shawn wasn't overreacting and that something was wrong. Nola and Rafe were going to have to see to that if they weren't too late already. Nola had no doubt that someone had learned Dean had gone to the DA. She should have set up security for him. If something happened to him, it was on her.

Nola pulled the Beretta from her holster and looked at Rafe. "You ready?"

He chambered around in the shotgun and nodded. "I'm ready."

Both of them stayed silent as they set off in the direction of the main house. The woods were quiet with only the sounds of nature surrounding them. An occasional bunny or squirrel would scurry through the brush, but there was no sound of any larger mammals.

Nola tapped her mic after five minutes. "You got anything?"

"Coming up on the house now. Hold on," Bishop replied.

Nola waited, cutting through the trees and seeing grass in the distance.

Rafe let out a low whistle, and Nola looked over. He nodded to a camera up in a tree. Then Rafe reached up and quickly disconnected the wires. He nodded at Nola.

They'd gotten the schematics on the security from Bishop. For a guy who'd spent millions of dollars on a home, he'd really skimped out on the security measures. There were only four cameras on the exterior of the house, each covering one-fourth of the yard. By taking out this one camera, they'd be able to reach the house without anybody noticing them. That was, of course, as long as nobody was monitoring the feeds.

Nola had a feeling that Tommy had skimped on that aspect as well and that they should be good to go. They crept toward the edge of the tree line, staring out over the manicured lawn.

Bishop's voice cut through her headset just as Nola was about to step out onto the grass. "There's movement at the back of the house." Bishop sucked in a breath. "They've got two people with them ropes around both their arms. One's got a head wound. I think it's your guy Dean."

"He's hurt?" Nola asked.

"Hurt but walking. The other one's that Hartigan guy. Looks like there're about four security guys plus Tommy. They're heading toward the dock. You need to move, Nola. I don't like how this is shaping up."

Nola's heart rate picked up. Rafe nodded. He'd heard everything through his own earpiece. And then the two of them took off through the trees, heading for the water, and Nola hoped that they got there in time.

Chapter Fifty-Six

TOMMY

The glare from the lake was nearly blinding. Tommy slipped his sunglasses on as they headed to the dock situated right on the water's edge next to the boathouse. He smiled at the structure. It held his powerboat, Jet Skis, and all things needed to have a little fun on the water. He always thought a boathouse was classy, and now he had one of the classiest ones on the lake.

"What the hell you doing, man?" Chris yelled at him from behind. Two of the security guards had tied him up and now walked him in front of them, their guns trained on him. For a big allegedly tough, guy, he hadn't put up much of a fight. His men had pulled their guns, and Chris had immediately raised his hands. Not that Tommy was surprised. Chris was the type who only got into a fight he could win.

Tommy ignored the boy's yells.

The other kid, Dean, was quiet, although not by choice. The blow he'd taken to the head obviously had given him a concussion, and he didn't really seem like he was all there.

That was probably for the best. He almost felt bad for the kid. Granted, he'd tried to take them all down, even if he didn't realize how much trouble opening that door would lead to. But he was probably a good kid who thought he was doing the right thing.

It might even be some solace for the kid as he went to meet his maker.

Hartigan, however, he had absolutely zero compassion for. The kid had been a disaster for the last year. He'd gotten more and more reckless. If he'd just been able to pull it back a little bit, they could have had a long-term lucrative arrangement. But the kid had to go and blow it all up when he killed that Blevins girl.

Stepping onto the dock, Tommy headed toward the heavy chain attached to the third mooring. He waved the men who were holding Dean over. The two dragged Dean, his shoes scuffing along the wooden surface. Without any concern, they dropped the kid to the deck.

Tommy winced as the football player hit hard, falling onto his side. Tommy's guy Marco reached over and rolled him onto his stomach and then looped the chain through his through the ropes on his arms. He snapped a combination lock at the end of the chain and then pulled on it twice, making sure it was secure. "All good."

"Where's the phone?" Tommy asked.

Marco pulled it from his pocket and handed it to Tommy, who was wearing gloves. All his guys were. Tommy grabbed the phone and then dropped it to the deck. He smiled. The cops would trace it here eventually. God, he felt like he was some sort of crime conductor right now, telling everybody what part they should play. This was fun.

Chris stared at Dean, who now sat up with that dazed expression, then turned to face Tommy. "What are you doing, man?" he asked again.

Wiping his hands on his pants, Tommy stood. "Like I said in the house, I'm not doing anything. You are."

He held his hand out, and Marco handed over his sidearm. Without hesitation, Tommy leveled it at Chris and pulled the trigger.

Chris grunted as the bullet entered just above his belly button. He crashed to his knees, hunching forward. Still on his knees, his eyes were wide in shock. He stared down at the growing bloodstain on his chest. He looked up, his face red, confusion in his eyes. "What . . . why'd you do that?"

Tommy threw the gun into the water. "I didn't do it. Dean here just shot you."

"Wh-what?" Chris stammered.

Tommy smiled. "It was horrible. Dean here fell in love with you. But you spurned his advances. So he kind of lost his mind, brought you up to my house, shot you, and then killed himself. It really is a tragedy all around."

"This hurts, man. Call a doctor."

The kid really was stupid. Tommy shook his head. "That's really not going to help with my little scenario. Toss him in." Tommy turned to head back to the house. It should take a few minutes for this to all be wrapped up. He was hungry and in the mood for pizza. He'd head over to that little joint about ten miles away. He needed to make himself scarce anyway.

A gunshot rang out, but it had come from the wrong direction. Tommy's head jolted up, and he darted a look over his shoulder as a gurgle sounded. Marco grabbed his neck. Blood seeped through his fingers.

A second gunshot rang out, followed by a third and a fourth. Tommy ducked down, shoving Dean into the water before sprinting for the boathouse.

Chapter Fifty-Seven

NOLA

"He's in the water!" Bishop yelled.

Nola tore across the open space. She'd missed Tommy by a hair as he ducked behind the boathouse. But the other four security guards were down. One leaned up, raising his gun from the ground, and Nola didn't hesitate to send a bullet right through the middle of his forehead.

She didn't even pause or flinch as she leapt over him. Rafe stopped at each of the security guards and kicked their weapons out of the way.

Stripping off her bulletproof vest and dropping it to the ground, Nola reached the end of the dock and quickly removed all of her weapons save the knife at her thigh. Kicking off her boots, she dove into the water.

She strode with steady, even strokes toward the bottom. The farther from the surface she got, the darker and murkier the water became. She really needed a light, but she had none.

She simply had to trust that Dean wouldn't have drifted very far, not with that heavy chain dragging him down. So she continued her strokes down to the bottom. And she lucked out: below her, she could make out movement. She swam quickly toward it. Her chest was feeling tight, and she desperately wanted to suck in more oxygen. She tamped down that need and focused on Dean, whose head shot up, his eyes focused on Nola.

Dean struggled frantically, trying to pull himself toward the surface. But the chain kept him down.

Swimming toward him, she pulled the knife from the sheath at her thigh. Dean's frantic struggles slowed and stopped as she reached him. *Hold on, Dean. Hold on.*

Nola grabbed his arms and quickly sawed through the rope. The chain slipped between his arms. She grabbed him around the waist and started to kick for the surface. He was dead weight in her arms. She prayed that she made it in time. Each stroke required more energy, more focus. *Come on. Come on.*

Finally, she burst through the surface. "Rafe!" she yelled.

But he was already there on the edge of the dock, reaching for Dean. She hefted Dean up as much as she could. Grabbing him under the arms, Rafe hauled him onto the deck.

Taking a deep breath, she braced herself on the edge of the dock before vaulting herself over and landing on her side. She rolled herself onto her back, breathing deep. Spots had started to appear around the edge of her vision from the lack of oxygen. She closed her eyes, breathing, and then slowly pulled herself up to her hands and knees.

Rafe was giving Dean CPR, pounding away on his chest.

Nola reached over for her boots and slipped them on, grabbing her discarded Beretta as her vision cleared, although her lungs still ached. She got to her feet. "Keep working on him. I'm going after Briggs."

Without waiting for a reply, she took off in the direction that Tommy had fled, praying that the bastard put up a fight when she caught up with him.

As she darted past Chris Hartigan, he latched onto her ankle. She winced, disgust filling her.

His face incredibly pale, one hand held the wound in his stomach as blood seeped into the dock while the other held Nola's pants leg. "Help me."

She looked into his face and then kicked his hand away. "No."

Chapter Fifty-Eight

TOMMY

Heart pounding, Tommy grabbed onto a tree as his breaths came out in pants. His whole body felt like it was covered in a thick layer of sweat.

Who the hell were those two? When the shots had first rung out , he thought it was one of his security guards and that maybe Chris had reached for one of their guns. But then those two people had burst out of the trees. He'd never seen either of them before, but from the practiced way they moved, his gut told him they were cops of some sort.

He didn't know where they were now. Hopefully they were too busy dealing with his security and Dean to come after him.

Bending over at the waist, he sucked in air, trying to fill up his lungs, which had started to burn. He'd really let himself go. When he was a football player, a little run like the one he'd just done would have been nothing. His blood pressure would barely have risen—now he felt like he was on the verge of a heart attack.

He pushed off the tree and stumbled forward. He couldn't stop. He needed to get away. He needed to call his lawyer. He'd figure out some way to spin this. He'd say . . . what could he say?

Maybe that his security turned on him. It was some sort of ransom thing. Chris and Dean had shown up, and then in all the craziness, he'd bumped into Dean, accidentally pushing him into the water.

Yeah, that could work. Tommy didn't have a record, and he could get O'Neil to back him up, be some sort of character witness.

O'Neil. He pulled out his phone and quickly called him, shifting from a jog to a fast walk. The phone rang and rang, and then O'Neil's voicemail picked up. Again.

A sense of foreboding ran through Tommy, but he pushed it away.

No. It was fine. O'Neil was just out somewhere or busy or something. The campus security chief would testify on his behalf if it came down to that. They could spin this whole thing to go back to Tommy's security. A couple of those guys had some pretty nasty records. It would be believable.

Despite feeling relieved at having a plan, his nerves were still strung tight. But the more he walked, the more his mind eased. It was entirely possible those two hadn't even seen him or at least hadn't gotten a good look at him. He could get a good lawyer, who'd argue mistaken identity. He could definitely find someone who he could pay enough to say he was with them when this all went down.

And Dean would be dead. Chris would be dead, and then there'd be no one to testify against him. No jury would believe his security against him. After all, he was a well-respected businessman.

Feeling even better at his chances, he picked up his pace, hearing the sounds of kids' laughter up ahead. He tapped the gun at his side. He'd grabbed it off one of the security guards when they went down. He could do this. He just needed to get away from here.

Chapter Fifty-Nine

NOLA

Nola tore through the trees. Normally, if she were tracking someone, she'd have to slow down a little bit to make sure that she could find their trail. But Tommy had left a trail a mile wide. It looked like a rhinoceros had come through here. He must have grabbed onto every branch and tree shrub along his way.

She barely had to slow to keep an eye on the direction he'd headed. Plus, he'd run across more than a few mud puddles, leaving even more evidence of his passing.

Obviously, the guy was in a panic.

Good.

Nola kept replaying him shoving Dean into the water. He had people moving in on him, and he still was trying to tie up loose ends. He probably thought there was some way he could buy or talk his way out of everything.

But Nola was going to make sure that didn't happen.

And with the feed from Bishop's drone, they would be able to do just that. Now she just needed to catch the bastard.

Nola hurried along, sure that she was getting close.

She wasn't exactly running quietly either, but she was betting on the fact that with the blood pounding in Tommy's ears, he wouldn't hear her coming. It was not an easy run. She was soaked, and every step she took, her clothes squished. Plus, her lungs weren't yet at a hundred percent, and the deep dive hadn't helped with that.

She was reaching the end of his property, which meant she'd have to catch up to him soon. The last thing she wanted was for him to—

A scream cut through the air.

Nola put on a burst of speed, knowing that Tommy must have come across one of his neighbors.

She burst out from the trees as Tommy stumbled across a grassy lawn. There was a trailer in the distance and two kids on a swing set. A mother sprinted across the yard toward her kids. "What are you doing here? Get out of here!"

Tommy stumbled forward, the gun in his hand.

Nola wasn't even sure if he realized he had it. Which meant he definitely wouldn't be taking care with it.

Putting on another burst of speed, she tackled him around the waist. He let out an oof as the two of them fell forward. His head slammed into the ground.

Nola looked up at the mother. "Get them in the house."

The mother didn't need to be told twice as she grabbed the little girl and yanked the boy from the swings, carrying them both into the trailer.

The little boy looked over his shoulder, his big eyes wide as he stared at Nola. She waited until the door closed and then slammed her fist into Tommy's ribs. Keeping her knee on his back, she climbed off and then rolled him over.

He stared up at her, his mouth gaping like a fish on land. He grabbed his left arm. "Heart . . . attack."

Nola stood up and just looked down at him.

"Help me," he panted out, just like Chris had.

Nola leaned down and looked him straight in the face. "Don't worry, Tommy boy. It can't be a heart attack. You don't have a heart."

Chapter Sixty

It had been a long day and night. The cops had shown up, called by Bishop, along with an ambulance. Restraining Tommy, Nola had called Bishop and had them divert one cop car and ambulance to the trailer where Tommy lay in the dirt. She stayed there, making sure they knew he was the one responsible for everything before she let them take him in the ambulance.

Chris Hartigan was rushed into emergency surgery and managed to pull through. Rafe managed to get Dean breathing again, but they kept him overnight for observation. Detectives and the district attorney had been in and out of his room for hours, taking down his statement.

Bishop had forwarded the video from the drone to the police and to the feds.

The woman whose home Tommy had stumbled into also swore out a statement about him holding a gun and heading for her children.

Nola and Rafe had to make a few statements. Ileana

managed to intervene with Rafe and clear up any confusion about his appearance at the scene.

Now back at the rental house, Nola grabbed the last of her clothes and placed them in her bag. It hadn't taken long to pack. She hadn't really unpacked.

Despite being ready to go, she'd decided that they weren't going to leave until the next morning. There were still a few more things that had to be done, and neither she nor Rafe had gotten much sleep last night. They hadn't even gotten home till four. The dog had been waiting anxiously for them. After letting her out and feeding her, she had curled up on the bed with Nola and gone right to sleep.

Nola hadn't been as lucky. She'd tossed and turned, thinking about all of the lives that Chris Hartigan, Tommy Briggs, and all the others that had let them go unchecked had destroyed.

She was just reaching for her coffee mug on the side table to try to keep herself awake when she heard the knock at the front door. She walked out, her eyebrows rising at the familiar face looking at her through the screen door.

"Come on in," she said.

Jack opened the door and stepped inside just as Rafe appeared from the kitchen with the dog right behind him. Those two seemed to have made their peace.

Nola nodded toward the door. "Rafe, this is Jack DiMeola, Cindy's uncle. He's a former colleague and friend."

"I hope she means current friend," Jack said with a smile as he held out his hand.

"Nice to meet you," Rafe said.

Jack looked down at the dog. "You got a dog?"

Nola shrugged. "So it seems."

Rafe grabbed the leash on the table by the door. "And

actually, I was just about to take her out for a walk. I'm trying to win her over."

"How's it going?" Jack asked.

"Well, she likes me plenty when I'm holding food." Rafe snapped the leash on the dog collar and headed to the door. "Nice to meet you, Jack."

"Yeah, you too."

Once Rafe was through the door, Nola nodded down the hall. "Coffee?"

"Always."

The two of them headed to the kitchen. Jack took a seat at the rickety table while Nola filled up a mug, added two sugars, and handed it over. Jack took a big sip and let out a sigh. "I needed that."

Taking a seat across from him, Nola asked. "How'd you find me?"

"I still have my ways."

Raising an eyebrow, Nola grinned. "Ileana."

Jack returned the smile. "She is my way."

"So what are you doing here?" She asked.

His smile faded away like it had never been. "I saw what went down on the news and drove all night. I wanted to see for myself that this was really happening."

Feeling the pain of the strong man across from her, she spoke softly. "It's really happening. Hartigan's going away for a good long time."

"So he's the one?" Jack asked quietly.

"He is," she confirmed. "And Cindy wasn't his only victim."

Jack let out a shaky breath.

"But he wasn't the only one responsible. Tommy Briggs will be spending some quality time in a state-appointed facility."

"He's the big booster?"

Nola nodded. "Yeah, and I just heard that the university president has resigned, along with six board members. The dominoes in this are going to continue to fall. The security chief of the university is supposedly singing like a canary. He's turning on everyone, trying to get himself a lighter sentence."

"Will it work?"

"To a certain extent, but he's dirty, and the courts aren't going to be able to let him off too easy. He knew about the Blevins girl and then arranged for her body to be dumped in the reservoir."

"What happened with her?"

"Apparently Chris strangled her after having sex with her. He freaked out and told some of his teammates. They're also being interviewed by the police and are lawyering up. If they're smart, they'll turn on Chris in a second."

Jack shook his head. "I had no idea it was going to get this big when I asked you to look into it. I never would have—"

She cut him off. "Don't say that. I'm glad that we put this guy away. He would have gone on hurting people until someone stopped him. Or maybe he just would have gone on, and no one would have ever stopped him. So I don't regret coming here at all. I'm glad I could help. Hopefully now Cindy can rest easy."

"I'm not sure if that's an option for her."

Nola said nothing, knowing that Jack and his family were staunch Catholics, and within Catholicism, suicide was a mortal sin. They no doubt believed that meant Cindy was doomed for an afterlife of horror and pain.

Nola didn't subscribe to that notion. People who were

driven to suicide, they'd already experienced a lifetime of pain, and if there was any sort of God, he certainly wouldn't require that they continue on in that horrific existence after death.

Jack hunched forward over his mug. "You're going to stay around for a little bit?"

"I was hoping I could leave tomorrow, but I have a feeling I'm going to have to stay and fill out a few more reports."

"And I know how much you love that." Jack said, forcing a smile to his face.

"It does give my life meaning," Nola said grinning back at him before the levity slipped from her face. "But it's worth it to make sure that everything gets done right."

"And the DA in charge of this, they're going to make sure that the charges stick?"

Nola paused for a moment. The DA for the county had actually taken a leave of absence. Nola had a feeling that he was going to get caught up in this corruption scandal as well. Lord knew how many people would be caught in the web by the time this thing finished spiraling.

But Leticia had been placed as interim DA, and Nola had every confidence that she would make sure that everyone who deserved to be punished was. "Yes, the DA will make sure that the charges stick."

"And then what about you? You heading on to another case?"

Normally the answer would be yes. But not this time. "Not right away. There's something else I need to do first."

Chapter Sixty-One

NOLA
ONE WEEK LATER

The reverend closed his Bible. The mourners at the back of the service started to peel away and head toward their cars in groups of two or three. A light drizzle fell, and the mourners were split in half between individuals holding umbrellas and those just letting the rain fall on them.

Nola was in the latter category.

She always felt it was right when it rained during a funeral. The world shouldn't be bright and sunny when people were saying their final goodbyes.

She started to turn away as Amy and Mike Blevins stood up from where they had sat for the funeral of their daughter. Amy looked over her shoulder and caught Nola's eye. Their gazes held for a long moment, and then Amy gave her a nod.

Chris Hartigan had been charged with Julie's death. The charges had just been announced yesterday.

He was looking at twenty-five to life for that count alone. His teammates had indeed turned on him. His case was looking like a slam dunk, but Nola knew that nothing was guaranteed.

But if the system failed to punish him, she would step in.

Ducking her head against the rain, she turned and walked slowly through the tombstones. She hadn't parked near the rest of the mourners. Instead, she'd placed her car on the far side of the cemetery.

An older woman stood in front of a grave, her head bowed. A man who was probably her son stood holding an umbrella over the two of them. The woman held onto her son's arm as tears rolled down her cheeks.

Nola turned her gaze away, not wanting to intrude on the private moment of grief.

As she walked, she looked at all of the names that she passed, people who had someone that cared enough about them to place them in the ground and erect a statue to tell the world that they were once there. Within a generation, though, the graves would be unvisited, with people wondering who they had once been.

Two rows over was a giant statue of an angel on top of a tombstone. Nola veered over to it, knowing what she was going to find. She turned and looked at the name on the grave. Todd Mabel, born 1960, died 1968. No matter what cemetery one went to, it seemed that children always got the largest markers. It was fitting. Their deaths were always accompanied by the largest amount of grief.

From the corner of her eye, Nola noticed the girl with the long brown hair walking parallel with her a few rows over, the same girl she'd seen on campus and throughout this case.

Nola didn't look over toward her or call out. She just

walked quietly, letting the girl walk with her. The two of them walked across the cemetery, and Nola read each of the names as she passed. It was silly, but she felt like it was respectful to at least acknowledge their existence.

By the time she'd reached her truck, her trench coat was soaked, and so was her hair. But it didn't bother her. Opening up the car, Nola slid off her coat, dropping it in the backseat before sliding into the driver's seat.

The dog picked her head up from the passenger seat and then leaned toward her, giving a wag of her tail.

Nola reached over and rubbed behind her ears. "Hey, girl."

Rafe had headed back to the estate, but Nola had decided to take the dog with her. She would head there now and see how the dog got along with Rafe's two kids. Hopefully, it would be a good match, and then they could pick a name for her.

The dog let out a little whine, looking out the window past Nola.

Taking a deep breath, Nola turned. The girl with the long hair stood only ten feet away. The rain didn't seem to affect her at all. She walked toward the car, her gaze focused on Nola.

Nola looked up into her eyes as she came to a stop right outside her window. The girl reached up and placed her hand against the glass.

Reaching over, Nola placed her hand on the inside of the glass against the girl's. The old wound pulsing with hurt, she whispered, "Hi Beth."

Beth gave her a small smile and then faded into nothing.

Taking a deep breath, Nola fished her keys out of her pocket and turned on the car, blasting the heat to try to ward off the chill that had slipped into her bones.

Her phone beeped, and she pulled it out. It was a text from Bishop. *How did it go?*

All right. Just finished.

Three dots appeared for a long few seconds before Bishop responded. *Are you looking for another case?*

Nola paused, her fingers hovering above the phone. She glanced at the dog, who looked back at her with her big brown eyes. Nola smiled, then turned her attention back to the phone. *No. I think I'm going to take a little time.*

Really?!!!

Before Nola could type a response, Bishop did.

Actually, scrap that, pretend I didn't text it. You already said you're coming home. I'm holding you to it. ☺

Nola grinned and then placed the phone in the cup holder between the seats. She reached over and rubbed behind the dog's ears. "You'd like that, wouldn't you, girl? Go and stay home for a little while?"

She leaned into Nola, and Nola took that as a yes.

Putting the car in gear, she headed for the exit of the cemetery and began her journey home.

Next in The Nola James Series

www.vinci-books.com/return-fear

When the hunt turns personal, Nola James faces her darkest battle yet.

Driven to the edge by a threat to someone she loves, Nola James must confront a ruthless predator on his terms, risking everything —even her life—to see justice through.

Turn the page for a free preview…

Return the Fear: Chapter One

NOLA

The yellow Corvette roared into the parking lot of Hudson's Hideaway. The family-owned seafood chain was located a few blocks down from the beach on First Street and saw a lot of pedestrian traffic from the sun-worshiping crowd.

It was too early for the beachgoers, though, as the restaurant didn't open for lunch until twelve. At ten a.m., the parking lot was empty save for the "look at me!" sports car and the rented jeep in the back of the lot.

The driver of the Corvette was Tyler Hudson, the owner of the Hudson's Hideaway chain. At forty-eight years old, Tyler looked like he was no older than forty-five, and that small achievement was only accomplished through regular visits to a not-so-reputable plastic surgeon. Deeply tanned with bright white-blond hair and pale brown eyes, Tyler was a fan of hard living, and his body, despite all the advances of the medical community, was unable to stave off the effects of his hard drinking and late nights.

But the drugs that he dabbled in recreationally seemed to, at the very least, keep the weight off. He wasn't quite meth-head skinny, but he was getting there.

Nola sat in the jeep watching as Tyler Hudson tried to hoist himself from the driver's seat. It took two attempts. The first time, he didn't use enough muscle as he pushed off the steering wheel. The second time, he braced his legs against the door frame to give himself leverage. The Corvette was so low to the ground, it was impossible to get out any other way. Once Tyler had extricated himself from the car, his face now red from the exertion, or maybe anger, he ran for the front doors of the restaurant.

Nola shook her head at the spectacle. She never understood why people got cars that they had trouble getting in and out of. You might look good driving down the highway, but the illusion was ruined when you had to contort yourself or get a push to get out of the thing once you'd stopped.

Linus Redfield sat next to her in the passenger seat, fidgeting, his agitation growing as he watched Tyler reach the door. Tyler pulled on the handle, but it stayed closed. He knocked loudly on the glass, but no one appeared from inside to allow him entrance.

"I need to go to work," Linus said.

Nola reached out a hand and placed it on Linus's forearm. "It's all right, Linus. He can't see you."

Linus shook his head, starting to rock from side to side. "That's Mr. Tyler. He's going to be mad. I need to go back to my room. The restaurant should be open now."

"The restaurant's not going to open today, Linus. Remember I told you about that? Today's a holiday. The restaurant is going to be closed."

Across the lot, Tyler was fumbling with his keys, looking

for the ones that opened the lock. Linus rocked faster in the passenger seat. The anger inside Nola burned even brighter.

Linus was fifty years old, but he had the mental capacity of an eight-year-old. He and Tyler had actually gone to school together. Linus was supposed to be two years ahead of him, but due to his cognitive deficits, he'd ended up in the same grade as Tyler. From what Nola and Bishop had been able to cobble together, Tyler had been none too kind about the boy who'd been mainstreamed into the public school.

Tyler's father, Tristan, however, had been a different story. He'd taken a shine to Linus and had hired him to work in the first Hudson's Hideaway in Venice, Florida. It had been a good relationship by all accounts. In fact, it had been one of the most stable and positive ones in young Linus's life. He'd worked for Tristan for thirty-one years until Tristan passed away unexpectedly from a heart attack three years ago.

Tyler had inherited the family business and kept Linus on, but with one major difference: he no longer paid him.

After his father's death, Tyler had expanded the restaurant business. Tristan had begun the expansion, but Tyler had taken it to a whole new level, adding two new restaurants in the same year: one in Key West and this one in Miami.

It was too much too soon, and his bank accounts were showing serious strain. Plus, Tyler had picked up the property at a low price, thinking he had gotten an incredible deal.

Apparently, he forgot about the impact of climate change on Miami. Because when the rains came in, the restaurant was more likely than not to flood. So the Miami

Hudson's Hideaway was underwater in more ways than one.

Across the lot, Tyler finally managed to get the front door open. He yanked it open and stormed inside. The front door slammed back, and Tyler disappeared from view.

"I need to go to work," Linus repeated.

"It's okay, Linus. You won't be working today. You've got the day off."

He shook his head at her. "I don't get a day off."

It wasn't a lie. Tyler had taken Linus from Venice to the Miami location and set him up in the small, cramped space above the restaurant. It couldn't really be considered an apartment. It was one room with no window. The only bathroom access was a bucket in the corner and a wash sink. Tyler locked Linus in each night.

His employees didn't say anything because most of them were illegal or had family members who were illegal, and Tyler threatened to call the authorities on anyone who stepped out of line.

Nola reached into the back seat and pulled over an iPad. She quickly brought up the first episode of *Gilligan's Island* and handed it to Linus. "Your grandmother said that you like this show."

Linus's eyes widened, and a smile slipped across his face. "Gilligan."

Automatically, Linus looked about twenty years younger, if not more. And it made Nola wonder if Tyler had ever tried smiling as a way to retain his youth.

"Now, Linus, I have to go into the restaurant for just a minute. I'll be back. Don't get out of the car, okay?" she asked.

Linus nodded but kept his eyes glued to the screen as he laughed. "It's not going to be a three-hour tour."

"No, it's not," Nola said, thinking the same had been true for Linus. Tyler had told him that he was bringing him to check out the new restaurant, and then he never let him leave.

It was modern-day slavery.

At the time of Linus's abduction, his grandmother had been in the hospital and had been unable to follow up on Linus's disappearance for two weeks. By that time, the uninterested police had faced a cold trail for the disappearance of a mentally challenged adult. They put out calls for information in the Venice area, but there had been no responses.

Tyler had even spoken with police and sworn that he had no idea where Linus had disappeared to. And that was essentially the end of the official search for Linus Redfield. But the grandmother kept trying. And recently, one of her granddaughters created a website asking for any information. Bishop had come across it, and that brought Nola into Tyler Hudson's life.

From the background report Bishop compiled, it was clear that Tyler Hudson had been a bully in high school who'd made Linus a common target of his cruelty. When his father passed, he'd taken the chance to take that cruelty up to a truly despicable level. The workers Nola had spoken with described horrific physical abuse that Tyler subjected Linus to.

It was so bad that Nola was a little worried that when she got her hands on Tyler, she wouldn't be able to pull herself back from the edge she always tiptoed up to in these cases.

But she'd come up with a plan to deal with that.

A search of social media photos taken at the restaurant had shown a few with Linus in the background. If the police in Venice had done a more thorough job, they should have been able to track down Linus. But apparently, he hadn't been much of a concern for them.

With one last look at Linus, who was still staring fixatedly at the screen, her anger burning hotter with each step, Nola headed across the parking lot to have a little chat with the Hudson's Hideaway owner.

Return the Fear: Chapter Two

The air inside Hudson's Hideaway was cool as Nola pulled open the glass door and stepped inside. So cool, in fact, that a chill broke out along her skin. The restaurant had a nautical theme with boats, sharks, and other seafaring accoutrements lining the walls.

A hostess station stood straight ahead with a red-and-white life preserver attached to its face. The floors were a dark polished wood, and the booths were a combination of bright white and blue.

Nola had to admit it was actually a nice-looking restaurant.

And that was part of the problem. Apparently, Tyler figured if he was going to Miami, he might as well go big and had splurged, hiring a ridiculously expensive interior designer to update the look. The result was incredibly attractive but also came with a hefty price tag that Tyler was still paying off.

"Linus! Linus, where are you?" Tyler's angry voice called from the back of the restaurant.

Nola wended her way through the tables and the booths and slipped through the swinging doors into the kitchen. She wrinkled her nose as she stepped inside.

How this place had ever passed inspection was beyond her. While the exterior of the restaurant looked beautiful, the kitchen left a great deal to be desired. Fruit sat rotting in a corner, stacked up in gray bins. A few pans were in the sink, which was loaded with dirty dishes.

Nola knew it wasn't the staff that had left the place looking like this. Tyler had decided to have a few friends over last night and had had Linus serve them.

The plan had originally been for Nola to show up this morning and set up some cameras inside to catch him in the act. But Bishop realized they didn't have to: Tyler had his own camera system set up that stored the files on an off-site server. It hadn't taken Bishop all that long to tap into the feed and start recording. And it had taken only a few hours to get everything they needed from the live feed. Bishop had also downloaded older recordings, which no doubt had just as much on them as the few hours they had already seen.

Once Nola had seen the footage, it had taken everything in her not to bust in and pull Linus right then. But she'd been a few hours away at the time, setting up the special surprise guests for this morning. She'd had to wait so that they had enough to charge Tyler with when they brought everything to the cops.

And last night, he had implicated a couple of other business leaders by having them take part in the illegal poker game in the back of the restaurant.

Tyler came stomping down the stairs that led to Linus's apartment and stopped still when he caught sight of Nola. "We're not open yet."

"It doesn't look like you're going to be open at all," Nola said, looking around the empty kitchen.

"Just a small staffing issue. But I'll be happy to give you a free appetizer if you come back again later. Let me show you to the door."

Nola planted her feet. "I'm afraid I'm not going anywhere. You, however, are going somewhere rather unpleasant."

Tyler stopped, narrowing his already small eyes. "What are you talking about? Who are you?"

Nola smiled. "I'm a friend of Linus's."

Fear flashed across Tyler's face before he took on a neutral expression. "Linus? Who's Linus?"

Nola scoffed. "If that's going to be your legal defense, I strongly encourage you to come up with a better one. You know exactly who he is. You went to school with him since kindergarten. And what, were you mad that Daddy dearest was better to Linus than he was to you? Or was it just the fact that he was decent to Linus that bothered you so much?"

"I don't know what you're talking about, lady, but you need to get out of here. You're trespassing."

"Oh, yes, and you're such a stickler for the law, aren't you? Tell me: How much do you pay your employees? And how often do you threaten to turn them in to the authorities if they complain?"

His face red, Tyler grabbed a ladle from the rack to his right and slammed it onto the silver counter. "You don't know what you're talking about. Now, I said you need to get out of here."

Nola raised an eyebrow at the kitchen utensil. "What do you think you're going to do with that?"

Tyler smiled. "Show you that you can't just come in here and make threats."

Nola shook her head. She'd seen a few of the recordings that showed Tyler using just such a kitchen tool on more than a few of his employees, and definitely on Linus more than a few times.

Her vision turned red as she pictured Linus crying in the corner as Tyler beat him. And the reason? Linus had been found making himself a sandwich in the back of the kitchen.

Nola took a step forward. "You're going to pay for what you did to Linus."

"I didn't do anything to Linus."

"Really? Because five minutes ago, you didn't even know who I was talking about. You really need to be a little more consistent with your lies. That's where people get tripped up."

His face screwed up in anger. Tyler glared. "You need to get out of here."

"Actually, that's probably a good idea."

The kitchen door behind her swung open. Two big and muscular men stepped inside. Tyler paled considerably when he saw them. "Vinnie. Jose. What are you guys doing here?"

Her arms crossed over her chest, Nola stepped to the side to give Tyler a better view of his visitors. "Oh, they came because I told them that you don't have the money you need to pay them back for the bet you placed on last week's game."

Tyler's eyes widened as he stared at Nola, and then he looked over at the two men. "She's lying. I've got the money. I was . . . I was just on my way to go pay you guys. You can tell Randall that I'll have the money to him in an hour, tops."

Nola shook her head again. "Oh, Tyler. They know that you don't have the money. I showed them your books. They didn't realize how underwater the restaurant was. Using it as collateral doesn't actually help when it owes more than it's worth. So yeah, Randall's not real happy with you."

Backing away, Tyler held up his hands. "You don't know what they'll do to me."

"Actually, I know exactly what they'll do to you. That's why I called them." *And better them than me this time*, she thought.

The two men strode forward. Jose stopped and looked at Nola. "You probably should get going."

As much as Nola wanted to see Tyler get his comeuppance, she didn't want to leave Linus in the car on his own for too long. She smiled over at Tyler. "Well, Tyler, I hope you enjoy the rest of your afternoon. Gentlemen," she said, nodding to the two enforcers.

She slipped through the kitchen doors as the first cry of pain came from the kitchen. And she smiled at the sound of Tyler finally getting a small sliver of what he deserved as she crossed the dining room and let herself out of the restaurant.

Grab your copy…
www.vinci-books.com/return-fear

About the Author

Author, Criminologist, Terrorism Expert, Jeet Kune Do Black Sash, Runner, Dog Lover.

Amazon best-selling author R.D. Brady writes supernatural and science fiction thrillers. Her thrillers include ancient mysteries, unusual facts, non-stop action, and fierce women with heart.

Prior to beginning her writing career, R.D. Brady was a criminologist who specialized in life-course criminology and international terrorism. She's lectured and written numerous academic articles on the genetic influence on criminal behavior, factors that influence terrorist ideology, and delinquent behavior formation.

After visiting counter-terrorism units in Israel, R.D. returned home with a sabbatical in front of her and decided to write that book she'd been thinking about. Four years later she left academia with the publication of her first book, *The Belial Stone*, and hasn't looked back.

9 781036 700898